T0065647

ESMOND IN INDIA

RUTH PRAWER JHABVALA

A FIRESIDE BOOK
Published by Simon & Schuster Inc.
NEW YORK · LONDON · TORONTO · SYDNEY · TOKYO

F

FIRESIDE
Simon & Schuster Building
Rockefeller Center
1230 Avenue of the Americas
New York, New York 10020

This book is a work of fiction. Names, characters, places
and incidents are either the product of the author's
imagination or are used fictitiously. Any resemblance to
actual events or locales or persons, living or dead, is
entirely coincidental.

Copyright © 1958 by Ruth Prawer Jhabvala

All rights reserved
including the right of reproduction
in whole or in part in any form.
First Fireside Edition, 1990
Published by arrangement with the author
Originally published in Great Britain by George Allen & Unwin.
FIRESIDE and colophon are registered trademarks
of Simon & Schuster Inc.
Manufactured in the United States of America

10 9 8 7 6 5 4 3 2 1 Pbk.

Library of Congress Cataloging in Publication Data

Jhabvala, Ruth Prawer, 1927–
    Esmond in India/Ruth Prawer Jhabvala.—1st Fireside ed.
      p.   cm.
    "A Fireside book."
    "Originally published in Great Britain by George Allen &
Unwin"—Verso t.p.
    I. Title
PR9499.3.J5E8   1990   89-39391
823—dc20   CIP
ISBN 978-0-671-68339-9

For C. S. H. Jhabvala

CHARACTERS

Har Dayal
Madhuri, *his wife*
Shakuntala, *his daughter*
Amrit, *his son*
Indira, *Amrit's wife*
Ram Nath
Lakshmi, *his wife*
Uma, *his sister*
Gulab, *Uma's daughter*
Ravi, *Gulab's little son*
Bachani, *Uma's woman servant*
Esmond Stillwood, *Gulab's English husband*
Betty, *Esmond's English friend*

All the characters are entirely fictitious. If a name
has been used that may suggest a reference to any
real person, it has been used quite inadvertently.

1

Ever since she had come home, Shakuntala had felt happy and excited all day long. She was very glad to be home now, for good. Not that she had not liked the College; she had, very much. It had been such fun living in the hostel with all the other girls. Sharing a room with three special friends, getting up with them in the morning, going to classes together, to tennis, boating, swimming, to the Debating Club – and always at the back of their minds the private jokes they shared, which no one else could understand and which would suddenly by some chance allusion or perhaps without any allusion at all, just like that without any reason, come jumping up into their thoughts, so that all four of them would then and there dissolve into laughter the more delicious because inexplicable to everyone else. But often also they would be serious, especially late at night when they would sit and eat nuts and raisins and confide in one another all they felt and what they hoped for out of life. Then a great lovely sadness which was also happiness would fill them.

Now that was done with and she was home for good. She was grown up, no longer a College student but a finished B.A. She often wrote her name to see what it looked like with the B.A. after it. She had no regrets about her finished College life; because now a new life was starting for her, her real life, her grown-up life, for which up to now she had been only preparing. That was why she felt so excited and happy all day long. She expected exciting things to happen to her. She did not know what those things were going to be and that made them all the more exciting. Sometimes she felt herself bubbling over with such a flood of unexplained happiness that, in her exuberance, she would snatch up some cushion and waltz round the room with it and squeeze it tight, tight against her breast; but even afterwards, after she lay laughing and panting with the effort, she still felt a great residue of emotion left in her.

The room was filled with early morning sun. It swam with clear pale yellow light. All the vases were overflowing with flowers fresh from the garden. When she looked out, the garden was like an extension of the room: sunlight and flowers. Only instead of rugs and cushions and bolsters there was the smooth stretch of well-watered lawn. And her father in his golden dressing-gown. He was standing talking to the gardener. She could see that the gardener was not listening: probably Daddyji was lecturing to him about the beauties of nature, he was waving his arms so that the wide sleeves of the dressing-gown fell back from his wrists. Bye and bye he would forget that he was talking to the gardener and break into sonorous English, quoting Keats or Wordsworth.

Her sister-in-law came into the room and said, 'What are you doing today, Shak ın?' This question was very pleasing to her because it brought home to her the fact that the whole day was hers and she could do whatever she liked with it. And anything might happen during the course of it. It was a fact brought home to her anew every morning, and every morning newly exciting.

'Because I am going to do some shopping; are you coming?' said Indira.

That was one possibility: she might go shopping with Indira. Or she might not, as she pleased. She did not find her sister-in-law very interesting but she loved shopping. They would go and look at saris in some little stall. The shopman would unfurl rivers of silk before them, she would dig her hand in and feel the soft texture lapping over her skin. Yellow, orange, purple – a rich world. And she would perhaps bargain with the shopman who would be so courteous and tell her how she was his daughter and that was why he was giving her such a low price, for how can a man ask a high price from his daughter, 'When you and I are one.' But in the end he would take much less, and he would be very good-humoured, and so would she, smiling as she left the shop with her parcel under her arm.

'I have to go to the Anand Stores,' Indira said. 'I must buy a wedding present.'

Shakuntala failed to ask for whom. She was thinking that of course, Indira was the type of girl to prefer going to a store in the fashionable shopping centre, where there was no squatting on a tiny bench, no rivers of silk flowing over the white sheet spread on the floor, no casual eating betel-leaf or drinking Coca-Cola; and no bargaining. On the other hand – this also was nice – there would be many fashionable ladies in exquisite saris, with long red fingernails and pursed lips, and the salesmen would be deferential instead of, like the independent little shopkeepers, elaborately courteous. One could feel grown-up and a lady. Probably that was what Indira liked, to feel grown-up and a lady; she had not been married very long so she liked to feel her new dignity as much as possible. And Shakuntala, who was not married at all, had to admit that she too liked to be made to feel dignified and married. It was like slipping on a new and untried personality, and she always liked to experiment with new personalities.

'What shall I buy?' Indira said.

'What shall you . . .?'

'For the wedding present.' And though Shakuntala still had not asked whom it was for, she explained, 'It is for a girl who went to College with me. She is marrying an army officer, Captain Srivastava.'

'Would you like to marry an army officer?' Shakuntala asked, adjusting flowers which had looked better before she touched them.

Indira looked at her and gave an uncertain little laugh. So then Shakuntala realized that her question had been silly, because of course Indira no longer had any choice in what sort of person she might or might not like to marry. How dull it must be to have no longer any choice; all possibilities to be irrecoverably lost in the certainty of a man like Amrit.

'I do not know if I would like it,' Shakuntala said, at least considering the possibility for herself, who still had the power. 'One has to be polite to so many Brigadiers and their wives. Though of course one gets posted to all sorts of places, and if there is a war – '

'Do you think she would like perhaps a clock for her mantelpiece?'

'How do you know she will have a mantelpiece? Soldiers live mostly in barracks and sometimes also in tents.'

'Or a silver fruit-bowl? Though this will come very expensive.'

'What sort of girl is she?' Shakuntala asked, with genuine interest because she always liked to hear about other people, even if there was little chance of her ever meeting them. 'Is she an extrovert or an introvert? Does she read poetry? Does she play tennis? Does she swim? Does she laugh a lot and smoke cigarettes?'

'What questions you ask,' Indira said with another uneasy laugh.

'But I must know if I am to advise about her wedding present.' But she had already lost interest. She picked up a magazine lying on a little carved occasional table by a jasper vase brimming with white roses. A rose petal, still wet with dew, had fallen on the magazine and Shakuntala picked it off and rubbed it against her cheek. The magazine was called *Advance: A monthly review of the Arts.* It looked very interesting. She fluttered the pages; some time when she was free she would read it. Daddyji would advise her which articles to read first.

'I thought if we go to the Anand Stores and look around, perhaps we shall see something ... though of course it is better to go with some definite idea in one's mind.' Indira was beginning to sound rather worried, but Shakuntala, who had now lost interest entirely, only said casually, 'You had better ask Mummyji.'

'Yes,' Indira said, for indeed her mother-in-law would have better ideas on this subject than anyone else in the house. But just then her father-in-law came stepping in from the garden in his golden dressing-gown and it seemed only polite to consult him too.

'Ah yes,' Har Dayal replied; 'wedding presents.' He smiled, his extraordinarily sweet mouth curling slyly upwards. 'Useless objects despairingly bought and despairingly received.' But it was not, he realized, neat enough for a *mot*. Shakuntala came and stuck a rose into his great bush of grey hair.

'And what will my darling do today?' he asked her. At once she was overwhelmed again by all the possibilities open to her.

'We are going to do shopping,' Indira said. 'For the wedding present. But please, Daddyji, advise us – '

'Yes, perhaps I will go with Indira,' Shakuntala said. But there were so many other things. Now, with her father there, she thought of quite different things: for instance, she might like to do a little painting; or put on the gramophone and practise Bharata Natyam; or read poetry.

'A Captain Srivastava,' Indira was saying. 'They are an old military family.'

'What shall we suggest for the future Mrs Captain Srivastava?' Har Dayal asked of Shakuntala. The rose was still in his hair.

'Perhaps six fishforks,' Indira said, but she did not sound happy about it.

'Shall I go with Indira?' Shakuntala said. 'Or what shall I do?' Perhaps her father would take her somewhere; or perhaps someone exciting was coming to see him this morning, and then she would sit and listen to the conversation. Exciting people were always coming to see Daddyji – visiting American professors, Urdu poets, young painters from Bombay.

'Oh, but Shakun,' Indira protested, 'You said you would come. You must help me. Afterwards we will have chilled coffee in Sharmaji's.'

The servant brought in the mail on a round silver tray. All the mail was for Har Dayal, except for Amrit's monthly copy of *Reader's Digest*, of which Indira took solicitous charge.

Shakuntala looked over her father's shoulder as he opened his letters. He sat on the broad divan, leaning against a bolster; the letters lay scattered in his lap. He pushed his big black-rimmed spectacles to the end of his nose in order to read over the top of them. There were three invitations: one was for a solo veena recital, one for a lecture by a visiting UN expert on 'The Role of the Student in the World Today', and one for a cocktail party. Only the invitation to the veena recital was in Hindi – a very elaborate literary Hindi, for the recital was to take place at the house of a Minister who was an ardent advocate of the immediate abandonment of English in favour of Hindi. She thought the invitation to the cocktail party very cute – 'Poldi and Putzi Schlesing would love you to come and have cocktails with them' – with caricatures of Poldi and Putzi, a fashionable young Austrian couple. Shakuntala looked lovingly at these invitation cards. Daddyji received so many of them and they lay scattered about the house, just where he had happened to open them: invitations to exhibitions, recitals, plays, parties, lectures. Shakuntala found them all so exciting, for they made her feel that she was really living in the midst of great cultural activity.

Har Dayal read out the sonorous high-flown Hindi invitation. He read it very beautifully but still managed to make it sound ridiculous.

'Amrit says,' Indira informed them, 'that it is silly to try and make us change English for Hindi.'

'Is Amrit sending the car back for you?' Shakuntala asked.

'You can have mine,' said Har Dayal. 'I am not going out.'

'Someone is coming to see you?' Shakuntala asked with interest.

He passed his hand over his hair which nevertheless did not lie down. 'I have to write an article for *Forward*, I have been promising Dhanraj so long.'

'If only you could suggest something,' Indira said. She bit her lip, she was so deep in thought. Perhaps a clock for the mantelpiece was after all the best idea. One could get very good-looking clocks nowadays, and not too expensive.

A servant brought black coffee for Har Dayal and the gardener came in with more flowers from the garden. Shakuntala said, 'There are no more vases.' She blinked, for the sun came into her eyes. Out on the veranda another servant arranged the day's papers on a white cane table and flicked vigorously with a duster. At that moment Shakuntala's mother was giving instructions to the cook for the night's dinner; she ordered egg curry, for this was a dish of which her son Amrit was very fond. The old woman servant, wearing a very clean white sari with a blue border, relaxed in the sun outside the kitchen and drank sweet and milky tea out of a brass tumbler; in five minutes' time she had to prepare her mistress' bath, set out the Olde English soap, the talcum powder, the oil for massage. A blue parrot put out to enjoy the early morning sun on the veranda pecked at a chili stuck through the bars of his brightly polished cage.

Shakuntala stretched her arms above her head and said lazily, 'I am going to change my sari. I want to wear green this morning.'

'It is a green morning,' Har Dayal murmured in a voice like honey.

'You will be ready by eleven?' Indira anxiously asked. 'You *are* coming?'

Shakuntala did not commit herself. She went up to her bedroom and unwrapped herself from her sari. She left it lying on the floor as it had fallen. Suddenly she was in a very contemplative mood. She took out her gramophone – her own old gramophone which had been with her to College, which had played at parties in the hostel and at picnics – she wound it, she put on Sibelius' 'The Swan of Tuonela', which had now displaced Liszt's 'Liebestraum' as her favourite accompaniment to her contemplative moods. She sat down on her new Kashmiri rug – leaf-green creepers twining among pink and yellow flowers and bright red birds – she clasped her arms about her knees shimmering with the silk petticoat and prepared to give herself over to a mood.

The music flowed over her and filled her with vague but strong emotions. She wondered what things were going to happen to her in fulfilment of her great longing and anticipation. She would like to have been a great dancer, a famous exponent of Bharata Natyam, but she did not think she had enough talent or training for this. Perhaps she would be a poet and the revered companion of great men, like Sarojini Naidu. How proud Daddyji would be of her. Her poems would be full of nature and emotion. Or if not a poet, then a painter of landscapes: she glanced at her water-colours framed on the wall but did not feel quite satisfied.

So she thought of other things: of all the people she would meet. She tried also to think of the man with whom she would fall in love, but this was more difficult. Though she could well imagine herself falling in love, she could not imagine herself doing so with anyone in particular. Young men were so inadequate; she could not imagine how other girls managed to be satisfied with them. How Indira, for instance, managed to be satisfied with someone as ordinary as Amrit. But then she thought of Gulab, who was to have married Amrit but now was Gulab Stillwood. Strange, that it should be Gulab, whom as a child she had always laughed at and would perhaps even have despised if it had not been for her great beauty – that now it should be Gulab of whom she thought with admiration and perhaps even some envy, because Gulab had been so brave and had refused to let herself be satisfied with the ordinary.

Here 'The Swan of Tuonela' swept over her with a particularly moving phrase and all her thoughts were swamped in a great flood of feeling which assured her that life was very very beautiful and all open before her.

12

2

Gulab, on waking up in the morning, had no expectations at all. She had never, it is true, had any very great ones; but while she had still lived in her mother's house, she had waked up at least with equanimity and the knowledge that the day would pass for her in agreeable calm. She had never anticipated much; and she did not anticipate now. But whereas then her unconcern for the future, based as it was on a great and unquestioning confidence, had been instinctive, now it was more deliberate. She did not want to know or think about what the day held in store for her, so she merely let herself sink into the languor of first waking. When Esmond was not at home, she would stay on her bed for hours and hours; for there was really no reason for getting up. The only thoughts she allowed to come to her were – one, when would Esmond be away from home during the day and for how long; and two, was there any possibility of meeting her mother. If the answers to these two questions were favourable to her, she continued to lie there and feel comfortable and tranquil. If it was unfavourable, she also continued to lie and at any rate to look comfortable and tranquil.

Her favourite days were Wednesday and Friday. Esmond had early morning lessons to give on those days and, unless he was feeling very cross, he would leave the house without coming into her room. Sometimes – this was the best of all – she did not even wake up until he had gone and then it would be Ravi who woke her. He would come snuggling into her bed and at once, even though fast asleep, she would turn to him and cover his face with kisses. 'My soul,' she said, 'my life, my little tiny sweetmeat.' Ravi kissed her back again ardently. Both felt very happy. Of course, they knew this was forbidden by Esmond; perhaps that was why neither of them ever mentioned him. Ravi was only three and a half, but he was very intelligent.

Today they had a new servant. Having a new servant was nothing new to them, for they had one practically once a month. Esmond was very impatient with servants, so they never stayed long. The one who had stayed the longest had been old Bachani, who had come with Gulab from home. Esmond could swear and shout at her as much as he liked, she never even heard him: she had eyes and ears only for Gulab, and afterwards for the baby Ravi. Esmond had thrown her out three times but she had always somehow come back; until at last even she could stay no longer and had to return home to Gulab's mother. Then the long succession of new servants had started.

The latest new servant was not very promising. He was from the hills and did not seem to understand what was said to him. He stood stupidly in the doorway and stared at Gulab and Ravi in bed kissing one another. They took no notice of him until they decided that they would like to drink milk, so they sent him to get it. It was nice to be able to send someone again. They had been without a servant for quite a stretch of time now, which had been rather uncomfortable for Gulab, for she did not care for housework. She had somehow managed, as she had managed on previous such occasions, but – again as on previous such occasions – Esmond had been bad-tempered all the time.

The milk the servant brought them did not have enough sugar in it, so they sent him to put in more; they both liked things to be very very sweet. Half-way through Gulab thought it would be nice to flavour the remainder with rose essence to vary the taste. When they had finished, both had white milk-moustaches and they had a good laugh at one another before Gulab wiped their mouths, first lovingly his then carelessly her own, with the end of her sari. The new servant, since he had nothing else to do, continued to watch them. Ravi tickled Gulab and then Gulab tickled Ravi. She yawned, she stretched herself, she felt content. Ravi sat on her and rode her as a horse and she laughed. The new servant also laughed, an animal sound, and Gulab lifted her head to ask him what did he want, had he nothing better to do than to just stand there and look?

'What am I to get from the bazaar?' he said.

Gulab thought about what they would eat today. These were pleasant thoughts and she dwelt on them at some length, while the servant stood in the doorway and waited. But she did not decide on anything because today was Wednesday and her mother, knowing that Esmond would be away in the morning, might send something or even bring it herself. If not, she could always open a tin in time for lunch.

The possibility of seeing her mother or of eating food from her mother's house made her feel good enough to want to get up. She did so, very slowly and languorously, and had a luxuriant stretch. The sari slipped from her shoulder, suddenly revealing her magnificent breasts, two vast round moons tightly encased in a shimmering blouse which was split under the arm-hole. With a slow and lazy gesture she replaced her sari and said to the servant who still stood in the doorway, 'Go away,' though it hardly sounded like that for it was stifled in another great yawn.

Ravi skipped through all the four rooms of the flat and sang at the top of his voice. He sang the Hindi hymns he had learnt from his mother and his grandmother and which were the only things he could ever remember, although his father tried so hard to teach him English nursery-rhymes. Gulab loved to hear him sing and sometimes she joined in. They both felt very free, as they did every Wednesday and Friday morning. Then old Bachani came and at first Gulab was a little cross with her, because she had hoped to see her mother. She sat and looked sulky, pushing out her full lower lip.

'She could not come,' Bachani said placidly. 'She had to go and see Him.'

'Why?' Gulab said. She knew that by 'Him' Bachani meant not God but Ram Nath, her mother's brother.

'What do I know?' Bachani said, and now it was she who sounded cross. 'She tells me nothing.'

Gulab was too anxious to know what Bachani had brought to sulk any longer. Ravi was already taking the paper off the little earthenware pots. 'Carrot halwa!' he cried. Gulab looked pleased, her large melancholy eyes flashed for an instant with a wonderful fire. In the other pots were gram, tomatoes and potatoes swimming in red curry, and chunks of meat soaked in curds. Everything would be very highly spiced: Gulab smiled with pleasure.

'And I will make you parathas,' Bachani said. Even the flour she had brought from Uma's house; she would take nothing from Esmond's. In the kitchen she found the new servant; he was crouching in a corner staring in front of him. She gave him a look of disgust and called to Gulab, 'Where did you find this?'

'He is new,' Gulab replied placidly. She lay on the floor of the living-room and debated whether to paint her toenails this morning or not.

Bachani snorted contemptuously and then snarled at the servant, 'You can go, I am here now.' She lit the fire herself and grumbled as she did so.

Gulab, lying on the floor, felt as comfortable as she ever felt in that flat. It was not really convenient to her way of living. In her mother's house she had been used to vast rooms and little furniture, so that she had been able to lie on an old stringbed in the middle of an otherwise empty room, floating as on a great sea of cracked marble flooring under a high, high ceiling fretted – a sky with clouds – with flaking frescoes. But here, in her husband's flat, she was hemmed in by furniture, there was no room to lie down, no room to move at her ease. Oh yes, everybody said what nice furniture it was and how clever Esmond was to make so much of that small flat. He had utilized every corner, fitted in divans and shelves and coffee-tables, all very low and modern and, so they said, attractive. But Gulab could not see any purpose for so much furniture; it only prevented one from being comfortable.

However, with Bachani there and the smell of frying parathas, it was not so bad. If she shut her eyes, Gulab could almost imagine that she was at home. Though this took rather more imagination than she had: especially since shut eyes alone could not conjure up her mother, just as shut eyes alone or shut ears could not make her disappear. Uma's presence pervaded whatever place she was in and there was no substitute for it. Not even Bachani and parathas and the thought of spicy food to follow.

'Always these new servant people,' Bachani grumbled in the kitchen. 'God alone knows where they come from and what diseases they bring with them.'

'Oh you old woman,' Gulab said happily, 'stop your chattering.'

'You can scold me,' Bachani said, 'but one day you will be sorry you did not hear me. The day when all your jewellery which you have from your mother and every piece of clothing and every anna you have in the house will disappear with one of these devils.'

Gulab laughed and kissed Ravi, who sat beside her and played with her hair. It was still braided in two rather untidy plaits – her night-coiffure – for she had not yet worked up enough energy to comb it and put it up. Nor had she as yet worked up enough energy to have a bath and change her clothes. She was still in the sari which she wore at night; it was crumpled and torn, but she felt at ease in it. It had been different when Esmond had made her wear those flimsy transparent nightdresses with lace and ruffles and ribbons; then she had put on her clothes the moment she had got out of bed for she had felt so indecent. She had felt indecent in the night too. Nowadays, fortunately, Esmond no longer bothered about what she wore.

'And worse!' Bachani continued to shout from the kitchen, at the same time her hands were very dextrously patting and pounding the dough. 'They will steal the very skin off my Ravi Baba!'

'Do not listen to that old one,' Gulab said with another laugh and kissed him again.

'Do not listen – yes, now you can talk,' Bachani said ominously. 'And what about yourself? Is it right that you should be all alone, with no woman to look after you? Perhaps if you were ugly and black, then you could sit here with nothing to fear . . .'

'Go, my little bird,' Gulab told Ravi, 'get Mamma's scent bottles.'

'But with a face, a body such as God has given to you – '

'Enough now!' Gulab cried.

Ravi reverently carried in the little oblong box with the stoppered glass bottles which Uma had brought from Lucknow. Gulab raised herself on her elbow and took the stopper off one bottle after another. First there was jasmine, then rose, khas, lilac, sandalwood; the heavily concentrated perfumes spread a thick pall, heavy and ancient and very much at variance with the smart good taste of Esmond's interior decorating.

'It is not right,' Bachani muttered in the kitchen, 'not right for her to be alone.'

'Please give me rose,' Ravi said, so Gulab shut all the other bottles and applied a few drops of rose scent on his forehead. He was very pleased with himself, and with her when he watched her sprinkling it rather liberally into the cleft between her breasts. They sniffed one another and laughed with delight. Gulab hoped she would remember to wash both him and herself before Esmond came home.

At eleven o'clock she sat down to eat. She sat on the floor and ate with her fingers. She always did so, whenever Esmond was out, for that was the way she enjoyed her food most.

Bachani said, 'Yesterday she prayed and prayed.'

Gulab went on eating but she listened carefully. She knew that now Bachani would begin to tell her all the news from home.

'All morning she prayed,' Bachani said, 'at four o'clock she got up and she walked over the whole house and the garden and into the quarters at the back, praying. She would not talk with anyone.'

Gulab knew that once her mother started praying, she did not usually stop for many hours. And next day she would arrive at some new decision.

'Afterwards she went down to the Jumna to bathe, and how she prayed as she sprinkled the water! God surely must have heard her, she prayed so loud.'

'Eat and live, my heart,' Gulab said as she took a morsel of food out of her mouth and popped it into Ravi's.

'And all day she would touch no food. I said to her, "What are you doing? Perhaps you have no intestines that you can go without food?" But when,' Bachani said with sad resignation, 'has she ever listened to me or to anyone.'

'So then?' Gulab said, and picked out a luscious piece of meat between her thumb and middle finger.

'So then in the night she sang hymns with Swamiji, she played the harmonium and for two hours they sang together. Is the meat tender enough for you, daughter?'

'Give me another chili.'

'And after she had sung with him, she came down and she ate. She ate very well then.'

Gulab's strong white teeth met with relish over a chili – her third. It was very green, juicy, and pungent, and her palate and tongue burnt agreeably. There was no one like Bachani for picking out good chilis.

'After she had eaten, straightaway she lay down to sleep. She lay in the big room on a mat – she would not even sleep on a bed though I told her, "Are you a servant that you have to sleep on the floor?" '

'Water,' Gulab said and stretched out her hand for the glass which was just out of her reach. Her meal was finished, she burped richly and again tasted the flavour of the highly spiced food she had eaten. Ravi ate up all the carrot halwa and afterwards he licked the dish with his tongue.

'And this morning when she got up, the first thing she did she prepared the food which I brought for you. With her own hands she prepared it, she would not let any of us help her. When is that one coming back?'

'At twelve-thirty,' Gulab said. Bachani never referred to Esmond as anything but *that one*. 'Go and make cheese salad ready for him, he will want to eat when he comes.'

'What sort of man is that,' Bachani said, for she had always entertained the greatest contempt for Esmond's dainty light lunches, 'who eats grass for his food.'

'But why did she not come herself to bring it to me?' Gulab said and looked a little sulky again.

'I told you, she went to see Him. She said to me, "Old Woman, take this to my child and tell her I will be with her when I can, but today I have to go to my brother." '

'Why did she have to go to Uncle?'

'Why, why, why – as if she would tell me,' Bachani said crossly. 'But this I know – there is something new she is thinking of now, she cannot hide her mind from me. It is not for nothing that I have tended her for thirty-five years.'

Gulab yawned and scratched herself under the armpit, where her blouse was torn. Uma was always thinking of something new, she had more energy than her daughter could encompass in her thoughts. So Gulab had never bothered even to wonder what new schemes her mother might be working on.

'Salad!' Bachani said as she viciously cut up the leaves for Esmond's lunch. But Gulab said, 'Hurry now, hurry,' for he would soon be home and by then everything must be cleaned up and Bachani gone. At the thought of the flat its empty smart self again, Gulab felt rather strange; she always felt like that after a visit from home. But she never dwelt on it, nor explained it to herself. She did not like to be sad. So she only said, 'Hurry now, hurry, why are you always so slow.'

3

Indira had been right, it was from her mother-in-law that she got sounder advice than from anyone else about the wedding present. It was the sort of problem to appeal to Madhuri; and she tackled it with a seriousness which neither Shakuntala nor Har Dayal had been disposed to give it. 'Now, please let me think,' she said and proceeded to do so, while Indira settled down happily on a stool at her feet.

Madhuri lay in a chaise-longue on the upstairs veranda, propped up by several cushions and her hands folded in her lap. She looked like a charming and much-cherished invalid, which, however, she was not. It had been her good fortune all through life to look delicate while actually enjoying perfect health.

She said, 'What about a beautiful rug?' When she said 'beautiful rug', Indira could see it exactly: deep, soft, subdued in pattern and very expensive.

But Madhuri was also practical. 'How much do you expect to spend?' she asked. When Indira told her, she nodded understandingly: it seemed to her a sensible figure to spend on an old schoolfriend. Indira was indeed a sensible girl.

'Then we shall have to think of something else,' she said. There was no question of buying a cheaper rug: one bought the best of whatever one did buy, even if it was only for a present for someone else. 'A military family, you say?'

'Yes, she is the daughter of Lieutenant-General Saxena and she is to marry Captain Srivastava who is the son of Brigadier Srivastava.'

Madhuri was pleased. She knew, vaguely, the Saxenas and the Srivastavas and knew them to be respectable families of the right class. That was the sort of thing about which one could trust a girl like Indira: she would make friends only with girls of the right class. Not, Madhuri thought ruefully, like her own Shakuntala, who had been sent to the best schools and the best College, where she had formed her firmest friendships with the daughter of a newly-rich Sindi mill-owner, the daughter of a disreputable Maharaja, and the daughter of a high Government official who was now serving a sentence for embezzlement of public funds.

'Where is Shakuntala, what is she doing?'

'She is playing the gramophone in her room,' Indira said a little resentfully. 'She has promised to come with me but she has not even put her clothes on. She is sitting on the floor in blouse and petticoat.'

'Yes,' Madhuri said, 'you must take her with you.' Indira was the best possible company for Shakuntala: so nice, so sensible, such good manners. She was a little vague about Indira's virtues but she was aware that they were there; all the virtues she had been disappointed in not discovering in her own daughter. 'What do you think of a pretty painted coffee-set?'

'That sounds lovely,' Indira said. It did, as spoken by Madhuri. She could see her mother-in-law sipping out of a tiny vermilion coffee-cup, the little finger ever so slightly crooked. Madhuri was so very refined, everything she spoke about or did, Indira thought, at once took on her aura of refinement.

And Har Dayal, as he came up the stairs to the upper veranda to bring his wife's morning cup of chocolate, felt it too, that air of elegance and refinement that she distilled so that it pervaded the whole house, all the downstairs rooms, the verandas, the carpeted staircase, growing more and more concentrated the nearer one drew into her presence. There she lay, in her chaise-longue, after her bath, fresh and fragrant with talcum powder and cologne water and wearing one of her exquisite silk saris which never seemed to fade or fray because she kept them so beautifully.

'Madame's chocolate is served,' said Har Dayal. He always said either this or 'Votre chocolat, Madame.'

Indira laughed: she thought it was the most charming thing in a charming household the way Har Dayal brought Madhuri her morning drink (hot chocolate in the colder weather, iced lime-water in the heat, every day at eleven o'clock sharp). He was the most attentive of husbands, she had never seen anything so sweet. Unfortunately Amrit had not inherited this trait from his father or did not care to imitate it; he was, his wife lovingly excused him, rather too masculine to cultivate these little attentions.

'Why is Shakuntala playing the gramophone?' Madhuri asked. It worried her, it did not seem the right thing to do at this time of morning.

'The Swan of Tuonela,' Har Dayal said; which meant nothing to his wife. She had never cared to follow her husband and daughter's cultural interests, she was only vaguely aware of them in the background. She supposed they were all right, though sometimes they did bring rather strange and not altogether desirable people into the house.

'She had promised ...' Indira said. 'Mummyji, really I think the coffee-set sounds nice.'

'We are choosing a wedding present for a schoolfriend of Indira's,' Madhuri explained to Har Dayal, rather absently for her thoughts were still fixed on Shakuntala sitting on the floor in blouse and petticoat and playing the gramophone.

'I know,' Har Dayal said. 'Shakuntala and I also gave our advice.'

Indira wanted to protest that they had done nothing of the sort. She had consulted them but they had not made a single sensible suggestion. And Shakuntala, who had promised to come with her, was now sitting playing the gramophone and would not answer when spoken to.

'Has she nothing else to do?' Madhuri said. 'I am sure other young girls . . .'

Har Dayal said, 'Shakuntala is not like other young girls.'

Madhuri suppressed a sigh: that was the trouble. She herself, as a young girl, had always been very much like other young girls. She had stitched samplers and taken singing lessons. remaining secluded in the women's quarter of her father's house.

'She has such an artistic temperament,' Har Dayal said proudly. She was his own daughter, inheriting from him what his two sons had unfortunately missed.

'Oh no!' his wife exclaimed. She did not know quite what he meant by artistic temperament but she had a most disconcerting vision of a painted girl with garlands round her neck and bells on her ankles stamping out a wild rhythm.

'There was a girl in my class at College,' Indira contributed, 'who wanted to be an artist.'

'Oh nonsense,' Madhuri said with feeling. 'Shakuntala never has such thoughts, I know.'

Har Dayal said, 'She has a strong sense for words and for colour.'

That sounded harmless enough but Madhuri still felt suspicious, till Indira said, 'But afterwards the girl in my class was married to an Under-Secretary in the Ministry of External Affairs and now she has a baby and lives on Aurangzeb Road, I think at number eighty-seven. Mummyji, do you think a clock *would* be better?'

'A clock?' Madhuri said. Her thoughts shifted from Shakuntala to Raj, her younger son. She never worried about one thing for long at a stretch; perhaps that was how she had managed to stay so well-preserved.

'Shakuntala says army officers do not have mantelpieces, but clocks do not *have* to stand on mantelpieces, that is just silly.'

'Of course not, I always keep my clock on my table. Why has there been no letter from Raj for over two weeks?' she asked her husband.

'My dear one,' he said with a little reminiscent smile, 'young men at Cambridge have so many better things to do than to write letters home.'

'Amrit wrote every week, he missed only twice and that was just before his examinations when he was very worried.'

'Oh no,' Indira laughed, 'how can you say Amrit was worried about examinations – he never worries, he is so calm.' Her big strong new husband, calm and sensible like an Englishman; sometimes he also smoked a pipe.

'His letters were always very short,' Har Dayal said rather wistfully. So were Raj's. He had hoped that through his sons he would be able to live his own wonderful Cambridge days all over again, but this hope had been disappointed.

'He was very worried about his examinations,' Madhuri assured her daughter-in-law. 'He studied hard for them – naturally, what else did we send him to Cambridge for.'

'Oh, for many many other things,' Har Dayal said with a gay laugh. He thought of the other things. But strangely enough, his sons did not seem to have enjoyed them the way he had; they really, as his wife said, thought mostly about their examinations.

'Of course for other things also,' Madhuri gravely agreed. For instance, so that he could come back a gentleman with the sort of nice manners that boys only seemed to acquire abroad. She was a great believer in going abroad. Though she did not believe in staying there for good. Europe, England, even America, were all right for education or sightseeing but one always had to come back to one's own dear India. It was here that one's roots were, here that one could get the best positions, here that one enjoyed one's money and property and one's proper social status. It was safe here, comfortable.

'It is strange,' said Indira, 'but one can always tell if a man has been to an English university or not. If Amrit had not been abroad . . .' She did not finish, because it was needless to finish. An Amrit who had not been abroad, had not acquired an English polish, would simply not have been Amrit; not her Amrit. 'I think,' she added, for she did not want it to be thought she could consider no one and nothing but her husband, 'that Raj also will come back quite different.'

'Quite different from what?' asked Shakuntala, who at this point stepped on to the veranda.

'From what he was before,' Indira said. 'You are not even dressed yet and you promised you would come.'

'You should not walk round the house in this way,' Madhuri said. 'Not with the servants, and what if someone should come?' For Shakuntala had thrown only a housecoat, which she had not even bothered to button in the front, over her blouse and petticoat.

'But I am very respectable,' Shakuntala said. 'Look at Daddyji, he is wearing only his dressing-gown, not even blouse and petticoat.' Har

Dayal laughed his high-pitched laugh, sometimes called silvery, but Madhuri's lips tightened; Indira, too, thought it was not a nice thing to say.

'Why were you talking about Raj becoming different?' Shakuntala asked and leaned comfortably against the balustrade of the veranda, crossing her arms and her feet at the ankles.

'We were discussing the effects of an English education,' her father told her. He smiled reminiscently. 'Oh yes, certainly it changes us. Before I went what a callow youth I was: I had read nothing, I spoke a terrible babu English and wore very tight suits with waists in which anyway I did not feel at all comfortable. At home I had always worn kurta-pyjama or a dhoti and I hated sitting on a chair instead of on the floor or eating with anything but my fingers.' He smiled again and looked at his wife. 'How shocked you must have been with me, you must have asked yourself, "to what sort of man have they married me, is it to be with this that I have had to leave my home?"'

'Of course not,' Madhuri said a trifle primly; she did not think it was quite right to talk in this way, especially not before Indira, who was herself newly married.

'You were so young,' Har Dayal said, looking at her fondly. She had been fifteen, he nineteen. In those days it had been thought expedient to marry young men before they left for their studies abroad. Nowadays it was different, one took the risk even of a foreign daughter-in-law.

'You can get very pretty coffee-sets nowadays,' Madhuri, who did not like reminiscent talk, told Indira.

'But not everybody comes back different,' Shakuntala said. She had a rather strident voice which sounded almost defiant and – thought her mother who herself spoke only in a low sweet voice – very unwomanly. 'Look at Ram Nath Uncle, for instance.'

'Ah but Ram Nath was not always so,' Har Dayal told her. He thought of Ram Nath at Cambridge; indeed the two thoughts, Ram Nath and Cambridge, were for him always intertwined.

'How was he then?' Shakuntala asked.

'Oh different, different, very different ...' Har Dayal pushed his spectacles up on to his forehead, then took them off and held them away from himself at arm's length, shutting one eye: yes, they needed cleaning. 'He was – how shall I say? – very lively, very gay, oh very Cambridge. Always there was a party in his rooms and always he overspent his allowance –'

'Ram Nath Uncle?' Shakuntala said with a little incredulous laugh.

'Yes, yes, who else,' her father said, briskly wiping his spectacles with a corner of his golden dressing-gown. He sounded excited; talking, thinking of those days always made him excited, pitched his voice even higher than usual. 'He drank, he smoked, he read so much English poetry, had so many English friends and wore such stylish English clothes.'

'He wore English clothes?' Shakuntala said and sounded even more incredulous than before.

'The most fashionable cuts, with waistcoats and flowing neckties and when he went into the country – often we went tramping on long hikes – he wore plus-fours, and white flannels and a blazer for boating.'

'Of course,' Madhuri said, 'this was before he joined the Congress.' She said it quite calmly, without reproach, for the Congress had long since become respectable.

'How I loved him, how I loved him,' said Har Dayal, waving his spectacles in the air, love trembling in his voice.

'Do young men in Cambridge still wear white flannels and a blazer for boating?' Indira asked with interest. She tried to imagine Amrit in white flannels and a blazer, and the vision she conjured up was pleasing to her.

Shakuntala asked her father, 'He was your very best friend?'

'Friend – he was more to me than a friend, more than a brother. He went to Cambridge a year or two before I did, so when I came it was he who showed me everything and taught me everything. All things I love and value in life,' he said in an emotional voice, 'I learned about first from him.'

'What things, Daddyji?' Shakuntala asked eagerly. This was the sort of conversation she loved – about fundamentals, about the things one loved and valued in life.

'Have you seen the Japanese coffee-sets?' Indira asked Madhuri. 'They are so pretty.'

'My darling,' said Har Dayal, but he was pleased, 'what a large, large question.'

'You mean poetry and art and music – '

'And for instance a gracious way of living,' Har Dayal said. Shakuntala thought of the invitation to the cocktail party – Poldi and Putzi Schlesing would love you to come ... 'But Ram Nath Uncle does not – ' she said.

'Now he has changed,' Har Dayal said in a voice which was rather sad and almost flat, and he replaced his large intellectual spectacles. 'His sister also ...'

'Uma Auntie? She is also very different now? Was she as beautiful as Gulab?'

Madhuri's fingers began delicately but insistently to drum on the side of her chaise-longue. She thought it was in the very worst possible taste to mention Gulab, especially in front of Indira, who after all was filling the position which was to have been Gulab's. Anger dilated her fine nostrils when she thought of it, of the slight to her son Amrit and indeed to all of them.

'No,' said Har Dayal, who had no such feelings, 'not as beautiful as her daughter but she had – ah, such spirit in her, such fire, to go near her was to be kindled by her.'

Shakuntala said, 'But she is still very lively, even though she is old. And her husband, how was he?'

'What words can I find for him? He was a giant – in body and in mind and in spirit, a giant...'

'How you always exaggerate,' Madhuri said in a sharp, clipped voice.

'Oh, I wish I could have known him!' cried Shakuntala.

Indira took a pin out of her neat coil of hair and stuck it into her mouth, while her fingers deftly arranged a few strands of hair. 'He is dead now?' she asked and replaced the pin.

'But of course,' Shakuntala said. 'Everybody knows how he died of the hunger strike in prison.'

'Please, Shakun,' Indira said, 'get dressed and come with me, it is getting so late.'

'Yes,' Madhuri said, 'get dressed and go with Indira.' She looked at her daughter, still leaning in a not very ladylike manner against the balustrade, her housecoat wide open, her hair straggling over her shoulders very wild and free. And from her she looked at Indira, so neat and charming in a sari with a pattern of tiny green and red checks and blouse to match, her smooth hair meticulously parted in the centre. Madhuri was pleased to see her daughter-in-law so well-groomed; but less pleased by the contrast she presented to her own daughter.

'But we have all changed,' Har Dayal said with a deep and melancholy sentitiousness. 'We have all grown old.'

'What do you expect,' Madhuri said rather tartly, which made Shakuntala laugh. Har Dayal ruefully smiled.

'I think the coffee-set is best,' Indira said. 'I think it is a very good idea, thank you, Mummyji.'

'She always has good ideas,' Har Dayal said, and tenderly took his wife's hand. 'She can solve all problems.' He wanted to apologize to her for having suggested that she too had grown old. Her hand was very small and delicate and yellow, the skin finely wrinkled; evidently it had always been treated only to the best and most expensive soaps.

'The Japanese ones are very pretty, you are right,' Madhuri said, withdrawing her hand out of Har Dayal's. 'I have seen a charming set in black with red dragons.'

4

Ram Nath's wife Lakshmi sat in the courtyard and pounded spices. She enjoyed doing this but if anyone had asked her why she was doing it, she would have pulled down the corners of her mouth and replied, 'What else should a poor man's wife do?'

However, her sister-in-law did not ask her, she only stood and looked at her and said, 'It is pleasant to sit out here in the open.' Lakshmi did not like this because it suggested that she was sitting idle and enjoying herself. She looked up at Uma resentfully. Uma was wearing an old and not very clean cotton sari but even in this she looked rather splendid. 'Is he at home?' she asked.

'Where should he go,' Lakshmi said half scornfully and half bitterly; and added 'poor old man,' though not in a pitying way.

Uma laughed; she threw back her head and laughed so heartily that Lakshmi could see the vibration in her throat. It annoyed her, this healthy laughter, so she turned her head and yelled for the servant.

'No,' Uma said on her last laugh, 'that he is not.'

'What else then?' Lakshmi said. She sounded cross, but really she was beginning to feel more cheerful: she enjoyed discussing her husband.

Uma, however, did not answer her. She was looking up and greeting the other tenants who, attracted by her laughter, were beginning to gather on the open verandas overlooking the courtyard. These verandas ran all the way round the house, forming two tiers of galleries from which one could get a perfect view of the courtyard. The courtyard belonged to Lakshmi, since she lived downstairs, and she certainly did not care to be overseen in this way. She considered the other tenants, and especially their wives, considerably beneath her. They were very ordinary lower-middle-class people, government clerks, teachers in primary schools, municipal inspectors, salaried salesmen. Whereas she herself came from a wealthy, well-known family, and had it not been for misfortune and an obstinate husband, would certainly have lived – as she often assured herself and her neighbours – in a large house of her own with many servants.

'Where is he?' Uma asked. She greeted the other tenants only perfunctorily, though they were smiling down at her with great pleasure, ready for a long talk. But she was in a hurry to speak to her brother and was incapable of simulating an interest in others which she did not at the moment feel.

'In his room, where else would he be,' Lakshmi replied. 'Hearing nothing, seeing nothing — I can fall down dead with a stroke while he is sitting there, what would he care? He would not even know.' She remembered that she had called the servant and he had not yet appeared, so she called again, very loudly and shrilly.

Ram Nath was sitting in his room with all the windows closed. The walls were lined with large, dark old books, his table was full of little piles of papers.

'How can you sit like this,' Uma said, 'without air, how can you breathe?' She flung the windows open; one of them stuck but she soon got it open with a wrench of her muscular arm. 'You will die like this,' she told him, 'you cannot keep in good health without air.' She herself could never bear to sit in a closed room. Even in the summer heat she preferred the shade of a tree to an air-conditioned room.

He was glad to see her. He was even glad that she had opened the windows, though he would never have done so of his own accord nor allowed his wife to do so. But it was good now, with the windows open, and her there, filling the room, large and strong with her square shoulders, her broad hips, her head held erect on a round, full, firm neck.

'I have been told,' she said, 'that you are a poor old man.'

He hunched his face between his shoulders and giggled. 'Quite right,' he said. 'I am certainly old and even more certainly poor.' He giggled again and it was such an old man's giggle that she felt sad and thought, yes it is true, he has grown old. He was small and dried-up and looked weak with the weakness of age.

She felt more protective than ever towards him, so she said in a bullying tone, 'And you do not look after yourself, you do not eat enough, sleep enough and you sit in this room . . .'

'Please,' he said, spreading his hands and looking at her with an expression which was both appealing and amused, 'Let me live in comfort.'

'Comfort,' she blustered, 'you dried-up little thorn of a man, you do not even know what it is to live in comfort . . .' but suddenly her expression changed; she became very serious and said, 'Today I prayed.'

'And what was the answer of your God?'

'I prayed all day for guidance,' she continued as if he had not interrupted; indeed, probably she had not heard him, she was so intent on herself and yesterday's experience. 'I sang hymns with Swamiji and

27

I went down to the Jumna and then in the night I knew what we have to do. I am sure now,' she said and looked at him significantly.

'About what?' he said, a little sharply, for he did not like such cloudy talk.

'The Lord has helped me and instructed me as he did Arjun on the battlefield,' she said with rapt and wide-open eyes. She was very much impressed. But he made a gesture of impatience and clicked his tongue; and when she still did not answer his question but continued to stare with unfocused eyes into the distance, he shifted the book open before him a little nearer and began to read.

'About Gulab,' she said then. 'About my child,' and he looked up again.

'She must leave him,' she said with passion. Ram Nath kept silent. 'She must come back to me. I know now.'

He said quite seriously, 'You must have prayed very long and hard,' for he knew his sister.

'I did, oh I did. And for how long now,' she said, 'have I thought and battled here,' and she beat her chest with her fist in a histrionic but convincing manner. 'How I have thought this way and that way – oh, brother, no one knows the days and nights I have spent trying to find the right path.'

Ram Nath pushed his book away. He said, 'You did not tell me.'

'What was there to tell?' she said. 'I could speak only to God in my prayers, no one else knows what moves in a mother's soul.'

Though he disliked her manner of speaking, he knew it was not needlessly inflated; the grief had been real. He looked up and saw that large slow tears were running out of her eyes and flowing down her cheeks, into her bosom; she held her head very erect and let them flow unchecked. He looked down again quickly. I am a useless, ineffective old man, he thought, and looked at his hands laid palm upwards on the table.

But what could he have told her? For him the solution was so much easier than for her. For him it was simply, 'Gulab must go away from her husband, today, at once, because he is making her unhappy.' His logical, emancipated mind saw no obstacle. But he knew that for his sister it was different. She was a free, bold, courageous woman; when she thought something was right, she allowed nothing to stand in her way. But the old traditions were in her, and often it took her a long and hard time to overcome them. Then no one could help her.

'So you have decided that Gulab must leave her husband,' he said. He said it so bluntly because that was the way she wanted to hear it. After her day's prayer she was now quite clear and certain and nothing would be able to turn her back. She had, for Gulab's sake,

28

stifled the habit of thought, the inbred instinct, that told her a woman's husband is her God.

'Yes,' Uma said, her head held high, 'now it is enough. Now it is time she came back to me.'

Ram Nath sat and slowly nodded his head up and down.

'Why,' Uma said on a sudden wave of passion, 'did she do it, why?' It was the first time she had asked this question for five years. Though, five years ago, then, they had all asked it, and constantly: why did Gulab, so soft, so tractable, so indolent, insist with an obstinacy she had never shown either before or since on marrying Esmond? She hardly knew him; none of them knew him. He had given one or two lectures in the College which she had for a short time attended – that was all any of them knew about him. But Gulab had been quite certain that she wanted to marry him: though everything had already been fixed for her, and they had all been so happy about it; she herself had shown herself happy about it, about marrying Har Dayal's son Amrit. He would have given her such a comfortable life, such a beautiful home, his whole family would have welcomed her and at last their two families, who had always been so close in friendship, would have been united. Uma had been most satisfied about the prospect of that marriage. Her own life had been far from comfortable, so she wanted more than anything that her daughter's should be: easy and conventional. And so it would have been, if Gulab had not suddenly come and asked could she please marry Esmond; and in reply to their protests had alternately smiled and looked sad, while remaining immovable, like someone very fat and indolent who refuses to be pushed off the bed on which he has chosen to lie.

'Why did she want it so?' Uma now asked – after five years during which almost everything she had feared had happened and she had never said a word because of a woman's husband being her God.

Ram Nath knew no answer and was not inclined to fabricate one. Instead he was practical and said, 'What about the boy?'

'My Ravi?' Uma said and looked at him with astonished eyes. 'He will come to live with me too, why not? Both will come and I will look after them.'

'But the father may claim him,' her brother pointed out.

'Tcha,' Uma said with decisive contempt, 'what nonsense you talk.' And perhaps she was going on to tell him how in that case she would deal with Esmond (now that he was no longer Gulab's God), but just then Lakshmi came in with a suspicious face and alert eyes.

'You sit with him all the time,' Lakshmi said, 'Why don't you ever come and speak with me?' She looked round the room and said resentfully, 'You have opened the windows.'

'He must have air to breathe,' Uma explained.

'Of course, that's what I tell him every day, but he doesn't hear me.' This was quite true: Ram Nath no longer heard his wife, nor saw her. Now that she had come he continued quietly to read his book where he had left off on his sister's arrival.

'And next time you come,' Lakshmi said on a louder note, 'perhaps you will also see to it that the servant can come in to clean this room and throw away all the papers which are no use to any man.' Ram Nath turned a page. 'And these books!' Lakshmi cried. 'What use are they in the house, what use have they ever been to him or to me!'

'I will stay to eat with you,' Uma said.

'. . . Or to our children,' Lakshmi said. 'You should have told me before, now what have I got in the house except a few miserable grains of rice and lentils which is all we ever eat. The servants in my father's house had better food than I eat with my husband. Look at him,' she said, 'how thin he is; when our children come home they will blame me and say I do not look after him well.'

'He was always so,' Uma said, and she also looked at Ram Nath, who sat peacefully reading his book. 'What news is there from Narayan, he is coming home?'

Lakshmi sighed, as she always did at mention of her son; and threw a reproachful look at her husband of which he remained entirely unaware. 'My poor boy,' she said; 'when does he ever have the time to come home to his mother?'

'It is always so when children grow up,' Uma said. 'A mother pines to see them.'

'When I think of other doctors,' Lakshmi said, her eyes fixed on her husband who at this moment turned a page, 'how easy their work is, how much they earn, they live comfortably here in Delhi with their families, they eat well, they sleep in soft beds, they drive round in big cars and go often to the cinema. And my poor son, who is the best and cleverest of them all, has to spend his life among dirty peasants and villagers, far away from his own family, work all day and also in the night and he is paid hardly enough for his needs. And what prospects has he? Who will help him in life? Must he stay there for ever and starve and overwork himself and no respectable person to speak with?' Ram Nath, glancing up for a moment, gathered that his wife was speaking about Narayan. She caught him as he looked up and repeated more plaintively, 'Must he stay there for ever?'

'Why not,' Ram Nath said. He thought that was what his son wanted. Narayan had never made any elaborate avowal of principle but his father had gathered that he wished more to work among the poor and the backward and the really needy than to set up a fashionable practice.

'Why not!' Lakshmi repeated in an incredulous shout.

'He does such good work,' Uma put in. 'It is men like him that Our Country needs at this time.' She spoke this in the special voice she kept only for exalted patriotic matters (different from the special voice which she kept for exalted religious matters).

'And have I not made enough sacrifices,' Lakshmi said, 'that now I must also give my son?'

'In life there must always be sacrifice,' Uma said. 'It is in this way that we acquire virtue.' She would at that point have liked to remember an appropriate quotation from the *Gita* or some other sacred writing, but it did not come to her.

'Yes,' Lakshmi said bitterly, 'this is all I will ever acquire.'

Ram Nath thought that was really funny, he began to cackle, hee-hee-hee he went and gleefully rubbed his hands, which drove his wife into a frenzy of irritation.

'Be quiet now,' Uma told him in an attempt at soothing her sister-in-law. 'Are you an old hen that you must sit there like that.'

'Let him!' Lakshmi shouted. 'This is all he is good for – to sit and laugh at his wife after he has stripped her of everything and ruined her life! Where are the jewels I brought from my father's house, where is my gold chain, my diamond necklace with earrings and bracelets to match, my ruby clasp, my sapphire ring which alone has been valued at 2,000 rupees? Look at me,' she cried and held up her arms, 'even my gold bangles have gone, I have to wear glass bangles like a sweeper woman!'

Ram Nath clicked his tongue in a pitying way, he looked quite mischievous, like a gnome.

'Ah, sister,' Uma said, 'we have all of us given all we had. But has it not been worth it, for Our Country, for Our Cause; how else would we have achieved Swaraj if we had not been ready to give all we had, even our lives and the lives of our dearest ones . . .'

'Yes, but now?' Lakshmi cried. 'Now that it is all finished and you have what you want?' She still said, 'what *you* want' for she had always stubbornly disassociated herself from her husband's and her sister-in-law's patriotic activities. 'Why is there nothing for us when all the others are now getting the prizes? All of them – look at Meher Chand, who comes from a not very good family and his wife from even worse, now he is a Minister, they have given him a big house in New Delhi with a sentry standing outside and he has a large car so his wife thinks now she is very great – my mother would not have taken her as a servant in her house – what has he given more than we have?

On the contrary, it was my husband who spent more years in prison than he did, leaving me alone and helpless all that time with my children . . .'

She caught new breath but was too excited to notice that Ram Nath had gone back to his reading, while Uma was getting restless; she wanted to talk to her brother alone, about Gulab.

'And those who just sat quiet and did nothing, what did they lose? Look at Har Dayal and Madhuri – what did they ever do, what jewels did she have to sell, has he ever seen a prison even from the outside? And yet now they sit there, with all their houses and all their lands and all their jewels, and laugh at us who have given everything and received nothing in return . . . if you are really staying to eat with us,' she told Uma, 'I will send out for meat koftas and nan. When we are alone, what is the use of sending for these things, he never eats so I too have to starve with him.'

5

Bachani had cleared up and gone. The flat was its own neat modern cosmopolitan self again; it smelt of DDT which Gulab had sprayed to get rid of the smell of the food which Bachani had cooked for them. She knew Esmond would not object to the smell of DDT – on the contrary, he was always insisting that things should be sprayed thoroughly and frequently. She had put Ravi to sleep, and now she lounged about in her own room, where she felt bored and uncomfortable. She would like to have lain down on the floor and gone to sleep, but Esmond might come in and then he would be annoyed. She could not paint her toenails either, as she had been intending to do all morning, because he did not like the smell of the polish she used. So she merely sat or aimlessly strolled about and felt caged in because the room was, by her standards, so small. She picked up yesterday's brassière which lay trailing over a chair and dropped it again absent-mindedly to trail over another chair, she yawned a vast uninhibited yawn which showed all her teeth, strong and white and quite perfect like those of an animal, and the luscious pink of her tongue and palate. She kept as quiet as she could because, if he heard her moving about, Esmond might take it into his head to come in and say something to her. She hoped he would be going out again soon.

He sat alone at his smart little dining-table in his smart little dining-corner and ate his cheese salad. Everything on the table was colourful and modern – the bright table-mats, the painted drinking-glass, the earthenware plates of a rich dark green – so that it looked rather like a beautifully photographed full-page advertisement in an American magazine. It was very different from Gulab's spicy meal eaten on the floor out of brass bowls.

When he had finished eating, Esmond called 'Bearer!' very imperiously. The new servant, who had never before worked in a household refined enough to call him bearer, continued to squat in the kitchen and stare in front of him with blank and melancholy eyes.

'Bearer!' Esmond called, even louder, and then again 'Bearer!' so thunderously, at the same time crashing his fist down on the table, that the servant jumped with shock and came rushing out of the kitchen to see what had happened. Gulab in her room gave another deep yawn and began slowly to unfasten one of her plaits.

'In my house,' Esmond explained to the servant in his very bad but very careful Hindustani, 'I expect absolute and immediate obedience . . .' The servant began slowly and clumsily to clear the table. He might have been seventeen or thirty-seven years old; he wore the indeterminate clothing of the poor (ragged shirt over ragged pyjama trousers once gaily striped in pink and green but now faded with age and poverty); he looked exactly like all the other nameless, faceless servants Esmond had employed. 'When I call, I want you here on the instant,' Esmond told him. The servant wondered what the Sahib was saying; he could not even identify the language he was talking. Esmond, who rather enjoyed listening to himself speaking in Hindustani, gave him a long and sonorous lecture on his duties.

Afterwards he sat down on his gaily striped little divan and telephoned. He telephoned to several ladies of his acquaintance, all of them the wives of foreign diplomats. When he spoke to them, his face took on a gay and bantering expression, he leaned on one elbow and crossed his legs and smiled down at the telephone. He enjoyed talking to them and they, he knew, enjoyed talking to him; which was fortunate for him, since his living depended on them. He lived by giving private tuitions, and it was these foreign ladies who mostly engaged him. He taught them whatever they wished to learn: Hindustani or the History of Indian Art or the History of Indian Literature. He had worked out a complete course on Indian culture, which was very useful to ladies who were only in the country for a short time but wished to take strong impressions back with them. He also sometimes acted as a kind of very superior guide, taking small parties to the Red Fort or the Juma Masjid, or to Kutb where in the winter they sat down to picnic lunches.

During the course of his telephoning, he made various appointments and picked up two invitations to lunch and one to dinner.

These invitations were meant for himself alone: his friends had long since given up asking Gulab out. In the beginning, five years ago when they were first married, he had taken her everywhere. She hated going out, he knew, but he had forced her – *gently* forced her, then – to accompany him to all his parties. He had thought it would be good for her. But she had always been so miserable – had sat there, silent, with downcast eyes, defeating all attempts at conversation which the intrepid English and American ladies had made with her, so obviously unhappy and uncomfortable and only waiting to go home – that in the end he had excused her and gone alone. He found that her absence was far more impressive than her presence. It gave him the opportunity of implying that real Indian ladies, from the best old Indian families, still stayed secluded at home; which thrilled his foreign friends by giving them a glimpse of the India they thought they had so far missed: the India of veiled women sitting together in marbled courtyards where perhaps a fountain plashed and a sprightly maid-servant engaged them in bantering conversation in between singing love lyrics to a lute. Esmond tended to foster the impression by giving evasive or distant replies when questioned about his wife; suggesting that the internal arrangements of his household were too private and oriental to be discussed.

When he had finished telephoning, he remembered Ravi (he was always remembering Ravi; he was a conscientious father), so he went to have a look at him. The boy was sleeping in the brightly-painted cot which stood under the window; Esmond's own sleeping-couch was against the opposite wall. He had insisted that Ravi should sleep in his room. He knew that if the child slept with Gulab, there would be far too much petting and unhygienic sharing of beds. He had now trained Ravi not to wake up in the night; or if he did wake, to keep quite still and not disturb his father. He looked down at the boy. Ravi was as dark as his mother, he looked completely Indian. At first, when Ravi was born, Esmond had been very happy about this: he had wanted an Indian son, a real piece of India, as he had wanted an Indian wife. Now, however, he thought wistfully of fair sturdy little boys with blue eyes and pink cheeks. Angels not Angles, he often found himself murmuring, quite out of context; Angels not Angles. He could see them. But Ravi was definitely dark.

He stooped towards his sleeping son. He sniffed; he sniffed again: yes, it was unmistakably that strong Indian scent which Gulab had so liked before he had forbidden her the use of it. He straightened himself up· his lips tightened but he looked triumphant rather than angry.

He entered her room so quietly that she did not hear him coming in. She was sitting on the edge of the bed, yawning and scratching her thigh. Her head was turned away from the door, so that all he saw of it was the outline of one full cheek. She sat in an old sari and a tight blouse torn under the armpit; obviously she had not yet had a bath. The room was thick with her own peculiar smell; and mixed with this, unmistakably, the smell of that scent.

'Gulab,' he said, very very quietly. She was startled, her head turned and for a moment she looked straight into his face. She saw his compressed lips and the triumphant look which made his nose seem sharper, his eyes more cold and blue. His brow was lofty under the wave of golden hair and his chin very pointed. She dropped her eyes again immediately, feeling awkward and ashamed and rather shaken. She always avoided looking at him directly. She had always done so: in the beginning because she had loved him so much, it had not seemed decent to her to look directly at someone one loved so much.

'The child went to sleep?' he asked.

'Yes, he . . .'

'What did you give him for lunch?'

'Spinach soup and carrots with potatoes,' Gulab replied. If Esmond tried to corroborate this later from Ravi himself, the boy would say that he had forgotten what he had eaten. He always said that he had forgotten after taking food from his grandmother's house. Nobody had told him to say this; indeed, no word on the subject had ever passed between him and his mother.

'Hmm,' Esmond said non-committally. 'And you gave him his bath in the morning?' She felt him looking at her very fixedly; she was uncomfortably aware that she herself had not yet had her bath.

'Of course.'

'He smells,' Esmond said, 'very peculiarly.' Then she remembered that she had forgotten to wash him after applying the scent. Also herself: she sniffed a little, trying to make out whether Esmond would be able to detect it on her too. He said, 'There's the same smell in this room.'

'Yes,' Gulab answered in her calm lazy way, 'poor Ravi by mistake spilt some of my scent. A little of it fell on him too. I was so angry with him, I told him you know your father cannot bear this smell, it is even bad for his health, what will he say when he comes home?'

'Why don't you throw the horrible stuff away? I've told you hundreds of times.' He knew very well that she was lying. But Ravi was asleep and could not be called in as witness. Perhaps later . . . but Gulab lied so often, it was difficult always to follow her up.

'Mama would be so hurt. You know it was she who gave it to me, every time she comes she asks me where is the scent I brought you from Lucknow.' She lifted both arms to the coil of hair which she wore wound at the back of her head. Her fingers poked ineffectively at hairpins.

Esmond walked round the room. He picked things up here and there, her brassière, an old blouse, very gingerly between forefinger and thumb, pointing his disgust. She kept her eyes lowered and wished he would go. She knew her room was not very clean; she knew she herself was not very clean; but that was the way she lived. However, he said nothing, only walked superciliously round. He was tall and slim and somehow pointed; his whole figure could express superciliousness.

'I'm out for dinner tonight,' he said at last.

She did not answer, but she looked down more intently as she did not want him to see how pleased she was. He might then – though this was unlikely because he so much enjoyed going out to dinner – stay at home, out of spite. Or come home unexpectedly early, to see what she was up to: it had happened before.

'Would you like to come with me?' he suddenly asked and swung round, his hands in his pockets, his long body slightly bent towards her from the waist; though she did not look at him, she knew he was smiling a little derisive smile.

But she answered him quite calmly. 'I cannot leave Ravi alone.'

'Otherwise I'm sure you'd have loved to come,' he said, getting cruder. He knew it was crude, but he could not help himself. Seeing her there, so languorous, so very placid, goaded him on. He wanted to rouse some response, some protest, in her, and though experience had taught him that this was not a feat he could achieve, ever, yet he always found himself trying again.

'You're such a social asset,' he said, a practised sneer in his voice and in his glance as he looked at her. 'You sit there and fascinate everyone with your brilliant conversation. Such a credit to me.'

She did not really understand him. Sarcasm was a form of humour entirely lost on her. But she gathered somehow that he was laughing at her – or scolding her, or both – for having been shy and awkward when he had taken her out. She was so happy that he allowed her to stay at home now. Because it had been very difficult for her. Sitting there in those bright, smart houses – as alien and uncomfortable as their own flat – among those bright, smart people: if only they had left her alone to drink her fruit-juice and follow her own thoughts till it was time to go home; but no, they had come to talk to her and she had hardly been able to understand what they were saying because they rattled so quickly in an unaccustomed different kind of English, and anyway they said such strange unexpected things; to which she had only been able to answer 'yes' or 'thank you' and this, she had sensed, was unsatisfying to them. She had been able to feel them getting uncomfortable beside her, sometimes even exasperated. But what could she do? She had been uncomfortable herself, and had only wished that they would go away.

'You'd be the original dumb blonde, if you were that,' he said, trying again and feeling the familiar irritation with her, and with himself, which he always experienced on such occasions. 'Were blonde, I mean.' But what was the use.

'Yes,' she said. There had been one thing at those parties to keep her, underneath all her social misery, buoyed up: the presence of Esmond. She would have felt it to be indelicate to follow him round with her eyes; but there had been no need to do that, because she had been able to sense him. And the sense of him had kept her radiant.

'Ah well,' he said with a sigh. 'Every man has his cross.' Only his was heavier than that of other men. He thought of himself as trapped – trapped in her stupidity, in her dull, heavy, alien mind, which could understand nothing: not him, not his way of life nor his way of thought. He sighed again and changed his ground: 'How's the new servant?'

'All right.'

'Like all the others, I expect – he cooked Ravi's lunch? You showed him?'

'Yes.'

'Hmmm ... well, I'll be home myself tomorrow to show him.' Gulab's spirits sagged for a moment. But she had the whole evening before her. She thought of what she was going to do with her free evening.

'Why don't you,' he said, looking round the room, 'get him to clear up this mess? Since you don't seem to be able to do it yourself.'

'Yes,' she said.

'Yes what?'

'Yes, I will ask him to clean here.'

'I should think so too. Smells like a bloody henhouse. Though you, I suppose, wouldn't notice a little thing like that.'

They would eat horseradish pancake at night. With pickles.

'You've got what I can only call a wonderful propensity to squalor. Tell me now, if pressed on the point, would you call yourself a slut?'

'Yes please?' she asked politely. Afterwards she and Ravi would get into bed together. She would sing to him, all the songs he loved. When he was asleep, she would watch over him for a little while before carrying him to his cot in his father's room.

'Oh never mind ... what are you going to give the child for his supper in the evening?'

'Spinach soup and carrots and potatoes,' she said without hesitation. The smell of the horseradish would deliciously float through the flat.

'That's what you said you gave him for lunch.'

'He liked so much.'

'What's that supposed to mean? He liked so much. What sort of language is that?' When they had first been married, he had sometimes tried to teach her a more idiomatic English, the English English that he himself spoke, But he had done so only very half-heartedly because he had – then – taken such delight in her Indian English. So when she, after such a lesson, had slipped comfortably back into her own expression, he had just kissed her nose and said, 'You sweet thing you.'

'I don't mind,' he said, 'what sort of babu English you choose to speak – I couldn't, as they say, care less – but that you might infect the boy with it too, that's what bothers me.'

'But always he hears you speak such good English,' she said. She said this in all innocence, he knew; she was too damn dumb, as he put it to himself, to try and get any kind of dig in at him.

'Oh go to hell,' he said, turning away.

'You are going?'

'Where?'

'To your dinner.'

He turned round again and faced her, arms akimbo. 'My dear woman,' he said, 'does one usually go out to dinner at four o'clock in the afternoon?'

'It is only four?' she murmured. She wished she had not spoken; she had been too eager. She had rather hoped that he would be gone before Ravi woke up from his afternoon sleep. It would have been such a nice surprise for Ravi too.

'You're not trying to get rid of me by any chance?'

'Please?' she said and gave a rather weak, uncomprehending little laugh.

'One never can tell with you. The moment my back's turned, God only knows what tricks you're up to.' Once he had come home unexpectedly early. He had found her and Ravi in bed together; she had been holding him right against her breast and singing to him. The whole flat had smelt of hot curried food; so had both their breaths. She, however, had denied that they had eaten any curry: and the boy had said he had forgotten what he had eaten.

'Today I will go to bed very early. I am so tired.' She yawned to demonstrate. 'First I will darn your socks.' There was of course always the risk that he might come home early; but one had to take that.

'Model little wife,' he said. But really, even though it was only four

38

o'clock, he did not feel like staying in the flat any longer. He had spent a lot of time and trouble and good taste over doing it up, but he had never felt at home in it. Not with her there; for though he had completely followed his own tastes in the furnishing and decorating of their home, so that outwardly it was all his, yet she had succeeded somehow in superimposing her presence, so that all the time that he was there he was aware of it, of her heavy smell and her languor, weighing him down, swallowing him up.

He decided to go and see Betty. He always, whenever he felt particularly oppressed by Gulab, went to see Betty. Her flat was so light, modern, and airy; she herself so light, modern, and airy. Being with her was almost as good as being in England – which was the one place where he wanted most passionately to be.

6

There was a committee meeting in Har Dayal's house. There were always committee meetings in his house. 'I will be so busy this morning,' he would say with a happy sigh. Shakuntala, on such occasions, would loiter round the study door or sit down on the stairs to watch the various committee members arriving. As they all came, one by one, driving up in their big cars, Daddyji would come rushing out of the study to greet them, full of affection and enthusiasm – 'My *dear* fellow!' And one he would embrace and another greet with joined hands, formally but radiantly courteous, and a third – a Minister perhaps – would be received with a self-deprecating deference which might even extend to the touching of feet ('such an honour', he would say with downcast eyes and a modest smile). Each new arrival seemed to plunge him into an ecstasy of happiness and he managed to make each one feel equally important and welcome. There was always an atmosphere as of an exciting party: the committee members, standing about in Har Dayal's study, joked and laughed with one another; even men who usually had very little to say to one another became, under the enthusiasm of his welcome, good friends. Shakuntala found all this very exciting. Sometimes her father, as he came rushing out to welcome another arrival, would draw her close, his arm affectionately about her shoulder, to say, 'Have you met my little girl, hm?' And he always managed to whisper something private and nice to her before disappearing again inside – '*So* busy, darling' or '*What* a morning,' casting his eyes up to the ceiling and then at once breaking again into a radiant smile for his visitors.

Even after the study door had closed and the meeting begun, Shakuntala continued to sit on the stairs. She thought about the various committee members who had come to attend today's meeting and wondered what they had done important enough to enable them to sit on committees. She knew one or two of them – for instance, Professor Bhatnagar, who had been a professor of literature at Allahabad University and who was now something very important in the Ministry of Education. Since becoming something very important in the Ministry of Education, Professor Bhatnagar had worn only Indian dress – tight white jodhpurs and a knee-length fitted coat buttoned high up to the neck; though Shakuntala could remember the time when he was always dressed very smartly and meticulously in London suits with a flower in his buttonhole. Daddyji too had changed his style of dressing, Like Professor Bhatnagar, he had once been very fond of good suits and shirts; but now he mostly wore Indian dress.

Indeed, so did almost all the committee members who came to the house for meetings – at any rate, the more important ones. It was a change which it had taken her quite some time to get used to. Before – before '47 – all her father's friends had looked just like English gentlemen: but now they all looked like Indian Congressmen. The only one who had remained the same was Ram Nath Uncle. Once he had looked rather odd, compared to those other well-dressed gentlemen, for he never wore anything but loose white clothes of handspun cotton with, in the winter, a blanket slung over his shoulders. Now, however, they all dressed in white clothes of handspun cotton and blankets round their shoulders in place of their well-cut overcoats. But Ram Nath Uncle did not come with them to committee meetings. He was, she supposed, not important enough.

It was strange, that he should not be important enough. She had always thought of him as being very important. Though important, she at once realized, was not really quite the word to use of him. He never had been important in the sense that Professor Bhatnagar was now important. She sat on the stairs, her elbows on her knees, her face between her hands, thinking what it was that had always impressed her so about Ram Nath Uncle. She frowned because she was trying to think very clearly and honestly (she and her girl-friends at College had made it a cult to consider things very clearly and honestly).

Really there had never been anything very impressive about him. He was not elegant and charming and witty and cultured like Daddyji. He was small and thin and old and spoke in a weak, piping voice; and his clothes were not only simple, they were even shabby. But everybody knew that he had spent many years in prison, had addressed huge meetings, led processions, been beaten up by the police. Of course, all that was history now; it had happened before '47, when everything had been different. Today Ram Nath Uncle did not address meetings and nobody kept him in prison. Nor did he sit on committees with people like Professor Bhatnagar who had become important. He was different, Shakuntala thought, very different from these people. Perhaps that was what impressed her so – his differentness. She had heard it said that in '47 he had been offered a high position in the Government and had – she did not know why – refused it. Ordinary people did not refuse such things. You had to have, she thought, very high ideals to refuse such honours. Ram Nath Uncle was an Idealist; and even if you were nobody, as he now was, it was always a great thing to be an Idealist. A great and wonderful thing, she thought.

But her mother, passing along the first-floor passage, was shocked to see her sitting on the stairs. She called down, softly but urgently, 'Shakuntala, what are you doing?' to which Shakuntala replied, 'I am thinking quite hard.'

Madhuri stood at the top of the stairs, small and frail and disapproving. She clicked her tongue, she said: 'Get up at once – people have come to see your father, what will they think if they see you sitting there?'

'Oh,' Shakuntala said, and laughed, 'they are too busy with their Committee to be able to think.' But she got up and began to walk up the stairs towards her mother. 'Mummyji,' she said, 'is it true that Ram Nath Uncle refused to become a Minister?'

'I have been looking at your saris,' Madhuri said. 'Almost all of them are unpressed and many of them are torn at the edge.'

'I know. They tear so quickly – I always get my foot caught.'

'*My* saris do not tear,' Madhuri said, at once proud and reproving.

'Of course not,' Shakuntala replied with much affection. 'One only has to look at you; at once one can tell – this lady's saris *never* tear.' This was true. Madhuri was so neat and elegant. Shakuntala, with her rather wild hair, her well-developed shoulders and bosom, her bold eyes set in a square, healthy face, looked almost rough beside her. And Shakuntala was much darker than her mother: this was one of the things Madhuri regretted most in life – that her daughter had not inherited her own fair complexion. Her complexion had always been a great pride to her. A friend who had been abroad had once said to her, 'If you went to Europe, no one would believe you are Indian – you would be taken for Italian or Spanish.' She often remembered that and dwelt on it with satisfaction. But no one could take Shakuntala for Italian or Spanish.

'But is it true,' Shakuntala said, 'about Ram Nath Uncle?'

'What do I know,' her mother replied a trifle crossly. 'At least you can give them to press, what is the use of having them lying in your almira unpressed?'

'Because if it is true, he must be a great Idealist. I admire people with high Ideals very much. I think it is better to be a great Idealist than a Minister.'

'Please ask your Uncle's wife which she thinks is better,' Madhuri said. 'You are often silly in your ideas, Shakuntala, I had hoped that now you have finished College you would be more sensible. And *so* untidy,' she sighed, thinking again of those crumpled, torn saris. 'I do not know what is the use of a College education if you cannot keep your clothes tidy.'

'Mummyji, you are very materialistic.'

'Please forgive me,' Madhuri said, 'I have not had College education, I do not understand your long words.'

'But why are you cross? What have I done?'

'If someone had come out and seen you sitting on the stairs . . .'

'But what does it matter!'

'To you, perhaps no. But I wouldn't like to have people go away from my house and say that my daughter sits on the stairs.'

Har Dayal in his study benignly presided over his committee meeting. He was used to presiding over such meetings – only yesterday they had had a meeting to consider schemes for the advancement of literature in the regional languages and early next week there was to be a meeting to discuss arrangements for an exhibition of folk-art from the backward states. Today they were considering the erection of a monument in a public garden. There were six of them considering – Har Dayal, Professor Bhatnagar from the Ministry of Education, the Secretary to the Board of Developments, an Under-Secretary from the Ministry of Information and Broadcasting, a man from the Treasury and a deputy from the Income Tax office who sat tugging at a loose tooth and said nothing at all.

Har Dayal was keenly interested in all cultural matters and he enjoyed presiding over committees. He made indeed an excellent chairman, for he gave courteous, even deferential attention to all proposals and always managed to keep a fine balance between conflicting points of view. He was very tactful. But sometimes he could not help feeling that the members of the various committees on which he served were not too well chosen. They did not seem to be very much interested in or knowledgeable about the cultural matters they were gathered to discuss. And their aesthetic sense, reluctantly he had to admit, was often at fault.

He listened to the Under-Secretary making a proposal; he listened with an expression of great interest and affability but doubt gnawed at his heart. The Under-Secretary wished to erect a giant statue of a recently dead statesman. The statue was to be hollow inside and there were stairs leading up into the head. People were to climb up the stairs and when they arrived at the top they were to discover that the face had been laid out as a charming promenade: winding walks along the lips and between the teeth, fountains in the eyes, grottos in the nostrils . . .

'Yes,' said Har Dayal, 'a charming idea.'

'Naturally,' the Under-Secretary said modestly, 'it will need more working out.'

The man from the Treasury rapped his blotting-paper with his fingernail and said, 'The expense also must be considered!' There were always men from the Treasury at these committee meetings and this was all they ever said.

Har Dayal smiled and said, 'Of course, there is always the expense'; he addressed himself mainly to the man from the Income Tax office in the hope of drawing some response from him.

When Amrit came home to lunch, the committee meeting was still going on. Amrit said, 'Well, I cannot wait, I have work to do.' He was an administrative officer in a large British firm of paint manufacturers who were grooming him for a high executive position. He was part of their policy of gradually replacing British executives by Indian ones; and indeed he was very suitable for this purpose, as he had attended an English university and was also very English in all other respects, except in his complexion.

'I will ask them to bring your lunch at once,' Indira said, feeling rather flustered.

Amrit, washing his hands, said, 'But quickly, one-two-march.'

Shakuntala came wandering in while he and Indira were sitting down to lunch. She said, 'You might have waited for Daddyji, you know he is busy with a meeting.'

'Drat his meetings,' Amrit said. 'None of you seem to realize that there is also important work to be done in the world.'

'I did not know,' Shakuntala said, 'that your work is so important.'

Indira felt uncomfortable but Amrit answered with placid good humour, 'Now I have told you,' while he cut a piece of meat from his chop (English food was always served at lunch-time, Indian food at dinner).

Madhuri came in and said, 'Oh good, I am glad you have begun our food, you cannot wait for your father and then eat in a hurry; his will only be bad for your health.'

'I have to meet a man in the office at 2.30,' Amrit said. 'Quite a big chap.' Indira looked proud as she passed him the bread.

'Quite a big chap,' Shakuntala said, 'how can anyone be quite a big chap in business?' Amrit laughed uproariously. 'Not like the people Daddyji meets,' Shakuntala said unperturbed.

'Yes, those people are very good to do the talking,' Amrit said.

'And selling paint is doing the acting,' Shakuntala said with deep scorn.

'Oh, Shakuntala,' Indira said reproachfully, anxious eyes fixed on her husband.

'Quite right,' Amrit said. He picked up the remains of a chop and began to gnaw it ('excuse fingers,' he murmured automatically as he did so).

'Why has there been no letter from Raj for so long,' Madhuri said. She sat sideways on a chair at the opposite end of the long dining-table, watching her son eat.

'Daddyji's committees,' Amrit said, 'and all this Art and Culture and fiddle-faddle – '

'Fiddle what!' Shakuntala cried.

' – are very nice to keep old gentlemen busy but why do we pretend they serve any useful purpose? Mustard, Indira.'

'Shakuntala, please do not shout so loud,' Madhuri said. 'It is not nice in a well brought up girl.'

'Really, Amrit,' Shakuntala said, 'I do not think you understand anything. And also you have no sense of proportion.'

'No what?'

Indira said, 'Do you like this mustard or the other in a bottle, Amrit? Last week in Anand Stores I saw such nice mustard all ready made up in a bottle. The bottle looked pretty, too.'

'You think selling your stupid paints is more important than the things Daddyji does. You understand absolutely nothing and yet you think you are so clever.'

'My little sister is giving me a good strong lecture,' Amrit said comfortably. He leaned back in his chair, for he had finished eating. He looked solid and well-fed; since his marriage his chest and stomach had started to become quite expansive.

'What can I say to you when you have no *idea*. You are simply not aware.' At College she and her friends had divided people into those who were aware and those who were not. By 'aware' they meant aware of certain values which they themselves considered the most important in life. They would not have been able to define these values, but only thought of them as being connected with art, poetry with culture. For Shakuntala her father was the most aware person in the world.

'Eh?' Amrit inquired. He winked at Indira, who smiled back at him.

'We have not heard from him for over two weeks,' Madhuri complained.

'Who, Raj?' Amrit said. 'Oh, he is busy swotting for his tripos.' He laughed in a rather superior manner, having all that safely behind him.

'You have no ideals,' Shakuntala told him.

'But he could write at least one line, he knows I am anxious.'

'Ideals?' Amrit said. 'No thank you, that is a luxury I cannot afford. Ideals we can leave to people who have nothing better to do in life.'

'Wonderful!' Shakuntala cried, throwing back her head, her eyes flashing.

'For instance,' Amrit said in his rich, self-assured voice, 'There is Ram Nath Uncle who, so they tell me, is full of ideals. And please just tell me where they have brought him?'

'It is true,' Shakuntala said with heavy sarcasm, 'they have not brought him to the honour of selling paints. But if Ram Nath Uncle – '

'Ram Nath Uncle, Ram Nath Uncle,' Madhuri said, 'what is the matter with you today, Shakuntala? All morning I have heard nothing but Ram Nath Uncle from you, now it is enough.' Reference to that family had such an irritating effect on her. After it had been more or less understood ... not that she valued Gulab particularly high – on the contrary, Indira was by far the nicer girl and her connections were very good – but the slight to her son, that was what she could not forgive.

Amrit, though it was he more than anyone who had been the injured party, bore no resentment. He had laughed the whole matter off with a shrug that was not in the least an assumed bravado: he was too sure of his own value to allow his vanity to be hurt. 'I grant you,' he said, 'Ram Nath Uncle may be quite a decent, harmless old stick, but if you ask what has he made of his life, then what answer can you give?'

'May I peel you an orange, Amrit? These are so nice and juicy.'

'If I told you the answer,' Shakuntala said haughtily, 'you would not understand. Because you cannot understand what it is people with ideals and high principles and culture want out of life. For you only the monthly income is important. That is also why you speak like that about Daddyji's committees: because he does not do them for a monthly income but because he and the other people do them out of love and conviction and because they know that art and culture are the only important things in life.'

'What long words my little sister knows,' Amrit said, accepting a piece of orange from Indira.

The committee meeting had drawn to an end; and as always on such occasions, whether anything had been settled or not, Har Dayal felt a sense of satisfaction The committee had sat, deliberated, and finally declared the meeting at an end. It had thus completely fulfilled its function. Har Dayal felt pleasantly ready for his lunch. He beamed at the other members, who also looked satisfied with themselves, even the man from the Income Tax office who all the way through had said nothing. For this, however, no one blamed him: because it was not what they said or decided that really mattered but the mere fact that they were there at all. A committee meeting of important people was an essential step in the erection of a monument in a public garden; and they were the important people without whose coming together nothing further could be done. Well, they had come together; now things could go ahead.

Har Dayal walked his visitors out of the house, one arm affectionately round the shoulders of Professor Bhatnagar, the other round those of the Under-Secretary. They were all in high good humour. Their chauffeurs jumped to open the doors of their cars for them. Har Dayal stood on the front veranda and waved and smiled sweetly. He felt a little tired – these committee meetings were always rather exhausting – but also exhilarated. As he turned back into the house, he hummed a little tune out of *Tosca*.

'At last,' Madhuri said to him.

Amrit said, 'We have been hearing all about your devotion to the Public Cause.'

Har Dayal laughed, but he was not ill-pleased. Nowadays he liked to think of himself as devoted to the Public Cause; just as before – before '47 – he had liked to think of himself as upholding private values in the face of too great a devotion to the Public Cause.

'From your daughter,' Amrit said.

Har Dayal shook his forefinger at Shakuntala: 'What have you been telling about me, you naughty darling?'

'Only how great and wonderful you are and what a silly duffer I am,' said Amrit.

'It is true, isn't it!' Shakuntala cried. But she was laughing. She felt safer and therefore less defiant now that her father was here; because he, she knew, was on her side, believed in the things she herself believed in.

46

'Darling, you must not be intolerant,' her father told her, smiling a conspiratorial little smile at her.

'She has been rating me very soundly,' Amrit said. Indira laughed, but she was feeling rather restless: she was keeping an eye on the clock and knew it was time for him to go back to the office. He must not miss his appointment with this big chap who was coming to see him; such appointments were important for their future.

Har Dayal clicked his tongue at Shakuntala and said, 'That is no way to treat an elder brother.' He caught her hand and pressed it: 'As a punishment I am going to take you with me tomorrow to a party at an American lady's house.'

'Oh, Daddyji,' Shakuntala said in high delight.

7

Ram Nath had a letter from his son which he did not wish to show to his wife. Unfortunately Lakshmi had already seen the envelope so when she gave Ram Nath his tea she asked at once, 'What does Narayan say?'

Ram Nath drank his tea, his eyes stared blankly ahead over the rim of the cup.

'Give me the letter,' Lakshmi said. He came out of what appeared to be a reverie to say, 'What letter?'

'What letter! My son's letter – what letter!'

'Yes,' Ram Nath said, drinking more tea. He thought about the letter. Narayan had written 'Please find me a wife.' That was why Lakshmi must not see it. 'I do not know where I have put it,' he said blankly.

'You do not know where – ' As so often, he left her speechless with indignation. They had been married for forty-five years, but she had never ceased to be bewildered by his vagaries and impertinences. In her youth she had appealed to his mother, to her mother: 'But why can he not behave like other people? What is it he wants?' and she had cried because she had not known what to do. Now that she was old, she no longer cried, but she still did not know what to do. Sometimes she would reach a conclusion of despair which she then imparted to Uma – 'He is simply mad. For the sins committed in my past lives, I am married to a madman.'

'Please go away now,' he said.

'First give me the letter.'

'I told you: I do not know where it is.'

'At least tell me what is written in it, what does my son say, you will tell me that at least?'

'But certainly. He says I am very well, I hope you also are very well, please give my respects to my noble mother.' But he felt sorry for her. He would like to have given her the letter: he knew it would have kept her happily brooding all day. She would have read it once, twice, three times (very slowly and laboriously because it was written in English and she knew little English). Then she would have read between the lines. She would have read there that Narayan was very unhappy and discontented, that he pitied himself and pitied his mother and cursed his father because he had done nothing for him. By night-time she would have worked herself up to a fine state of indignation and could have gone to bed quite happy.

'Oh!' Lakshmi cried in despair and rage. But she knew that, for the time being, it was hopeless. She would return to the attack later and then she would keep it up for days. She might or might not achieve her object that way, but at least pride would be partially satisfied. 'There is a man waiting to see you.'

'I do not wish to see him.'

'It was I who told him to come.'

'And it is I who tell him to go.'

'He has brought his son. He wants you to do something for his son.'

'Tell him,' Ram Nath said rather gleefully, for this was her own favourite weapon that he was using, 'that I cannot even do anything for my own son, what then shall I do for his.'

'There is no need to tell him so. All the world knows it, much to your and also my shame.' But she was always encouraging people who approached her to lay their problems before her husband. This soothed her vanity, for it proved that he was still, after all, someone important. Even though they were poor and lived in a shabby flat in a shabby lower-middle-class district and held no official position.

'Then let him go home. And you may go with him if you like.' Ram Nath did not like people to come to him to ask for letters of recommendation or favour for their relations or a word from him to secure them a job. He would say to them, 'Look, my friend, why should I do this thing for you when I do not even know you?' to which they would reply fervently, 'You are such a good man, such a great man, God will reward you for your kindness to us.' He was aware that a word or a letter from him might make a lot of difference to them. His name was known, and in a system which rested mostly on personalities and personal recommendations it could act at least as a passport to attention. But he disliked this system and saw no reason to support it.

48

'You have no heart,' Lakshmi told him. And she meant it: she was sure that he had no heart because he never listened to her wishes. Even when she had first come to him as a young bride, he had never listened to her wishes.

'That is why I thank God every day that he has given me such a good kind wife with so much heart.'

'How can I tell the poor man to go away when he is sitting there with his son asking for you?'

'Why did you tell him to come?'

'Because I had hoped that you might expiate your sin of not serving your own son by serving the sons of others at least.'

'I can only hope for expiation through the good deeds of my wife.' All the time he was thinking of Narayan's letter. 'Please find me a wife: I am beginning to discover that I need one rather urgently.' Narayan did not mean his mother to see this letter, Ram Nath knew. Lakshmi would go about it too vehemently, finding him the wrong kind of wife.

'And since you will not go away, I will,' he said, and got up. He wanted to go out, he wanted to think what to do about Narayan; perhaps he would go and see Uma.

'Where are you going?'

'I am retiring to the forest for contemplation. I feel my old age upon me.'

'This man is sitting with his son in the passage waiting for you.' She spoke triumphantly, for Ram Nath's room led straight out into the passage and he would not be able to avoid him.

The man jumped to his feet as soon as Ram Nath came out. The son remained seated, till his father gave him a sharp push. 'Good morning, brother,' Ram Nath said in a genuinely friendly voice and walked straight past him out into the street.

'What are you staring at!' Lakshmi shouted at the visitor. 'You cannot speak with him today – he is in contemplation, no one can reach him when he is like this.' She stood in the dark passage, furious with her husband, who seemed to win every time. In all their life together it had always been he who had won. That, she thought bitterly, was why she now had to live in this shabby dirty house with neighbours who were not only far beneath her in social status but, worse, did not even realize their inferiority. She stood in that little passage and seethed with indignation – first, against her husband, who had brought her to this, then against her neighbours, whose whole essence, so it seemed to her, was concentrated in the red stains of betelnut juice splashed on the wall, the raucous hymn-singing of a sweeper engaged in picking up squashed pieces of banana and orange-peel from the staircase, in the smell of South Indian cooking from the flat above.

The street was like the house: narrow, crowded, full of life and food. Everywhere there were little food-stalls – freshly made fritters, chunks of sweetmeats, fruit piled high – people stood around, drank tea out of brass tumblers, chewed betel leaves and spat the juice like blood, talked work and religion and philosophy, squatted on the pavement and threw dice. Ram Nath threaded his way through, frail and alone in his white cotton clothes. Everyone knew him and many respectfully greeted him. He was, however, too preoccupied to notice. He was thinking about the man who sat in his house with his son; many such men came to him with many such sons. The sons always seemed very large and very stupid; they stood with mouth open and huge hands dangling by their sides and pretended not to hear while their fathers were explaining what clever, talented boys they were. Sometimes they had to be nudged to show some signs of life.

Narayan was small and spare and quick. He had never asked his father to introduce him to anyone and would probably have refused if Ram Nath had offered to do so. He never consulted anyone about what he intended to do, but only announced his decisions when he had made them: 'I shall become a doctor,' had been the first; the second, 'I am joining a Community Health project and shall live and work in small villages in backward areas.' Now he wanted a wife; and asking his father to find one was, as far as Ram Nath could remember, the first thing he had ever asked him to do.

So naturally his father wanted to do the best he could. Only it was not easy, as Narayan himself had pointed out: 'I cannot offer a very easy or pleasant or amusing life here.' There would be no society of her own class and education for the girl; no modern comforts; and often she would be alone because Narayan's duties took him to a scattered series of outlying villages. She would have to live through long, hot, dusty, empty days and lie in the nights listening to the jackals howling on the barren plains. Yes, Ram Nath thought, he would have to choose the girl very carefully. She must be made fully aware of what sort of life was in store for her, so that she might be able to face it in imagination beforehand; consent, that is, to that life willingly and in full awareness, not find herself suddenly and unwillingly in it.

That was a hard thing for women, he thought, to have their lives warped by circumstances to which they could not submit because they could not or would not understand them. As his own wife's had been. When he thought about her like that, he felt quite tender towards her. She was one sad example of a girl who had been led into a marriage under false pretences. Only at that time who was to have known they were false? It had all been planned with such certainty: after their marriage, Ram Nath, then seventeen years old, was to go to Cambridge and when he came back he would start a lawyer's practice in which, with all the influence and great properties of his family behind him, he would do very well. His wife – that had been held for certain, his parents-in-law had been quite satisfied about it – would be able to lead the sort of life she and all her female relations had always led – live in a large house with many relatives and many servants, gossip and make pickles and bring up children, go to weddings in costly saris, weighed down with the jewellery she had brought from her father's house. That was what she had been prepared for; she had not been prepared for a husband who gave up his career before he had even entered on it, forfeited his property – and hers – and went in and out of prison for the sake of a cause for which she herself could find neither understanding nor sympathy.

Ram Nath got on a bus. He wanted to see Uma, discuss the problem of Narayan's wife with her. His sister was the one person with whom he ever consulted about anything. And that only recently. In his younger days he had been like Narayan: he had come to his decisions in solitude. But now he found it rather pleasant to talk to her; they knew one another so well, shared so many memories, it was almost like talking to himself. Or perhaps, he thought, he was getting self-indulgent; wanting to lean on someone else in his old age instead of standing upright and alone as he had done all his life; pampering himself with gossip instead of disciplining himself in solitary thought. He smiled a little at the thought, finding himself rather ridiculous.

Uma was not at home. He sat down on the stairs which were marble and had once, in the days of Uma's parents-in-law, been magnificent. Everything had been magnificent in those days: stained glass, rich heavy carpets, silk cushions, Moghul miniatures. Gradually, in the years between 1918 and 1947, as Uma and her husband went in and out of jail, forfeited most of their property to the Government, recklessly spent the rest in the course of campaigns and voluntary work, the furnishings of the house had disappeared, the house itself fallen into decay.

Ram Nath sat on the stairs. He felt rather tired and old, and perhaps also a little sad. He thought about his brother-in-law, Uma's husband. It was difficult not to think about him when one came into this house, though he had been dead now for many years.

Bachani came and said, 'Your Honour here? Sitting on the stairs? Oh,' she said, 'oh.' She really was shocked. She had always honoured him very highly and there he was, looking so alone and old and almost humble, like a poor man.

'I will sit here for a little while,' he said. Bachani, for him, was part of the house. Besides Uma, she was the only one who was left. It had been so different once. His memory did not regret, only stated a fact: the fact that once the house had been full of people and activity, there had been meetings and so much talk and business. They had had an office with a typewriter and a duplicator and cupboards full of files and forms and pamphlets. There had even been a regular secretary – a young man just passed from the M.A. class in College, very earnest and enthusiastic – who had sat there all day and often a good part of the night too; indeed, in the end he had brought his bed in because it had not been worth his while to go home.

'Let me bring tea for your Honour, tea and sweetmeats,' Bachani said, half pleading.

He gave no sign of having heard, only got up and began to wander about. He wandered into what in the days of Uma's parents-in-law had been the reception room, a room with a vast frescoed ceiling and carved marble pillars; it was now furnished with a few stringbeds and cane-stools and an earthenware water-cooler. In one corner a sadhu in an orange robe sat on a mat and ate with enjoyment from a brass tray.

Bachani whispered, 'He came yesterday from Nagpur, a very holy man.'

People were always coming to Uma's house. They came from all over India – old Congress workers, holy men, widows on pilgrimages, musicians from the South. They stayed a little while and then they went away again. Often Uma was hardly aware that they were there. The house was so large, it did not really matter if someone rolled out a mat in some corner to sleep on; and there was always enough atta and dal, what difference did it make if one person ate or ten?

Ram Nath thought of his brother-in-law. Uma's husband had been a very large man, and he loomed large in one's memory. He had been an intellectual, a skilled economist and a subtle political thinker, but it was difficult to think of him as such because he had always looked so much more like a dacoit chief from some wild mountain tribe. He had been a man of vast chest and thighs, with a wild crop of hair and a short, tough tangle of beard. Whenever he could, he wore nothing but an ankle-length cloth wrapped round his waist and huge farmer sandals on his feet.

'At least rest,' Bachani urged, walking behind him, 'sit down and rest – or else what will She say to me when She comes home and hears that your Honour did not even take rest in our house?'

Ram Nath absent-mindedly stirred his foot in a few flakes of plaster which had dropped from the ceiling and lay there on the floor. Bachani said, 'That sweeper fellow – he does nothing, never sweeps, never cleans, I do not know why we keep him in the house. O Pattu!' she called, energetically but not very hopefully for she knew the sweeper would be sitting under a tree in the garden listening to the cook reading from the *Ramayana*.

There had always been the clatter of the typewriter and voices raised in argument, feet up and down the stairs, quarrels and committee meetings, the telephone ringing; and always, booming through and above everything, the voice of Uma's husband, which was not so much a voice as – whether in laughter or anger, both of which were frequent with him – a roar.

From upstairs came the voice of the Swamiji, raised in song. He sang shakily but lustily and accompanied himself on the harmonium. The Swamiji had come to the house nine years ago and had never gone away again. He had a little room to himself and his food was sent to him very punctually. Uma found him a great spiritual comfort.

'Tell her,' Ram Nath said to Bachani, 'that I came to speak with her.' He did not want to stay any longer. There was really not much use in speaking to her about Narayan. His call for a wife, Ram Nath thought, is answered only by the prayers of the Swamiji; and he would not find that very satisfactory.

Bachani pleaded with him to sit, to eat, to drink, but Ram Nath did not even hear her. In this, thought Bachani with a sigh of resignation, they are alike, He and She: they are so obstinate, one can plead till one's tongue drops out and still they do not hear.

8

Uma had pushed armchairs and coffee-table out of the way, set the new servant to cooking in the kitchen and now sat cross-legged on the floor, singing to Gulab and Ravi. While she sang, she beat the rhythm out on her thigh; often she forgot the words and sometimes the tunes and then she would either improvise or pass without hesitation into another song. She thus passed quite naturally from lullaby to hymn to peasant folksong. Sometimes Ravi and Gulab also sang, and Uma would go into loud laughter and hug and kiss them both. Altogether, between his mother and his grandmother, Ravi was almost stifled with love; which he much enjoyed, his cheeks and large eyes glowed with happiness. Gulab also radiated a great contentment; stretched on the floor, supporting herself on one elbow, she looked sleek and luxurious with satisfaction.

'Mama,' Gulab said, when Uma had paused in her singing for a moment and was hugging Ravi's head against her bosom, 'why did you not come on Wednesday? I was so sad that you sent only Bachani. You know I always want to see you.'

'My darling, I had to go and see your Uncle.'

'Why, Mama? You know on Wednesdays he goes – on Wednesdays I like to see you here in the morning, why did you have to go to Uncle on a Wednesday?'

Uma kissed the back of Ravi's neck and then cradled him on her lap; she looked down into his face with great love. But her laughter had gone, she had become very serious.

'You can go to Uncle every day,' pouted Gulab.

'My daughter, I had to speak with him very particularly.'

'What about?'

'My sweetest,' Uma said gravely, 'about you.' The moment had now come.

Gulab, however, laughed. She could not understand why anyone should have to talk about her. 'Oh, Mama – ' she said protestingly and a little embarrassed. She put out her hand and tweaked Ravi's ear.

Uma remained grave. She said, 'I wanted to speak with Uncle before I came to see you today.'

Gulab became uneasy. She hoped nothing unpleasant had happened.

'Yes,' Uma said, 'today I must speak with you on a very important matter.'

Gulab was now more than uneasy. She hated to talk about important matters. All she wanted was to sit with her mother and be happy and comfortable – eating, singing a bit, languidly talking about nothing in particular.

Uma very gently removed Ravi from her lap. She got up and began to pace the room. There was a frown on her face; she said, 'This room is so small, and it has too much furniture.'

'Go, darling,' Gulab said, 'get Mama's comb, I want to comb your hair, my sweetest.'

'Now, my child,' Uma said, striking her fist in the palm of her hand just as she had done when she had addressed public meetings, 'why do you not come home with me, you and my Ravi?'

Ravi came back with the comb and sat down expectantly in front

54

of his mother. She began to comb his hair, making curls with her fingers.

'For today, you mean?' Gulab said. She hoped her mother meant only for today: she did not want to face any larger issues.

'No,' Uma said mercilessly, 'always.'

Gulab twisted a very fine fat curl and leaned back to study it; Ravi looked at her face, his eyes asked, 'Do I look nice?'

'You must come,' Uma said. 'I talked with your uncle and he also says you must come. It is so easy,' she lied. She knew it was not easy at all. It had been very difficult for her, it would be worse for Gulab

'You look beautiful, beautiful,' Gulab told Ravi. Uma also said, 'Such lovely hair, only my own sweet daughter had such lovely hair; never have I seen such hair on any other child.'

'Daddy says I must have a hair-cut,' Ravi announced complacently.

'What! before the Shaving Ceremony has been performed?'

'He does not wish for Ravi's head to be shaved,' Gulab said in a low voice.

'He does not wish,' her mother said. 'Who is he not to wish! Does he want my darling's beauty to be spoiled?'

'He says,' Gulab said, looking down into her lap, 'it is a barbaric custom.' She said this as a quote: she was not really sure what barbaric meant.

'Everyone knows that unless the head is shaved in youth the growth of the hair will not be luxuriant. And now he comes and tells us it is a barbaric custom.'

'Oh look, Mama,' Ravi cried, 'tears are coming from your eyes.' There were only three tears: three very large round ones, two out of one eye and one out of the other. They dropped slowly from Gulab's lashes on to Ravi's face. She wiped his cheek with her hand.

Uma knelt on the floor, her arms round Gulab. She rocked her to and fro rather violently and said, 'I told you it was easy, easy, so why do you cry?'

After a little while during which she let herself be rocked, Gulab said, 'Please go and see if the servant has finished cooking, I am so hungry.'

'Why do you cry?' Uma repeated. But she went out into the kitchen and, seizing the pan from the servant, said, 'He is just a fool.' Very expertly she tossed onions in ghee, then added potatoes with finely cut chilis. The servant stood by, with his arms hanging by his sides and a blank expression on his face. When Gulab came, in her tight orange blouse and blue sari, he stared at her fixedly but his expression remained blank.

'How beautiful it smells,' Gulab said, beginning to look happy again.

Uma told the servant, 'Now see you do not burn it.' Back in the living-room she said, 'Where do you find such servants? He is an idiot, what use is he to you.' And then she said, 'You need only pack your clothes and jewels and you can come with me, you and the little one.' It hurt her to see Gulab's face slipping out of contentment again, but she had to be ruthless.

'Where shall we come with you, Nani?' Ravi asked.

'There is no difficulty. I and your uncle too will look after you. No harm will ever come to you, we will see to this, and you will be happy.' She stroked her hand over Ravi's hair and then pressed his head against her thigh. 'You can come today, what is to stop you? I will help you now to pack and we will take a tonga and go away together.'

'No,' Gulab said in great agony.

'Why not? You do not love your mother any more, you do not care to come with her to your old home?' She knew very well that Gulab cared only too much, but she had to insist.

'Please, Mama,' Ravi said in excitement, 'let's go with Nani in a tonga.'

'You want her always to be alone in that house, with only servants and strangers, longing all day and night for her daughter and the little one?'

Gulab's face was turned away. She said nothing and wished she did not have to hear.

'Is this the love you have for your mother?' Uma said sternly. Ravi understood that something strange was going on, so he burst into tears and said, 'I want to go in a tonga.'

'Now see what you have done!' Gulab shouted at her mother. She jumped up and caught Ravi in her arms; she was very glad of an excuse for feigned anger.

'You *shall* go in a tonga, you shall,' Uma said, stamping her foot.

'Yes, tomorrow you shall go,' Gulab said, kneeling on the floor in front of him and holding him tight against her. 'Tomorrow I will take you – I will take you to India Gate; yes, we will go to India Gate and eat ice cream.' She looked over his shoulder but defiantly refused to meet her mother's eye.

'You shall come to your Nani's house,' Uma said, looking at them both from the other side of the room. 'Do you want to come to your Nani's house? I will buy you a big tub of ice cream, you shall eat it with a wooden spoon. Pistachio ice cream. Every day I will cook carrot halwa for you when you come to my house, and I will put a

56

swing in the garden so you can sit all day and Bachani will swing you.'

'Leave him alone!' Gulab cried. Ravi was sobbing loudly and uncontrollably by this time, past caring for tonga or ice cream or for swings in the garden.

'Is the child always to be shut up here in this chicken-house with nothing to look at but this *furniture*!' with which Uma angrily kicked the leg of the table.

'I told you – tomorrow I will take him to India Gate, just he and I will go, and we will be very happy!'

'Tcha!' Uma shouted in great contempt, 'happy! you know too well you will never be happy, not you nor the little one, till you leave here and come to live with me!'

Gulab got up from her knees and led Ravi into the bathroom where she washed his face. She pleaded, 'Please, sweet mine, please do not cry any more, Mama cannot bear it.' He tried hard to control himself, but the sobs came out of his chest in spite of him.

Uma sat down on Esmond's gaily striped little divan which was so dainty that it looked as if it must give way under her. She blew her nose very forcibly and frowned. But when Gulab came back, she spoke to her gently; she said, 'Not like that, daughter. We must not speak about it like that.'

Gulab pretended not to hear. She sat down on the floor and took down her hair for Ravi to play with.

'Why do you hurt yourself so?' Uma said in the same gentle tone. 'You know it is necessary for you to go away now, you cannot live here any longer. Please be brave, my darling. Come with me.'

Gulab pretended even harder not to hear. Her fingers fumbled with her heavy plait of hair, undoing the strands three by three.

'It is I your mother who am telling you this. Would I lead you into a sin?'

Gulab undid the last strand and then she shook her head, so that the hair opened out and came tumbling forward over her shoulders, cascading down her arms, wave upon blue-black wave.

'For a whole day I prayed and I bathed in the Jumna and then I had reassurance from God that it is no sin. On the contrary, it is your duty now to go.'

'Can we eat? I am hungry and my Ravi also.' She called the servant to spread a mat on the floor and bring the food. Ravi was playing with her hair, he crept underneath it and let it fall like a warm cloak over his face and body. It was very thick, strong, rather coarse hair, each wave shining separately with oil.

They ate in silence. The servant stood by the door and his eyes were fixed on Gulab's hair. When they had finished, he brought them water and they poured it over their hands, and it was only then that Uma started again.

'Listen, child, I will tell you the truth. Why should I not tell you the truth, since we are one, you and I. Listen, I also was afraid, just as you are, I thought it is not possible, she cannot leave him, he is her Husband, how can she leave him? But then after prayer and fasting and bathing in the Jumna I learned differently and now I know that it is your duty.'

'Leave me alone,' Gulab said in a low sulky voice. 'I am happy, why can you not leave me alone.'

'You are happy,' Uma repeated derisively.

'Of course I am happy.' She caught Ravi's face between her hands and kissed him on the eyes, nose, mouth. 'With this pearl, this jewel, this precious gift.'

'Yes, and how often can you enjoy him? For five minutes, for ten minutes, when his father is away from the house, you must steal your pleasure with him like a thief.'

'He is *my* child,' Gulab said almost fiercely. 'It is me he loves.'

'Can you take him into your bed in the night, can you give him the food on which he will grow strong, can you sing to him the hymns which he must learn?'

'He is my child.'

'He has to sleep in a bed like a cage and in the man's room – if he wakes and cries in the night, the mother cannot come to him. Is that the way for a child to grow up strong and healthy and happy!'

Gulab said almost in despair, 'But he is strong and healthy and happy; Mama, he is, you know he is.'

'I know nothing. And what is this food he is made to eat, *boiled* food that I would not give even to a pariah dog, and not a drop of pure ghee to be found in the house.'

'Ghee is too heavy for a child,' Gulab murmured, so unconvincingly that she expected nothing better than to be ignored.

'And he is never given massage with oil because the father does not wish it, and now also I hear that his head is not to be shaved as it should be . . .'

'These are all modern scientific ideas.'

'You are just an owl,' Uma said decisively.

Ravi gathered up all his mother's hair and walked round with it to bring it over one shoulder and so wind it round her throat.

'Who is he to come and teach us modern scientific ideas? What does he know about our children and how they have to be tended in our country and our climate?'

'Leave me alone,' Gulab said; 'leave me alone.'

'It is easy to say "leave me alone," but if you do not care for yourself and for your own health and happiness, at least think of your child. Why are you so selfish?'

'Why do you speak to me like that, Mama!' Then she called for the servant, though she did not want anything. When he came, she said, 'You have not dusted in this room today, everything is filthy,' which rather surprised him because before she had not cared about this. However, he began listlessly to flap a duster about the room.

Uma, sitting square and solid on the divan with her knees apart, reviewed the position. Perhaps she had gone too far: but then, she thought, it was always better to go too far than not far enough. So she decided to press on further, she said, 'And also, I am your mother, if you are selfish about your own child, I cannot be selfish about you – stop that now!' she shouted at the servant.

'Let him dust, the room must be clean.'

'If I had my way with this room, I would make it so clean that not one bit of furniture would remain in it. Then perhaps one could begin to live and breathe here. Go away, I told you!' The servant stood with the duster suspended and gazed dully into space.

'Perhaps it is not enough that he is an idiot, he is also deaf,' Uma said.

'Go, go,' Gulab shouted at him, 'go then, you heard what she said!'

'Do not let him upset you,' Uma said when he had gone. 'You should never let the servants upset you.'

'Mama, make it into a plait again,' Ravi said. She gathered her hair together and quickly her fingers worked down the length of it, folding the strands into each other. Her eyes were very large and melancholy, she stared straight ahead.

'If you do not care for yourself or for your son, then it is I who must care for you both. I will talk with your husband, I will tell him, "I am taking her away." '

Gulab looked at her, shocked and frightened, and she said in a low voice, 'You must not,' very intensely.

'What else is there for me to do? I cannot sit and see my children suffer because of him.'

'We do not suffer, you are wrong.'

'Please do not try to deceive your mother. My darling,' she said, becoming soft again, 'have I ever said one word to you before, have you ever before heard me speak against your husband?'

Gulab raised her eyes to her mother's face and she smouldered with defiance and unhappiness. 'Why should you speak against him?'

'Because,' Uma answered directly and loudly, throwing back her head, 'he is no good.'

Ravi said, 'Who is no good?'

'What has he ever done to you, he has taken nothing from you.'

'He has taken my daughter from me and made her unhappy, is that not enough?'

'Who, the servant?' Ravi said. 'I do not like him, he never puts enough sugar and he is not nice.'

'I am not, *not*,' Gulab said, urgently and unconvincingly.

'And we all know,' Uma went on ruthlessly, 'the whole world knows that he goes to other women.'

Gulab flashed, 'Only to white women,' before she could stop herself. She never, as far as she could help it, thought about Esmond's infidelities, but when she did she always quickly drew comfort from the fact that they were only with white women. This made it somehow less humiliating.

'Oh, my darling daughter, my child,' Uma said in a sudden passionate appeal, 'please do not talk any more but only come away with me, come away.' But she saw that it would not be easy to move Gulab. She was as blindly and as unreasonably adamant as she had been five years ago, when no one could stop her from marrying Esmond.

9

The lady who gave the party lived in a house which, in its interior decorating, very much resembled Esmond's. This was no wonder, for it was he who had helped her in doing it up. He helped all the ladies of his acquaintance with their interior decorating; he had such a flair for that sort of thing. He chose the textiles, the rugs, mats and carpets, the knick-knacks. The things he chose were all traditionally and typically Indian and gave just the right, the fashionable touch of folk-art to the drawing-room: bold bright motifs from Orissa for the textiles, South Indian grass-mats, huge Naga hats for lampshades, Tibetan anklets converted into ashtrays. And they were so wonderfully cheap, too, Esmond would say, 'Now, we won't go to any of these New Delhi shops, we'll go straight off to the city where with a bit of bargaining we can get everything ridiculously cheap.' Since Esmond did not possess a car of his own, the lady whom he was helping would send hers for him and off they would go. And what fun it all was. Esmond really did lead one right into the city, into narrow lanes crammed with stalls full of – oh, the loveliest loveliest things, and everything so very Indian and picturesque. It was all perhaps a little overwhelming – so much noise and smell, so many beggars, such *very* narrow lanes – and the ladies would not really have cared to find themselves there alone. But with Esmond along it was quite all right. He seemed perfectly at home here – of course, he had been in India a long time and had an Indian wife and spoke such fluent Hindustani. He could really talk to these people like one of themselves. And he didn't stand any nonsense about prices either. He was quite an expert bargainer, so that going out with him turned out to be a real saving. Afterwards, when they returned to New Delhi, tired but triumphant and laden with bargains, Esmond would usually be asked to stay for lunch.

Shakuntala, arriving at the party with her father, was much impressed by the way the room had been arranged. She could not at first take in all the details but she gathered a general impression of colour and gaiety. Everything, she saw at once, was very modern, just like the pictures of interiors she had seen in foreign magazines. She could not have imagined a more fitting background to a fashionable party.

Most of the people there seemed to be Europeans, large men in good suits and tall ladies with narrow hips and narrow faces, smoking cigarettes. There were also a few Indians, some of whom Shakuntala knew: for instance, the two Billimoria sisters, skinny, intense Parsi girls who dressed fashionably though rather untidily and talked very quickly in excited high-pitched voices. Shakuntala did not like them particularly. She felt at once that they were trying too hard to be popular, which jarred in contrast to the easy and almost casually friendly tone of the rest of the party. Daddyji, on the other hand, was just right. He must have been the oldest person there, but he was not in the least out of place or incongruous. He was the only one in Indian dress – long, buttoned coat and white jodhpurs – and this gave him a special distinction. All the ladies made a great fuss of him, he was surrounded by a little admiring circle, and of course he was as usual terribly polite and charming. 'I have brought my little girl along,' he kept saying, his arm in Shakuntala's, and even when he was swept away from her, he always managed to smile and wave at her from out of his circle of admirers. Shakuntala did not mind being left alone, she was far too interested in everything to feel shy or embarrassed; besides, there were always plenty of people who came up to talk to her, saying, 'So you are the great Har Dayal's daughter.'

There were cocktails, and Shakuntala, tasting one, thought she liked it. Someone also offered her a cigarette, which she took and smoked fairly successfully. She had smoked before, at College very secretly, but this was the first time in public. When Daddyji saw her, he shook his finger at her from the other side of the room and then he gave her a great sweet wink. All the ladies round him laughed, they looked from father to daughter and were delighted. Shakuntala also laughed and the man who had given her the cigarette, a large red Englishman now squatting informally on the side of her armchair, said, 'I hope I shan't be getting into trouble with your Daddy.'

The hostess came sweeping down on them with a plate of saltsticks and she told the Englishman, 'Now, can I rely on you to look after Miss – er – ?'

Shakuntala said, 'Please call me Shakuntala,' and the hostess, staring at her with great naked blue eyes like hard-boiled eggs, said, 'Isn't that sweet.'

The big red Englishman said, 'May I also call you Shak – Shak – '

'Shakuntala,' said Shakuntala with a laugh; 'if you like.' She was really enjoying herself, she loved this free atmosphere with men and women talking to one another quite naturally and everybody laughing and being witty. She thought, they know much better than we do how to enjoy themselves. But the most laughter always came from where Daddyji was.

'And what do you do with yourself nowadays, Shak – Shak – I don't think I'll ever get it.'

'I have just finished my College education – Shakuntala. I was named after a very famous heroine in Sanskrit drama, the "Shakuntala" of Kalidasa.'

'Well, that's something I've learned today, anyway,' said the Englishman.

'What have you learned?' asked another Englishman, leaning over from the other side of Shakuntala's chair.

The two Billimoria sisters swooped down on Shakuntala, shrieking, 'What a lovely sari, wherever did you get it!' Both were smoking cigarettes which they held far away from them, back from their bodies, their forefingers perpetually tapping to flick off ash.

'Yes, it is rather nice,' said the second Englishman, scrutinizing Shakuntala's sari.

'Lovely!' shrieked the two sisters and bared their teeth in a terrific smile at the Englishman who, however, did not respond.

'What I mean is,' said the big red Englishman, 'that we ought to be learning something all the time.'

'Of course,' Shakuntala said gravely. She wondered whether this was the beginning of an intellectual conversation.

'Like your name and this famous play,' said the Englishman. 'Here we are living in this country of yours and we just don't know a damn thing about it. I think that's a shame.'

'We have a very ancient Culture,' Shakuntala said.

The Billimoria sisters cried, 'These days, everybody must be modern, how else are we to make progress!'

'I'd like to learn something about it all,' said the Englishman, but before Shakuntala could answer, the hostess had stepped forward and clapped her hands for silence. She announced, 'One minute please, everybody! Our dear friend Mr Har Dayal has kindly consented to give us a recital of a poem he has translated himself from the Sanskrit!'

There was clapping as Daddyji got ready to recite, smiling all round first. The Billimoria sisters clapped the loudest, they stuck their cigarettes between their lips so as to have the use of both hands and clapped very briskly with hands held high in the air.

When Daddyji had smiled all round, he became quite serious. He waited for a short time till it was very very quiet, and then he began to recite:

> O swollen hath the mango, sprouted and budded and
>   bloomed!
> O swollen hath our love, sprouted and budded and
>   bloomed!

He recited, as always, beautifully, with much expression. And he looked so distinguished, with his bush of grey hair and his large horn-rimmed spectacles and the long coat which made him rather taller than he was. Shakuntala was very proud of him. She looked round the audience and saw that most of them were looking down at the tips of their own feet; she thought this was a pity because one ought to look at Daddyji as well as hear him when he was reciting, he put so much expression into his face and gestures to suit the words.

> And do thy thoughts, O Lord of hearts,
> Ne'er fly to me
> Who sit and long, and long for thee?
> Seduc'd by thy arts
> I pine in love's valley
> Where thou didst once dally,
> 'Midst orange blossoms that cloud the clear sky
> As the tears cloud my eye.

Of course, she knew the poem very well. Daddyji often recited it. There were four poems he had translated from the Sanskrit, and he usually recited one or another of them. Actually it was not he who had translated them (his Sanskrit had never been very good) but Ram Nath Uncle, many years ago when they were together at Cambridge; but it was Daddyji who had put it into proper English verse with rhyme and metre and everything.

O do not weep, my tender maid!
Lift thy tearstain'd cheek from thy slender palm
   that fondles it
And e'er this in memory keep:
Though the bee may rove and sip
The mango's bloom with thirsty lip,
Far will he never stray
From the jasmine's fragrant May
That hath ravish'd his heart away.

It was only when she looked round at the audience for the third time that she noticed Esmond. He was leaning with one elbow against a sideboard, his long legs at a slant, his feet crossed. He looked casual and elegant, and she wondered who he was.

When Daddyji had finished, there was a moment's silence because no one except Shakuntala realized that he had finished. It was only after he had stood for a while, smiling and with lowered eyes, that they applauded and some of them said 'Jolly good' in hoarse voices. Shakuntala looked at Esmond and saw that he had ever so slightly raised his eyebrows at a lady near to him.

She turned to one of the Englishmen next to her and asked, 'Who is that gentleman over there, the one in fawn trousers?' She wanted so much to know and could see no reason why she should not directly ask.

'That,' said the Englishman, 'is Mister Esmond Stillwood,' and he said it in rather an emphatic, funny way; however, she was too interested in the information itself to take much notice of the manner in which it was delivered.

She had always been very interested in Esmond Stillwood – ever since Gulab had married him. She had wondered what he could be like, this unknown Englishman who had come so suddenly and taken Gulab away from Amrit. She thought about him quite often. And now that she had at last met him, she did not neglect the opportunity of looking at him as much and as hard as she could. She decided at once that he was – yes, very handsome. Much more so than any of the other foreigners there. He was slim and graceful, and while they were red and rather raw, he was pale with golden hair and a fine pointed chin. He looked so sensitive, she thought, like a poet.

'I suppose your father is the man from whom to learn about Indian culture,' said the big red Englishman.

'Oh,' said Shakuntala, 'Daddyji knows an awful lot.' But she did not say it with her customary fervour. She was thinking that of course Esmond would have long slim hands. She looked at them and he had. Then she looked up into his face again and she met his eyes, which were very blue. It was Esmond who looked away: Shakuntala was too interested to think about being embarrassed.

'So does Mister Esmond Stillwood,' said the second Englishman.

'Oh yes,' laughed the first, 'he knows *every*thing there is to know about India.'

Shakuntala looked gravely from one to the other and said, 'Yes, I have heard he is clever.'

'*Tre*-mendously,' said the second Englishman, casting his eyes up to the ceiling.

'Didn't you know,' said the big red Englishman, 'he's come specially to India to teach you people all about your own country.'

Shakuntala did not quite know what they meant. However, she was not greatly interested. She was looking at Esmond and wondering why he should have chosen to marry, of all people, Gulab.

'I'd like to know your father better,' said the big red Englishman. 'I'm sure he'd be fascinating to listen to.'

'You must,' Shakuntala said absently, 'come and have tea at our house.' Then she got up, while the big red Englishman was still saying that there was nothing he would like better. She murmured, 'Will you please excuse me,' and crossed the room to join her father.

Har Dayal was talking to Esmond. He took Shakuntala's arm as she came to stand beside him and said, 'Have you met my little girl?'

Esmond gave a very faint little bow and said, 'How do you do?' But Shakuntala, behaving in the free and western manner she thought suitable to the party, held out her hand, which he then had to shake.

'Are you having a nice time, darling?' Har Dayal asked her, but then a lady came up to him and said, 'Mr Har Dayal, I thought that was a simply lovely poem, what was it called?'

'How is Gulab?' Shakuntala asked Esmond, who was about to turn away to talk to someone else.

The question took him aback for a moment: Gulab was the last person he expected to be asked about at a party like this. However, he answered quite smoothly.

'I have not seen her for – oh, for so long,' Shakuntala said. It must have been at least five years. She had not seen Gulab since her marriage. She wondered whether she had changed.

The hostess came up and said to Shakuntala, 'I haven't seen you eat or drink a thing, what *is* this?'

Shakuntala laughed, rather embarrassed, and said, 'Oh no – ' and to Esmond she said, 'You have a little girl, don't you?'

'Boy,' Esmond said.

'It's queer to think that our Esmond can be somebody's Daddy,' said the hostess. Esmond raised his eyebrows at her and said with an amused smile, 'And just what do you mean by that?'

'Don't take me amiss,' said the lady, with the same smile, before she turned away to someone else of whom she could be heard to ask, 'Why don't I see a glass in your hand?'

'Who does he look like?' Shakuntala asked with genuine interest, 'you or Gulab?'

Esmond replied shortly, 'Gulab,' sounding as if he had rather viciously bitten the word off with his teeth.

'She is so beautiful,' Shakuntala said with enthusiasm. She looked up into his face and her eyes shone, thinking of Gulab's beauty. 'Your little boy must be lovely.'

Esmond faintly smiled. He glanced over his shoulder to see if Betty was still standing there. He tried to catch her eye but all he managed to catch was that of a Billimoria sister who came and shouted into his ear, 'Isn't it a lovely party!' And before he had even time to reply, the second Billimoria sister grasped his arm and shouted into his other ear, 'Esmond, how long it is since we have seen you!'

Shakuntala felt quite ashamed. Esmond would be getting a very bad impression of Indian women.

'Far too long,' said Esmond, taking each sister by an arm. Delighted, they allowed themselves to be led off; but, Shakuntala noticed, he soon dropped them and began to talk to a pert and pretty European lady. She watched him from a distance; she thought the way he smiled down at the lady and raised his eyebrows at her was very attractive. He looked so much at his ease; and also so sensitive, so distinguished. Of course, she thought, Gulab *was* beautiful . . . she saw Esmond raise his hand and pass it very slowly over his forehead and then over his hair, in a thinker's – a poet's – gesture.

Daddyji came and put his arm round her shoulder. He said, 'You are not lonely?' and then the big red Englishman came up behind them and said, 'We've been having a most interesting conversation.'

'Oh good, good,' Daddyji said and beamed at him. The hostess said, 'Mr Har Dayal, I think your daughter's really charming,' smiling with long, narrow teeth at Shakuntala.

'She's been teaching me a lot,' said the big red Englishman. 'About Indian literature and things.'

'Oh no,' said Shakuntala with a deprecating laugh, but Daddyji patted her cheek and said, 'Good girl.'

'Which reminds me,' said the hostess, 'who's coming to Esmond's lecture on Indian poetry on Tuesday?'

'Count me out,' murmured the big Englishman, but very low.

'Why don't you come along, Shakuntala? I'm sure you'll enjoy it;

it's arranged by the W.W.O. – the Western Women's Organization – and besides Esmond's lecture there'll be some tea and chat.'

'Oh, those lovely W.W.O. teas,' said the Englishman, for which the hostess playfully pinched his arm.

'Mr Har Dayal,' she said, 'don't you think it's high time you gave us another lecture?'

Har Dayal answered only with his most charming smile.

'It's positively disgraceful the way you dodge us.'

'Daddyji is so busy,' Shakuntala said.

'Now don't you start standing up for him,' the hostess said, shaking a long thin wrinkled finger at her. 'He's such a very naughty man. It's ages since he's been to any of our meetings. Here,' she said, 'have a saltstick, they're rather nice even though it's me that says it.'

'What shouldn't,' said the big red Englishman. Shakuntala smiled uncertainly.

10

When Har Dayal saw Ram Nath standing on the veranda, his whole face lit up with delight and love. 'Please come,' he said, 'please come,' and took his friend's hands to draw him into his study.

He was really very happy. He always was, whenever Ram Nath came to see him: happy and excited. He was capable of a great deal of hero-worship and most of it, throughout his life, had been concentrated on Ram Nath. It was he himself now who was important – served on Committees, advised Ministers, sat on the platform at public functions and was garlanded, while Ram Nath was neglected and almost forgotten: but he still felt that he owed him some kind of homage.

'Will you sit?' he said, gently pressing Ram Nath into his own favourite armchair. 'Will you be comfortable there? May I bring another cushion for your back?' And he snatched up a cushion of burgundy velvet from one of the leather armchairs which stood round the study and were always drawn up to the desk whenever committee meetings were in progress. The desk was a massive piece of furniture, highly polished, and on it were laid out in a precise and orderly manner a silver paper-knife, blotting-paper in a crimson leather folder with a picture of the Taj Mahal in gold, and a presentation inkstand. Books bound in heavy leather with bright and precise gold lettering stood row upon row in glass-fronted cases.

Har Dayal danced about his friend, thinking how to do him good.

He would like to have been able to offer him sherbet, sweetmeats, biscuits, but he knew that Ram Nath never accepted anything except, in the heat, a glass of water. And now it was not hot, so that he could not even have the satisfaction of seeing him grow cool on iced water in his house. Always, when his friend came, his first impulse was to want to fling everything he had at his feet – 'please take my books, my furniture, my house, please take anything that pleases you!' he would like to have cried. Only of course he could not, because Ram Nath was hardly an easy receiver of gifts and would certainly not have been pleased at such irrational behaviour.

'My dear friend,' said Har Dayal, pressing the other's hands, 'I am so happy to see you, so happy,' and he pressed again; it was the only outlet he could get for his strong emotion.

Ram Nath looked down at his own feet. He was touched and also a little ashamed, because not only could he not return Har Dayal's ardent affection but he had also always rather laughed at him.

'You come to me so seldom these days,' Har Dayal complained. But their lives were so different, he knew, that the wonder was that Ram Nath came at all.

'How was I to come,' Ram Nath said with a gentle smile. 'It is rather far and I am an old man now.'

'Oh no-no-no-no,' Har Dayal said, putting up a hand as if it were himself he wanted to shield. 'You will never grow old.'

But it was true, Ram Nath did look old. There were only a few years between the two of them, but Ram Nath did look much older. Har Dayal's heart was wrung with love for him. Frustrated love too, for he would like to have cried, 'Then let me send my car for you, every day let me send it for you, so that you may go wherever you like!' but he had to restrain himself: not only would Ram Nath have been offended, but he himself felt it to be something of an affront that he should be in a position to make such an offer, while his friend – his far greater friend, as he thought of him – had to be in one where it could be made to him.

'You are giving me idle excuses,' he said affectionately. 'I know you do not come because you are too busy and have not even the grace to spare one day in a month for your old friend.'

'Yes,' said Ram Nath, smiling gently still, 'I am too busy killing my time.'

Har Dayal squeezed his hand as if to say, 'I know you lie.' Yet he knew nothing of the sort. Often he had to wonder what it was that Ram Nath did with himself now that he took no more part in public affairs; but then he usually comforted himself with the thought that probably the other was engaged in writing some momentous work. He greatly looked forward to its appearance. Certainly it was what he expected of his friend: he had always been convinced that Ram Nath was destined to some great achievement, and though it was getting rather late now, he still did not have any doubts about it.

'But it is you who have so much to do,' Ram Nath said.

Har Dayal sighed and ran his hand through his shock of hair. 'It is true,' he said, 'I am busy, but my work is so ephemeral.'

'So is all the world's,' Ram Nath said lightly.

'Yes, all the works of men ... "My name is Ozymandias, king of kings,"' he quoted rather solemnly. 'No, but often I feel – to you, my dear friend, I can speak freely – often I feel: what am I doing, why am I doing this, what purpose am I serving? It is true, my days are very full, there are always lectures and meetings and many things to be discussed and arranged: but when I ask myself this question, what purpose am I serving, then I do not know any answer.'

Ram Nath quite realized that it was a question Har Dayal did not very often ask himself. But he said, so soothingly and sympathetically that it hardly sounded ironic, 'Why trouble yourself with such questions? You are known to do much good work, and everywhere people speak in your praise.'

'Ah,' said Har Dayal, and he looked at his friend with his eyes stretched wide open in an impressive manner, his right hand spread dramatically on his chest, 'but can such work give the *spiritual* satisfaction that a man needs?'

'Well, well,' said Ram Nath, 'why not, it is good work.'

Har Dayal, though, shook his head. There was a sad and solemn expression on his face which made him look rather childish. He was, however, intrinsically too happy to be able to keep it up for long. Soon his mouth had curved into smiles again, his spectacles gleamed with love as they looked on Ram Nath.

'Come,' he said, 'let us go to Madhuri – how cross she will be when she hears I have been keeping you to myself all this time.' He knew that she would not be cross at all, but it was what he liked to think. Though usually he did not bring his visitors into Madhuri's presence, he always insisted on doing so with Ram Nath. He would have felt it an insult to his friend if he had not taken him right into the heart of the house, to its mistress.

Madhuri, warned by a servant of their approach, sat ready to receive them in the drawing-room. She sat on a wide, low divan which was piled with cushions and bolsters in highly-coloured Kashmiri patterns; she wore a purple sari of Benares silk with a deep silver border, and several rings on her very frail hands. When Ram Nath came in, she greeted him with her hands joined together, held close under her chin, and her eyes lowered. He returned her greeting in the same manner, looking down only at her feet. Har Dayal smiled from one to the other and felt happy.

'Well,' he said, 'our brother has at last condescended to come to our house.'

Madhuri still did not look up and her face remained quite expressionless. Ram Nath sat very still on the edge of a chair, his hands in his lap, his feet close together. Har Dayal beamed with satisfaction

And Shakuntala, bursting in, thought at once, seeing her mother and Ram Nath, they look like lovers. There was that air of constraint about them, as of lovers who have long struggled with their love and are suddenly confronted with one another in the presence of a third who must not know their secret. And there was something similar about them – perhaps because they were both small, both frail, both somehow exquisite – which made Daddyji between them, plumper and more solid, look rather out of place, almost an intruder.

'Oh, Uncleji,' Shakuntala cried, 'I did not know you were here!' She looked and sounded very enthusiastic, her eyes were brilliant with pleasure. Her mother found her lack of reticence displeasing; she was also sorry to note that Shakuntala looked, as usual, rather windblown – her hair loose about her shoulders, the sari not drawn discreetly enough over her well-developed breasts. But Har Dayal said, full of pride, 'She is home with us for good now, her College education is finished.'

'I am a B.A., Uncleji!' Shakuntala laughed. 'Though it is only a pass degree.' Ram Nath laughed also, his high-pitched cackle, he said, 'Oh good, good, very good,' as he did so; Har Dayal smiled radiantly, his arm about Shakuntala's shoulder and looking into her face with great tenderness.

'And now what shall I do, Uncleji?' she cried, gaily tossing her hair back from her face.

'Shall she be a poet, a dancer, a painter, what shall we make of her?' said Har Dayal, equally gay.

'Excellent,' Ram Nath cackled. 'She has so many talents?'

'*All* the talents!' Shakuntala laughed.

Madhuri said, 'How is your wife?' She spoke as always in a very low and gentle voice, but she managed to make herself heard at once.

Ram Nath said, 'I beg your pardon?' very courteously, though without looking at her.

'Yes, yes, how is Lakshmi,' said Har Dayal, 'how is she?' He felt a little conscience-stricken for not having asked before. He had simply forgotten; he always forgot about Lakshmi.

'Yes,' said Ram Nath, 'yes, she is very well.'

'And your daughters?' Madhuri inquired, politely if dispassionately.

And Shakuntala, always romantic, thought, perhaps then they do love one another and have all their lives had to suppress that love because of Daddyji. That would explain so much. It would, for instance, explain why her mother was being so cold and withdrawn, though they were all happy together; and it would explain why she was always somewhat irritated whenever Ram Nath was mentioned.

'They also, I think,' said Ram Nath, 'are well.'

'And your son?'

'Yes, Narayan?' Har Dayal asked. But just then Amrit came breezing in, with Indira behind him, and boomed very cheerfully at Ram Nath, 'Why hello, sir, haven't seen you in donkey's years.'

'You see,' said Har Dayal, 'they all miss you.'

'What are donkey's years?' Ram Nath inquired, which made Shakuntala laugh rather more lustily than her mother could approve of. But Indira earnestly explained, 'It is an English idiomatic expression,' after which she looked at her husband.

Ram Nath also looked at Amrit, who was now sitting next to his mother on the divan, his legs apart and hands planted on his knees. He had a soft, full, smooth face and wore well-cut clothes. Though young, he already looked prosperous and comfortably satisfied.

He asked, 'And how is old Narayan?' Not that Narayan had ever been a particular friend of his, but he felt well-disposed towards him; as indeed he felt towards almost everyone. Before Ram Nath, however, could answer his question, he continued, throwing one leg over the other, 'You know, I cannot understand him. He is such a clever chap, yet why does he go out there in the jungles, when other doctors are making a good pile in the cities and also leading a comfortable life among civilized people?'

'Yes,' Ram Nath said, 'you have a good point there. I must put it to him when next I write.'

'What I mean is,' said Amrit, 'he is wasting himself.'

'Of course,' Har Dayal said, 'Narayan could establish a very good practice in Delhi, or even in Bombay or Calcutta, if he cared to. We all know how brilliant he is.'

'It is not,' said Amrit, 'so much a question of being brilliant, as of knowing how to seize one's opportunities. Now, look at me.' He left a short pause, which was so intolerably smug that Shakuntala, quite ashamed before Ram Nath, burst out, 'Oh Amrit, how conceited you sound.'

'Not at all,' Ram Nath said courteously.

Madhuri said, 'Shakuntala, you may speak with a little more

respect to your elder brother.' She was much annoyed. She felt that Amrit was being made to look ridiculous before Ram Nath. She was, anyway, very sensitive for him: ever since Gulab's marriage, she had felt that the very existence of Ram Nath and his family was a slight to Amrit.

'As I was saying,' Amrit continued placidly, 'it is not a question of being brilliant. Now I have never been one of these brilliant chaps – '

'But?' Shakuntala meaningfully inquired.

'Do please let Amrit speak, Shakun,' Indira said.

'Not like Narayan,' Amrit said magnanimously; 'I am sure he has ten times the amount of grey matter that I have. But where has this got him in life?'

Har Dayal thought of Ram Nath at Cambridge: brilliant, full of promise, India's bright star, as they had all thought of him. And Har Dayal himself his humble admirer, who would never have dreamt of comparing himself with him. Yet now it had all worked out differently. He said, 'Narayan is gaining experience which is very valuable. Later on we shall hear great things of him.' As, later on, they would hear great things of the father too.

'What experience can you gain out there in the jungles?' Amrit said.

'Listen, I will tell you something,' Ram Nath said. 'Do you know, I have long suspected this, but I think my son has no ambition – is it not dreadful to have such a son?'

Har Dayal laughed, though a little uneasily, and patted Ram Nath's shoulder. 'Will you never change?' he said.

'For instance,' said Ram Nath, 'I have never seen him wear good clothes such as you, Amrit, are wearing; he possesses only a bicycle and his thoughts are so lowly that they will not let him do as much as even hope for a motor-car; he is a doctor but he dare not aspire to a fashionable practice; and worst of all, not only has he no money in the bank, he is not even ashamed of this fact. Have I not reason as a father to grieve for him?'

'You may laugh – ' said Amrit with a booming laugh of his own which, however, was not quite hearty enough. And, 'Indeed you may!' Shakuntala cried.

Their mother did not like the turn the conversation was taking. Why does he come here, she thought resentfully, why does he not leave us alone. For, contrary to Shakuntala's newly formed romantic notion, her attitude towards Ram Nath was dictated not by love but by dislike. She had always disliked him, even before Gulab's marriage, because she had always felt that he exerted an unsettling effect on her husband. And now he was bringing the same tactics to bear on her son. She said, 'Of course, different people take to different ways, it is so in life.'

'Who is to say,' Indira backed her up in a very grown-up and sensible fashion, 'which is best and which is worst.'

'Well, you know,' Amrit said, leaning back against a bolster and looking up at the ceiling from which two fans hung suspended like dead spiders, 'I have always been suspicious of this Simple-Living-High-Thinking sort of thing. What is wrong with having a motor-car, good clothes, a good bank-balance? Who would not accept these things if they came to him? It is only those to whom they do not come who say they would not.'

Madhuri was so pleased with her son that she at once stole a triumphant little look at Ram Nath. Thank Heavens, Amrit had more sense than his father; *he* was not to be so easily influenced. She was proud of him; it was good to have such a son. She wished her second son could also be here: Raj too, she was sure, would have been able to make an effective stand against Ram Nath and his insidious talk. For a moment, at the thought of Raj, the worry which had been nagging at her for weeks now came over her again: what was the matter with Raj, why had he not written for so long? But reassurance followed almost at once. He was all right, one could be sure of that, he was such a good sensible boy; like Amrit. Yes, it was good to have such sons. Especially when all one's life one had had to put up with an unstable husband like Har Dayal. He was unstable, really there was no other word for him. It had always been so easy for other people, people like Ram Nath, to influence him, to unsettle him.

As if in illustration of her thoughts, Har Dayal at that moment replied to Amrit, 'It is not so simple as that, my son,' in that rather embarrassed guilty voice which she knew came to him only when he had been talking to Ram Nath. She had always known when he had been seeing Ram Nath, because afterwards he had always been depressed and somehow self-abasing. He would say, 'What good am I doing in life, what purpose am I serving?' and she had then had to work hard to persuade him yet again that it was a far finer thing to be a scholar of leisure, a gentleman, respected and respectable, with several friends in British official circles, than to be a Congress worker without money or position and with a police record.

'Why not?' Amrit said. 'To me it sounds very simple. We have only one life, so why not get what we can out of it? That is my philosophy, take it or leave it. I am very frank, you see; please do not take offence, Uncleji.'

'Offence,' said Ram Nath with a quite unaffected laugh, 'why should I take offence? You tell me Narayan is a fool: very well, I agree with you: let us call him fool.'

'How can you talk so, Uncleji!' Shakuntala cried. 'When you know, we all know, that what Narayan is doing is great and wonderful!'

'Great and wonderful?' Ram Nath repeated in a puzzled, smiling tone.

'Of course, what else! Is it not one hundred thousand million times better to go out into the villages and give your life in the service of the sick and the poor and the ignorant than to sit in a fashionable practice in New Delhi and take fat fees from fat clients and yourself grow fat like a money-lender? A doctor must do good to people, this is his function in life; to be worthy of his profession he must be quite selfless and have no ambitions but only ideals.'

'There,' said Amrit; 'I was waiting for her favourite word, ideals.'

'All right, you may laugh at me if you please, but I know very well that a life without ideals is useless and worthless! But to lead a life such as Narayan is leading, to know that you are serving a purpose which is greater than yourself, this is wonderful, this is living. I would give up everything, gladly – but gladly – to serve such a purpose. What is the use of our motor-cars and nice clothes and jewels and all our servants if our lives are without purpose and we have no ideals to guide us? How happy I would be to give all these things up for the sake of a great Ideal!'

Ram Nath looked at her very observantly. He noted that, in spite of her high-flown language, she really looked as if she meant what she was saying. Her eyes were shining, her head very proud and erect. She was wearing a sleeveless blouse and out of this her arms came naked and strong, very energetic. She reminded him somewhat of Uma as she had been in her youth.

Har Dayal said, 'Darling, you are too enthusiastic.'

'And also she talks a great deal too much,' said Madhuri.

11

Uma walked round the house with fresh garlands on a tray. She was changing the garlands hung round the portraits of departed loved ones, but her mind was busy with other things. She was thinking about Gulab and the thought made her angry: not with Gulab but for her. What is the use, she thought, of giving a girl so much beauty and then afterwards making an unhappy life for her! She did not quite know whom she was blaming; logically it should have been God, but if this had been suggested to her, she would have denied it with horror.

A bride fit for the Lord Krishna, she told her husband as she adorned him with a fresh garland, and she has thrown herself away on that leprous one. Her husband, however, continued to stare impassively out of his frame; just as he had done five years ago when she came to him once, twice, three times every day to weep and complain how their daughter wanted to marry an Englishman. At that time she had taken almost a dislike to him; resenting the fact that he was only a photograph, and a very undistinguished one at that, looking like all other photographs of the dead, dim and remote and blurring off into nothing at the edges – when she had such great need of him. It was strange that he, of all people, should fail her. In his lifetime he had never failed her. Everything had been easy – the going to prison, the giving up of their property, the years of defeat – because he had been there. He had been so very big and very strong; his mere physical presence had been enough to keep all worries away from her. She had known that, whatever happened, she and Gulab were safe; he was there to carry them over everything. But now he was dead, and the concerns of his wife and daughter, she had to realize, were of no further interest to him.

She wandered gloomily about the house, so engrossed in bitter thoughts that she quite failed to notice her various visitors – a very pious widow from Madras who was still rolled up on her bedding in a corner of what had once been the dining-room, a professor from Lucknow reading an Urdu weekly on the front veranda and a conference delegate from a backward state who was busy cleaning his teeth under a tree in the garden. Bachani came running after her with a cup of tea, but she only said, 'Leave me alone,' and began meditatively to climb the stairs. Bachani shouted after her that of course it was no business of hers and that *she* did not care if Uma chose to starve herself to death, but what account was she to give afterwards to Uma's brother and her daughter and her little grandson who would blame her for not looking after their relative properly.

Uma did not listen. She continued to wander round the house and thought how nice it would be if she could have Gulab at home again. As a girl, before her marriage, Gulab had always been lying around in the house, stretched out on the floor or on the swinging sofa on the veranda, her arms under her head, quite oblivious of all the coming and going around her and radiating a quiet luxurious contentment. Uma had so loved bringing little surprises for her – a few sweetmeats freshly made in the kitchen, a bowl of creamy rice-pudding, a ripe and juicy mango. And now it would be better still, for there would be not only Gulab to enjoy these little offerings but also Ravi.

How happy Ravi would be in the house, running in and out of all the rooms, up and down the stairs, into the garden. She stepped out into the garden and thought perhaps later, when he was a little bigger, she would have the tennis court restored for him. And the pond, which now had only a little green slime at the bottom, should be gay with little fishes and the fountain should play all day long. But she would not cut down any of the shrubs and growths that had started up on the paths and round the statues; because it was more fun for a boy to play in a wild than in a cultivated garden. Though later, when he was grown up and brought home a wife, everything should be again as it had been: coloured lights in the trees, the well-laid paths, flowerbeds and rockeries, the statues repaired and restored; and in the house furniture and carpets and all the panes mended in the windows. She did not often think about her house -- she had hardly noticed that it had changed -- but now she was happy to have it, for Ravi's sake; though the next moment she was plunged again in gloom, when she thought what good is it to him when she will not bring him here to me, but he has to stay there in that flat with the furniture, where a mouse cannot move in comfort.

From the garden she wandered into the block of servants' quarters. It was a large, high construction with a tiny courtyard of its own. Since she herself had hardly any servants left, she let it out quarter by quarter, each at a rent of ten rupees a month; if this rent had been paid to her regularly or often, she would have had quite a nice little income. There was always a great deal of activity going on in this block, for it was very crowded. Each quarter held a family, and each family usually consisted of several brothers with their dependents; these always included a great many children, besides wives, old parents and widowed sisters-in-law. And as if this were not enough, many of the tenants had also sublet part of their quarter, the right-hand or the left-hand corner or the space under the window. At one time Uma had tried to stop this practice of subletting, but she had soon given up the attempt, realizing that there were always poor people desperately in need of a corner to live in.

She often came to visit here. She settled feuds that had arisen, attended a marriage ceremony or helped to mourn at a funeral, or just sat and talked with the other women in the courtyard. Today, however, she did not feel like talking. She wandered aimlessly around the courtyard where everyone was too used to her to take much notice. The women carried on quietly with what they were doing, lighting fires with the slabs of cowdung which served them as fuel, grinding atta, washing clothes, feeding their babies. They always enjoyed talking to Uma, but they noted that today she was too preoccupied and they respected her privacy. The children went on playing all round her, sometimes even bumping into her which, however, neither she nor they noticed. The pariah-dogs continued to sleep in their own favourite spots, from time to time twitching their ears. They are poor, thought Uma, wandering among her tenants, they have nothing except too many children, yet each of them is happier than my daughter; for at least they have company, they can sit here in the courtyard with one another enjoying the air and each other's conversation, their children run around free in the open. And she surged with indignation as she thought of her Gulab and her Ravi trapped like two chickens in Esmond's flat.

She went back into her house, for she felt she had to unburden herself to someone. She climbed the stairs to glance into the room where the swami usually stayed; but she saw that today she could not speak to him, for he was in contemplation. He sat in the Padmasana pose, his legs tucked under him, feet on his thighs, hands palm upwards on his knees, and his eyes wide open and unblinking stared straight through her. But she was not really sorry that she could not talk to him. Usually she enjoyed talking to him very much – she was always thanking God for sending him to her house – for he elevated and purified her mind. But for discussing a specific problem, like this of Gulab's, he was not really satisfactory. True, he would talk very wisely and very spiritually, but always in the abstract, in large philosophical terms; this was edifying but not what she wanted just now. For now she was too full of a real anger, concentrated on one real object, to be satisfied with abstractions. What she wanted was to rail against Esmond, deplore the fate of Gulab and her little Ravi, wring her hands over her daughter's obstinacy; and since there was no one else, she decided to go down and seek out Bachani. But just as she was about to descend the stairs, she saw, to her immense satisfaction, her brother standing at the bottom; and she called down to him in a ringing voice, 'What am I to do, she still refuses to leave that *monster!*'

'Please,' Ram Nath said, 'first come down and offer me a glass of water.'

Regally she descended the stairs. As she did so, she said, 'I talked with her and talked with her, how I talked with her, and still she would not hear me.'

Bachani came shuffling up and inquired, 'Shall I bring tea?'

'Tea, can you think of nothing but tea,' Uma said. 'Of this I am certain,' she told Ram Nath, 'I will not rest till I have got her away, if I have to carry her here with my own hands.' They went to sit side by side on the veranda. The Professor from Lucknow, who sat there reading his paper, greeted them very courteously with his hands joined and a modest smile on his face, but they failed to notice him.

'But you did not think,' said Ram Nath, 'that she would come away at your first word?'

'And why not?' Uma replied with hauteur. Yet it was an assumed hauteur: really she knew and had known all along that it would not be so easy. Gulab had the same instinctive inbred notions about a husband as she herself had; only Gulab did not have her courage and strength of will to overcome them.

'Why not,' Ram Nath repeated, 'because our women are so, what can you do with them?'

'Are so what?' said Uma, though she knew perfectly well what he meant.

'So like animals, like cows,' he said with sudden revulsion. 'Beat them, starve them, maltreat them how you like, they will sit and look with animal eyes and never raise a hand to defend themselves, saying do with me what you will, you are my husband, my God, it is my duty to submit to my God.'

'It is true, a husband is a woman's God, it is written so in all our old books. And please also see how Sita submitted to Ram, she followed him into the wilderness and afterwards, when he banished her, she turned and went without one word though she was innocent.'

'Please try to think rationally. This is the trouble with all of you, you must always bring in these primitive myths whose original meaning has long been lost or at least has no longer any bearing or significance for us, and you apply them or rather force them and squeeze them into every cranny of your lives.'

'So our Ancient Epics, which even foreigners everywhere read and admire, you now call primitive myths!'

'Excuse me,' said the Professor, who had been listening with great interest, 'this is a significant point on which it is worth while to dwell for a moment.'

'Every word that is written,' Uma cried, 'is true and full of virtue, and it is our duty to guide our lives on the principles that have been laid down for us. Only,' she said, 'in the present case it is an exception, with Gulab,' she persuaded herself; 'it is different because she is married to a foreigner.'

Ram Nath knew how hard she had struggled finally to persuade herself of this, so he made no further comment. 'Tell me,' he said, 'what do you know of Har Dayal's daughter?'

'Her name is Shakuntala. But what has she to do with my Gulab?'

78

'You see,' he said, and he drew it from his pocket, 'I had this letter from Narayan.'

After she had read it, she said, 'Of course it is time, he is past thirty.'

'I do not want to make a mistake.'

'Your Narayan,' said Uma, 'would not accept a mistake.'

'But what do you know of her, this Shakuntala?'

'Of course, she is not like her mother.' Uma said this regretfully: she had always had a great admiration for Madhuri.

'No,' said Ram Nath who certainly did not share this admiration. 'If she were, I would not be asking you.'

'It is true, Narayan does not require a wife like Madhuri, his life is too hard, poor boy. But how lovely she is, how delicate and such a fair skin ...' For forty years Uma had been talking about Madhuri in these glowing terms. She had always thought of her as her very dearest friend and had not realized that Madhuri had never by any means returned the sentiment; or if she had realized, it made no difference to the warmth of her own feelings.

The Professor quoted with a scholarly little smile: 'Her nether lip is like the cup of the flower where the bee sits and sips, the palm of her hand like the lotus blossom.'

Ram Nath said, 'But I am asking you about the daughter.'

'Of course, she is a good girl, a very sweet girl, I love her very much. Narayan could be happy with such a wife and also our two families would then be ...' Since she had always had this great admiration for Madhuri, she had wanted nothing better than to be united with her in some relationship. Part of her sorrow over Gulab's marriage had been caused by the fact that it put an end to their plans for a marriage with Amrit. Though she had never yet realized the depths of resentment Gulab's defection had stirred up in Madhuri.

'At least, she is very different from her brother,' Ram Nath said. 'That one seems to me a complete fool.'

'Amrit? But he too is a sweet boy, a charming boy. How I wish only that it had been he, as we had all planned ... how comfortable she would have been, how happy, my sweet child, in that house and with such a husband.' She sighed, but as it was not much in her nature to look backward, her sighing soon gave way to a sterner expression. She said, 'But I will get her away – she may be obstinate but she will find her mother is more obstinate. I will not stand by and keep silent when I see my children suffer.'

Ram Nath got up, ready to go. He said, 'Please think about this Shakuntala and tell me whether you decide it is a good idea. Go and see her, talk to her, if you will.'

12

On Tuesday evening Har Dayal had a meeting of his own, so he could not take Shakuntala to Esmond's lecture. But she was determined to go. She realized that it might be a little awkward to arrive there all alone, so she asked Indira whether she would like to come with her; but she did not ask with any great enthusiasm. Indira laughed and said what should she do at a lecture, she was glad to have finished with lectures now that she had left College and was married. This refusal was quite a relief to Shakuntala. She felt that the companionship of Indira would have been a hindrance rather than an asset: though, if she had thought about it, she would not have been able to say quite what it was that she did not want Indira to hinder her from.

The lecture was to take place on the terrace of someone's house. Chairs had been placed in rows, and at the sides there were tables covered with checked tablecloths from which coffee and sandwiches were served. It was sunset time, but it was quite warm; the season was changing, soon now it would be summer. The sky glowed with a large patch of orange against which roofs and the tops of trees were cut out in black. When Shakuntala arrived, quite a number of people had already gathered on the terrace; there was a lot of talk and laughter which sounded rather strange and disembodied in the darkness closing in. Then someone said, 'What *are* we doing? What's happened to the lights?' and when they were switched on, Shakuntala saw that most of the people there were ladies; even though this was a general evening of the Western Women's Organization, for which many invitations had been issued and husbands encouraged to come along. Shakuntala looked round to see whether the lecturer had arrived yet, but she could not see him. The Secretary came up to her and said how happy she was to see her and greeted her, to Shakuntala's surprise and somewhat to her embarrassment, with hands joined together in Indian style.

There were quite a number of ladies who had been to the party and who remembered her and asked after her father. They gave her coffee and a dainty little sandwich, and she stood and made conversation. She found it easy to make conversation, topics occurred to her quite naturally. She asked about the activities of the W.W.O. and she asked with such enthusiasm (she really wanted to know) that they could not but answer her back with enthusiasm. So she heard all about the lectures they arranged and the dramatics and fashion-shows in aid of charity, the musical evenings and the trips to places of historic interest. 'Oh, it *does* sound fun,' she said, so they smiled and asked why not join. She thought this a wonderful idea; 'May I really?' she said, and they called the Secretary, who at once gave her a form to fill in, and one lady sponsored her and another seconded her. The Billimoria sisters, waving skinny arms like cranes from sleeveless blouses of green net, cried, 'Hooray!' and told Shakuntala how happy they were to have her as a fellow-member. 'We joined *ages* ago,' they told her, 'and really we don't know *what* we would do without the good old W.W.O.'

'Isn't it getting rather late?' the ladies began to ask. Shakuntala thought so too, she kept looking round but there was still no sign of the lecturer. The Secretary looked rather worried, she said, 'Wherever's that Esmond?' It was quite dark now, the sky-scape of roofs had disappeared and there was only the lighted terrace with the ladies in pretty floral dresses and the sandwich plates on checked tablecloths.

'I'll go and telephone,' the Secretary said, but when she came back she looked more worried still: 'His wife says he hasn't been home at all since morning.' It took Shakuntala some time to realize that the wife who had said this was Gulab, and this seemed to her rather odd. It was difficult to connect Gulab with a gathering such as this. She was not at all surprised that Gulab had not come to hear her husband lecture; though she herself, she knew, would never have missed the occasion, had she had such a husband.

'Betty, have you any idea . . .?'

Betty shrugged one shoulder and said, 'Not the foggiest.' Shakuntala recognized her as the pert pretty lady to whom Esmond had talked a lot at the party. She wondered was she a relation of his or just a special friend.

Betty said, 'I'll go and put on a record.' Shakuntala watched her walk away. She really was very pretty. She was small, with fair wavy hair and a trim figure; she wore a pink dress buttoned high up to the neck in front but quite open at the back, exposing a stretch of smooth skin tanned golden-brown.

The gramophone started and Shakuntala said, 'How beautiful.'

'Lovely!' cried the Billimoria sisters.

'Mozart,' explained one of the ladies; 'I don't know if that means anything to you.'

'But of course,' Shakuntala said, quite shocked.

'*Eine Kleine*,' Betty said when she came back.

'I like "The Swan of Tuonela" by Sibelius very much,' Shakuntala said.

'Isn't it funny,' said another lady, 'that you should like *our* music when we can't make head or tail of yours.'

'Oh please,' cried the Billimoria sisters, 'you need not think that we enjoy that caterwauling any more than you do!'

Shakuntala frowned a little. 'Our music is also very beautiful, only of course one must learn to understand it.' The ladies beamed at her: 'But can one *learn* or does one have to be born to it?' and the Secretary said, 'Perhaps one evening you'd care to give us a talk on Indian music and how to enjoy it? Just an informal chat.'

Though she liked being there and enjoyed talking to these ladies, Shakuntala did hope that the lecture would not be cancelled. It was because of the lecture that she had come – the subject, as she had told her father, was very interesting to her – and she did not want to go home disappointed.

When they had finished their coffee and sandwiches, several people sat down in the rows of chairs ranged in front of the lecturer's table. The Secretary bit her lip and said, 'This isn't at all like Esmond.' But the audience did not seem to be much concerned. They sat quite calmly and turned round in their chairs to chat affably with their friends behind. *Eine Kleine Nachtmusik* provided a pleasant background. Two bearers walked round unhurriedly to collect the empty coffee-cups.

'He is not usually late?' Shakuntala asked.

'Oh no, he's so dependable,' said the Secretary.

Betty gave a rather secret little smile and said, 'Well, in some things maybe.'

And then, just as Mozart was at his most lyrical, Esmond came stepping up on to the terrace. Shakuntala saw him at once. He was dressed quite informally, in gabardine trousers and a cream-coloured shirt open at the neck. He looked cool and handsome and as distinguished as she had remembered him.

'I'm most awfully sorry,' he said, coming straight up to the Secretary, though not in any hurry.

'I should hope so,' she replied, with a great sigh of relief.

He nodded at the other ladies standing round, also at Shakuntala, who said, 'Good evening'; but from the way he looked at her, she realized that he did not remember.

Betty said, 'You know Har Dayal's daughter?'

'Of course,' he said absently; and looking round to see how big an audience there was, 'Shall we start, then?'

His subject was the Indian love lyric. He stood, apparently quite unselfconscious, behind the lecturer's table; sometimes he leant forward on it, supporting himself on both hands. He spoke with ease and

82

authority. Shakuntala was surprised to hear him speak names like Bhartrhari, Bilhana and Jayadeva so fluently: she had had no idea that an Englishman could know so much about Indian culture and was rather ashamed that she herself knew so little. The audience listened respectfully. Only Betty, who was sitting next to Shakuntala, kept whispering rather irreverently. She whispered, 'Goodness, what a tongue-twister,' or, 'Wonder how long it took him to master that one?' whenever Esmond pronounced a difficult Sanskrit name. Shakuntala forced a laugh, but really she wished the other would keep quiet. She wanted to concentrate on the lecture, it was so interesting. She kept her eyes fixed on Esmond and marked all his little gestures, the way he passed his hand over his hair or picked up a pencil from the table and balanced it for a moment between his two forefingers as he spoke to the audience. He was so calm and informal, he did not seem to be lecturing so much as talking. She had never before seen a lecturer lecture without notes: how clever he must be, she thought, and what a wonderful memory.

He ended with a quotation: ' "O wandering heart," ' he said, raising his eyebrows at the audience and smiling rather ironically, ' "stray not in the forest of woman's fair body, nor in the steeps which are her breasts, for there lurks Love, the highwayman." ' All the ladies laughed and Betty said, 'Coo,' quite loudly, and then there was clapping as Esmond sat down, leaning back in the chair and crossing his legs.

The audience was invited to ask questions, and after a short embarrassed pause one lady got up to ask did Esmond think that Indian poetry was unduly sensual. He answered her briefly but effectively, and then another lady said could not a parallel be drawn between the Indian lyricists and the Elizabethans? Betty made a face and whispered to Shakuntala, 'that's Intellectual Ida, trust *her*,' but Esmond drew the parallel very efficiently. After that there were a number of other questions to which, however, Shakuntala paid no attention as she was trying to summon up enough courage to ask one herself.

'Any more?' Esmond said, letting his eyes travel slowly over the rows of chairs, smiling and looking as if he were prepared to sit and answer questions for ever. There was a silence and Shakuntala tried to screw herself up; she told herself, '*Now*,' but it was too late, the Secretary was already proposing a vote of thanks, during which Esmond studied his nails.

There was really nothing to stay for, though people still hung about, having a last chat before parting with a gay, 'See you the day after then!' or 'Don't forget coffee at Sharmaji's tomorrow at ten!' Shakuntala also lingered; she did not really know what she was waiting for but she felt it would have been rather an anticlimax to go home right away. So she was very happy when Betty put her arm lightly round her shoulder and said, 'Come down and have a drink.' The Billimoria sisters called, 'Coming our way, Shakuntala?' across the terrace, but Betty called back, 'Not just yet!' and steered her down the stairs. 'They're good girls, I'm sure,' she said, 'but they do have rather loud voices, don't they?' which made Shakuntala feel very intimate.

It was only now she realized that this was Betty's house. They went into her sitting-room, an awfully sweet room, Shakuntala thought, with brightly coloured cushions and curtains and painted earthenware pots: in its decoration it was very much like the house to which she had gone for the party, but this did not detract from its charm. There were only a few other people, one of whom was Esmond. He sat on a sofa, looking quite at home and fluttering through the pages of a book. They all had cocktails and Shakuntala accepted a cigarette. She held it rather self-consciously between two fingers of her left hand while in her right hand she held her cocktail. In this manner she strolled over to Esmond's sofa and said, 'I did enjoy your lecture.'

He looked up and his eyes were quite vacant for a moment as he stared at her, but then he smiled: 'How nice of you to say so.'

'To say so what?' asked Betty, squatting down on the arm of the sofa.

'I told Mr Stillwood how much I enjoyed his lecture.'

'There you are, Mr Stillwood, you have an admirer, happy now?'

Esmond said, 'What makes you think I'm so badly in want of admiration?'

'Oh we all know our Mr Stillwood. Our own dear Percy Bysshe.'

'Our own dear nothing of the sort.'

'Only to his friends and admirers.' All the time they were smiling in a private manner.

'Please,' Shakuntala said, 'Percy Bysshe is the first name of Shelley, isn't it?'

'You *are* a well-read girl,' Esmond said. Betty tilted her glass and said, 'One cocktail going down Mr Stillwood's back.' Shakuntala laughed, but rather uncertainly.

'Do sit down,' Betty told her. 'Don't stand there like that, you look so uncomfortable.' And indeed she felt uncomfortable, with her cigarette and her cocktail, neither of which she wanted.

'Yes do,' said Esmond, casually but kindly, moving over a little way.

She laughed again, for no reason, and then thought why do I laugh, how silly I sound.

84

Betty said, 'Why did you like his lecture?'

'What a question,' Esmond said.

'Oh I thought it was very good,' Shakuntala replied with conviction.

'Yes, but why?'

Esmond said, 'That's enough now, whom are you trying to make a fool of?' He leaned towards Shakuntala and, indicating her cocktail glass, said with a very kind smile, 'May I hold it for you?'

She looked down at it and realized that she had been wishing for some time she could find somewhere to put it. She laughed, quite unselfconsciously this time, for she really was amused, 'No, I will drink it, what else is it for,' and proceeded to do so, very bravely and gaily.

The other people in the room were making ready to leave, they called ' 'Bye, Betty, 'bye, Esmond,' and to Shakuntala they said, 'Good-bye, do hope to see you again soon.' Now there were only the three of them left and Shakuntala said, 'I think it is time for me to go, too,' but rather reluctantly.

'Oh, pity,' Betty said, sounding as if she meant it but making no attempt to hold her back.

Shakuntala glanced at Esmond. She wondered whether he too was not leaving; she thought it was fitting for the last two guests to go together. But he made no move.

She said, 'How is Gulab?' for she remembered that she had not yet asked him and thought it was polite to do so.

'Oh, you know her?' Betty said with interest. She looked at Esmond out of the corner of her eye and smiled a bit.

'We were children together.'

Betty said, 'How interesting.' She looked at Esmond with the same smile as before and asked him, 'You never bring her anywhere these days, what's the matter?'

'Gulab must be very busy with her child,' Shakuntala said; though she thought how can he bring her anywhere, she would never know what to do or say. She looked at him again, trying to make out how it had come about that he was Gulab's husband.

'Yes, I expect that's it,' Betty said rather slyly. Esmond got up and walked over to the bookcase. He stood with his back to them, taking out books. None of them spoke, and in that moment of silence, Shakuntala, who was looking at Esmond's slender back, realized that he was unhappy.

She sensed it, she knew it, she was quite sure of it. At once it occurred to her that it was his marriage with Gulab that was making him so. And how indeed could a woman like Gulab ever hope to make such a man happy?

Betty was also looking at Esmond's back. She said in a rather mocking voice, 'Oh, to be in England ...' Both of them saw one shoulder raised up in a gesture which could have meant almost anything but seemed most expressive of a kind of hopeless resignation.

'You know that one?' Betty asked of Shakuntala.

'Is it Alfred, Lord Tennyson?'

'Well, nearly ...'

Esmond turned back to them. Shakuntala was watching his face keenly and she noted at once the lines of sadness marked on it. Sorrow, or what she interpreted as such, made him look more handsome than ever: so sensitive, so deeply spiritual in his suffering. She felt herself brimming over almost to the point of tears with a new sensation which was pity, yes, but also very much more than pity, so that she wanted nothing less than to fling down her own life to soothe the suffering in his.

Betty, however, was quite cheerful. She called to him, 'Come on now, sit down, you're making me quite nervous fidgeting about like that.'

Obediently he sat down next to her, and Shakuntala, though she was so full of strong feelings clamouring for some kind of expression, could only say in a weak voice: 'I think I must go.'

'You must come again soon,' Betty said. 'Very soon. Look here, I've got a tiny party on Thursday – just a few friends – how about it? I'm asking her for Thursday,' she explained, turning to Esmond who sat next to her with his head far back, resting against the wall behind him, his eyes shut and his fine sensitive chin jutting into the air, so that he looked like the Death Mask of a Poet, 'don't you think that's a good idea? She's so nice.'

13

Gulab did not like to go out of the house. Sometimes for days and even for weeks at a time she never stirred out of the flat; for though she did not feel comfortable there, she rarely had resolution enough to get up, get dressed, leave instructions with the servant and shut the door behind her. Besides, she hated going out into the streets, exposing herself to the eyes of strangers; it made her feel terrible. She would like to have travelled only in a closed car and because she did not have a closed car, nor any kind of a car at all, she preferred to stay in the flat.

But sometimes she could bear it no more, she had to go home and see her mother. She would wake in the morning and at once she would know that this was one of those days when she had to go home. Then she would be half glad and half afraid.

'Ravi,' she said when Esmond had gone, 'today we will go and see your Nani;' for this was one of those days. Ravi was terribly happy; for him there was only the joy of going to Nani's, he did not have to worry about leaving instructions with the servant and negotiating the transport. Gulab counted her money. She hoped there would be enough for a taxi or at least for a tonga, but found there was not. She was surprised how little there was left. But then, she was surprised by this in the middle of every month. Up to now, however, she had never asked Esmond for more: she always preferred to ask her mother.

But now that she had decided that she could no longer ask Uma for money, they had to go by bus. This she hated almost more than anything, almost more than walking in the street. She pulled her sari over her head, edged herself right into the corner of the seat and clung tight to Ravi. Soon the bus began to fill up, and she shrank further into her corner. It was a great relief to her when a woman came to sit next to her. A hard thin shrivelled peasant woman who smelt, but Gulab was happy to have her. Last time she had travelled in a bus, a huge fat Marwari had sat next to her, she had been able to hear him breathe and feel him very close and she had almost died of shame.

From the bus-stop there was still the walk to her mother's house but after that she could be safe and happy the whole day long, till it was time to go back again. Bachani was washing clothes by the pump, so she was the first to see her and she cried, 'At last they have come!' swinging a wet sari coiled like a snake.

Uma was sitting on the veranda, talking to Lakshmi who had come to see her to complain about Ram Nath. Ravi rushed straight into his grandmother's arms from which shelter he looked out with timid eyes at Lakshmi; who pronounced that he had got thinner than when she had last seen him, was Gulab not feeding him properly? Gulab flushed and said of course, meat every day and gram and all his food was cooked in pure ghee. She avoided her mother's eyes as she said this, but Uma backed her up with, 'Of course, only the best is good enough for our child,' pushing his face deep into her bosom.

Gulab stretched herself on the swinging sofa which hung on the veranda, while her mother thrust pillows under her to make her soft and comfortable. 'What are you doing!' Uma called to Bachani, 'can you not guess that my children are hungry!' Gulab softly swung herself to and fro, smiling to herself. Soon Bachani brought huge brass tumblers filled to the brim with buttermilk; layers of cream floated on top. 'And the sweetmeats?' Uma demanded angrily. 'How many hands have I to carry with,' Bachani said, but soon she returned, carrying a bowl full of sweetmeats studded with green pistachios and covered with silver-foil paper. 'Eat, child, eat,' Uma said, 'I will have special food prepared for your lunch.'

Lakshmi said, 'Where is your husband, why do we never see him?' but Gulab was so intent on her buttermilk, she did not even hear. 'He is too great for humble people like us,' Lakshmi said with bitterness, and she continued with a different kind of bitterness, 'Well perhaps he is right, why should he waste time with people like us who are nothing.'

'I sat in the bus,' Ravi told his grandmother.

Uma looked at Gulab and said, 'Why did you come in the bus?' For herself she had no objection to this mode of transport, indeed she hardly ever used any other; but she knew how much her daughter hated it, so she hated it for her too.

'I could not get a taxi,' said Gulab, who had thought it out long before and was ready. Her mother said nothing, but she was sad. Now it has come to this, she thought, she will not take money from me, she would rather lie to me to defend him.

'You should not come in a bus,' Lakshmi said. 'If you cannot get a taxi, then take a tonga. We who are poor people, we can travel in a bus, but *you* . . .' She was quite convinced that Esmond was rich. She thought that all white people in India were rich, and considered this as only right. She felt rather flattered to have a European in the family and frequently made reference to him when talking to her neighbours. 'Your husband should get a car, this would be more convenient for you and also for him.'

'Should I get you another pillow?' Uma asked and looked with satisfaction at Gulab swinging herself.

'Everybody nowadays has a car,' continued Lakshmi, 'even people who before rode in nothing better than bullock-carts. This is what is so painful to me,' she told Uma, 'that my Narayan who is a Doctor should not have a car but must sweat in the heat on a bicycle. When there are others – boys like Mrs R. P. Sud's Jagdish, for instance, who failed so often in his examination, he always had to appear again, while my Narayan came out first class, and now it is Jagdish who has a big car in which he visits his patients while my Narayan rides on a bicycle out there in the jungle.'

'How is Narayan?' Gulab sleepily asked. She was fond of her

cousin though he rather frightened her, he was so energetic and some-how impatient.

'How can he be,' her aunt gloomily replied.

'Of course he is well,' Uma said. 'He is happy, he is doing the work he wants.'

'Alone out there.'

'He need not be forever alone,' Uma said and thought of Shakun-tala.

'This too I wanted to talk with you about.'

'What do you mean, you want to get him married?' Gulab asked. Such talk was pleasing to her, she liked to listen to marriages being arranged, while she sat and contemplatively chewed betelnut.

'It is no use talking with his father, that one will never do anything for him, he does not even listen when I say is it not time you found a wife for your son.'

Gulab said, 'How I love this rocking, soon I shall be asleep.'

'After your food you shall sleep, you and the little one together. I will spread a mat in the long room for you, so that you will be cool. It gets very hot in the afternoons already, summer is nearly upon us.'

Lakshmi gave a great sigh. 'It is hard to have to bear the heat in the plains. As a girl, in my father's house, not one summer did we ever have to endure, we always went up to our house in Naini Tal, and also when I was first married and my husband was still – ' thinking a moment, she gave a laugh and then said with bitter satisfaction – 'yes, still sane.'

Gulab thought of all the summers she had known. Not the summers since she was married, she did not care to remember those. But the old ones, when she had slept out the noonday heat under the fan and afterwards, in the evening, she had bathed and eaten hot curry and then she had sat in the garden where the jasmine smelt so rich and sweet.

Uma said, 'A little heat more or less, what does it matter.' She really cared very little. Even in prison, in the hot bare hutments where the walls burnt and there was not a tree, not a blade of grass that was green and could throw a shade, even there she had cared very little.

'When I think of my poor boy out there in the plains with no electricity, no fan, nothing ... how can we find him a proper wife, what girl of good family will go out there to such a place?'

Gulab murmured, 'It will be difficult,' and certainly she herself would not care to have gone.

'Nonsense,' Uma said stoutly, 'for a young healthy girl it is nothing, on the contrary, she will even be happy to go there, she will feel that she is doing service for our India and her life will have purpose. If I were still a young girl and such a match were proposed for me, I would not hesitate one moment.'

'Even if the girl should be willing – who knows what ideas grow in the heads of young girls – is there any family that will consent to marry their child so unfavourably?'

'Of course, many will be happy to serve our country . . . And Narayan, such a handsome, clever, healthy boy.'

'Thanks be to God, but what is the use of all this to him when he must be out there, and his father – '

Uma called into the kitchen, 'How much longer do my children have to wait for their food?'

Gulab, whose lids were slowly sinking over her eyes, opened them again to say, 'It is time, I think.'

'I must go,' Lakshmi said.

'No,' Gulab said, surprisingly, 'please, why do you not stay to eat with us,' to which her aunt agreed at once.

Uma felt herself outwitted. She had been waiting to be alone with Gulab before starting on the topic of Esmond again; now Gulab had effectively prevented her. She has even acquired cunning, Uma thought, to fight against her mother and her happiness.

After food – a pilau with peas and browned onions and sultanas and almonds, a curry made of thick blocks of cream cheese, dark brown meat-balls, ladyfingers fried with onions in clarified butter – Gulab went to lie down on the floor in the long-room. Her mother saw to it that she was settled comfortably and even massaged her legs to make her quite contented and relaxed. Then she began with determination, for she was not going to let up; 'Daughter,' she said, and she looked at Gulab and saw that she was already asleep. Really asleep, not shamming; she had made up her mind to it and so she really slept. Uma sighed, knowing it was no use to try and wake her.

She sat down in the adjoining room, with Ravi on her lap. She rocked him and sang, 'We have made our bread and spread it with ghee'; soon he too was fast asleep. Lakshmi lay on a charpai, heavy with the good food she had eaten. A deaf and dumb ascetic, who had come walking all the way from the Himalayas, lay snoring in a corner.

'He is over thirty now,' Lakshmi said. She gave a good rich burp. 'It is a great worry to me.'

'Please do not worry. All will be well.'

'What mother would not . . . how he snores!' she said in disgust, glaring at the ascetic. 'Why do you allow such people into your house?'

Bachani appeared in the doorway from where she looked tenderly at Ravi asleep. 'How beautiful he is, our little one, may God bless him.' Uma rocked him to and fro and gazed into his face.

'He has taken nothing at all from his father,' Lakshmi said. 'He is as dark as a real Hindu child.'

'Thank God,' Uma said with passionate intensity.

'His skin is rather too dark, it is a pity.' Lakshmi threw another contemptuous look at the ascetic. 'You allow them to lie everywhere, have you no better use for the property your husband left for you?' It was a very sore point with her that her sister-in-law should have this spacious house while she and her husband had to live in an ugly rented flat in a tenement. 'We are her brother and sister,' she would often say to Ram Nath, 'is it not better that she should give two or three rooms to us than to allow all these pariahs to lie about at their ease?' She did not know how often Uma had tried to prevail on Ram Nath to give up his flat and come to live in her house; and how he always refused.

'See how he is lying there,' Lakshmi said, 'has he no shame to sleep in the same room where women are sitting?'

'Men or women, for one so holy it is all the same.' Uma sat and waited for Gulab to wake up. What shall I say to her, she thought. But she had said everything already.

When the worst of the afternoon heat was over, Lakshmi left. She said, 'Please think about what I have told you. We must find someone for my poor boy.'

Uma, with Ravi asleep in her arms, went to look at Gulab. She looked so peaceful, lying on her back, one arm laid across her waist, the other under her head. The lids of her closed eyes were large and smooth, with lashes like black satin.

'Child,' Uma said. Gulab opened her eyes and looked at her mother with Ravi in her arms.

'Child,' Uma said on a sudden inspiration, 'Why do you not stay here with me and never go back?' But she could see subterfuge at once clouding in her daughter's eyes which, coming out of sleep, had looked so liquid and innocent.

'Have I been sleeping long?' Gulab asked and sat up with a yawn.

'I will send for your things later or, if you like, I will go myself to take them and also tell him what we have decided.'

Gulab stretched herself and feigned a very deep and concentrated yawn.

'You need never go back there again. You need never see him again.' But it was no use because Gulab would not listen. She got up, perfunctorily arranged her hair and her sari and asked, 'Is there no tea for me?'

Again she sat and rocked herself on the veranda; she had tea and freshly-made fritters and some more sweetmeats. But it was not the same as it had been in the morning because she no longer had the whole day before her. Her face now was puckered slightly, it was not smooth and contented as it had been, though the fritters were very good, full of hot red chilis.

When Ravi woke up, he cried. He would not stop crying, though they did everything they could. At last he said, 'I do not want to go home, I want to stay with Nani,' and began to cry more stormily than ever. Gulab, driven almost beyond endurance, shouted at her mother, 'You taught him to say it! While I was asleep, you taught him!'

Uma, with a shocked expression on her face, put a hand to her heart and said, 'May God be my witness . . .' She took Ravi into her arms and told him, 'Listen, my darling, my sweet one, you will come again very soon to your Nani, a whole day you will come to her again and play and eat, very, very soon'; and she continued to murmur to him, to soothe him and comfort him, till he was quiet and sat and ate a whole rasgulla which she gave to him.

Gulab had meant to, she had really meant to go back as she had come – by bus. But the going back in itself was heavy enough for her. She stretched out her hand for another fritter and said as casually as she could, 'Please lend me money for a taxi, I have forgotten all my money at home.' She chewed her fritter for a while and then she added, 'Of course I will give it back to you.'

Uma lowered her head and looked down at her own hands, which were trembling slightly.

14

When the servant came to announce Uma, Madhuri made a very wry face. Her day was always very exactly apportioned. There was a set time for her bath, a set time for her accounts, a set time for her conversations with her husband; and of course, strictly dividing the day into three, set mealtimes. She hated to have her routine disturbed; and indeed, this very rarely happened. When she wanted to go out shopping, she would arrange to do so days beforehand; the chauffeur was given notice to have the car ready at a certain time, then she would sit in it to drive to she knew exactly what shops to make she knew exactly what purchases. Her social life was ordered in the same regular manner. On certain prearranged days she would sit in her car, dressed in one of her best saris, to call on ladies of her acquaintance;

or she would receive them in her house, sitting in the richly carpeted and cushioned drawing-room, while the servants passed round the dainty refreshments. She neither encouraged nor made chance visits, everything had to be fitted into her day beforehand.

Uma knew no such schedule. Her days were long and rambling and unpremeditated, full of possibilities. She rarely knew, when she woke up in the mornings, what she was going to do, whom she was going to see. Her visits, therefore, unexpected and unplanned-for, were always rather irritating to Madhuri, who shut her eyes wearily and told Indira, 'We shall have to finish this later.' They were making out a shopping list, for Madhuri had decided on a shopping expedition the day after tomorrow. Indira had been asked to accompany her: she found her daughter-in-law increasingly useful and indeed very pleasant, quiet company.

'How long it is since I have seen you,' Uma said at once, as soon as Madhuri came into the drawing-room. 'Too long, far, far too long;' and she embraced her and kissed her with great ardour. Madhuri submitted patiently; she knew this was inevitable with Uma.

'I always mean to come,' Uma said, 'but I do not know how it is, something always happens to prevent me.' It did not occur to her that Madhuri, who after all had a car, could as easily or more easily have come to see her. 'And Indira,' she said, kissing and embracing her too for good measure. She was so pleased to have come. 'Every time I see you,' she told Madhuri, 'you are more beautiful than ever.'

Madhuri smiled, rather painfully. 'At our age there can no longer be much talk of beauty.' Certainly, she thought, with Uma it has long gone. Not that she herself had ever granted her to have much. But now it was all gone; more than anything, Madhuri thought, through neglect. Uma had allowed herself to become too muscular and massive, and too dark and wrinkled in the sun. She seemed to take no care of her appearance at all: her hair which, Madhuri noted fully, was still quite black, straggled out of its pins; she wore a cotton sari of the cheapest millcloth bundled carelessly around her, and the sleeves of her blouse were too short, revealing far too much of her big muscular arms.

'Why so much ceremony with me,' Uma said, waving those same muscular arms right and left to indicate the room. 'I told the servant I will go up to her, I am not a stranger that I have to be made to sit on a chair in a fine room.'

Madhuri murmured, 'It is more comfortable for you here,' and was glad that she had such well-trained servants.

Indira, sitting demurely beside her mother-in-law, also made a very critical survey of their visitor. She was quite shocked by Uma's negligent attire: one would hardly think, she told herself, that she was a woman of our class.

'How lovely your home is,' Uma said with enthusiasm. Not that she usually noticed such things: but what delighted her about Madhuri's house was Madhuri's personality, which so daintily suffused it.

'How is Gulab?' Madhuri said. It cost her quite an effort to ask this, but etiquette demanded that the health of a visitor's nearest and dearest should be inquired after.

'I will bring her to you,' Uma promised, 'it is a long time since you have seen my child.' Madhuri thought this statement in very bad taste; certainly she had no desire ever to see or hear of Gulab again, and it seemed to her that if Uma had had any tact, she would have realized this.

'It is not right,' Uma said, 'that we who are as one should stay so long without seeing one another; when my daughter is your daughter and yours mine. Certainly I will bring her to you, soon, very soon.'

The worst of it was, Madhuri thought, that Uma really was capable of it. 'I hope you will,' she stiffly said.

Indira sat beside her mother-in-law, with her hands folded in her lap and her eyes demurely lowered. She was thinking, if only Uma would dress properly, she would look quite impressive. Of course, never dainty and charming like Madhuri, but with her powerful physique — her great height, her strong shoulders — impressive. And she carried herself well, one had to admit that.

'Marriage becomes you, daughter,' Uma said and smiled kindly at Indira, who gave a tinkling laugh.

'She is an excellent wife to my son and an excellent daughter-in-law to me,' Madhuri said very clearly and with ringing satisfaction.

'But of course!' Uma cried, quite failing to draw any inference.

Indira did not raise her eyes; her mouth was set in a prim line. She ought to wear black, she thought. A good black sari of heavy silk with perhaps a silver border; and a black blouse to match, sleeves reaching below the elbow. Or perhaps grey, all grey.

'Where is my Shakuntala?' Uma asked. 'I want so much to see her.' And she added, for it was true and she saw no reason for not saying it, 'It is her I have come most specially to see.'

'She is in her room, painting a picture with colours,' Indira said. And a few pieces of really good jewellery, she thought, speculatively fitting a necklace round Uma's strong sun-darkened neck, drop-earrings into her ears.

'Please, Indira, go and call her,' Madhuri said, feeling vaguely ashamed of her daughter's way of spending time.

'She has now finished her College, I think,' Uma said. 'It must be wonderful to have such a learned daughter, how proud you must be of her.' She spoke this without envy. She did not hanker after what she did not have. Gulab had been sent to College for a while – alas, that it had been so, for it was there that she had met Esmond – but it had always been evident that she had no aptitude for study.

'Girls must have a certain amount of education, this is the trend in modern times.'

'How true,' said Uma, nodding her head up and down and smiling blissfully.

One of Madhuri's well-trained bearers came in with a tray which, solemn and ceremonious, he placed on a carved little Kashmiri table. Uma leaned forward and saw lime-water in a cut-glass jug, cheese straws in one perforated silver bowl, thin arrowroot biscuits in another. She clapped her hands together and cried, 'You make everything look so nice, you are like a little queen!' gazing at her friend with great tenderness. Really, Madhuri thought testily, she is becoming childish in her middle age.

Shakuntala came running in, crying, 'Auntieji!' She wore a very professional smock splashed with paint over her sari, and there was also a streak of green paint along her cheek.

'Mmm!' said Uma with love and enthusiasm, unable to say more as her mouth was full with thin arrowroot biscuit. She got up and very heartily embraced Shakuntala, who equally heartily embraced her in return.

'Oh!' Shakuntala cried, drawing back, 'I am smearing you all over with paint!'

'Yes,' said Madhuri indignantly, 'I wonder, have you no shame to come in this manner before our visitor.' She was grateful at any rate that the visitor was only Uma and not one of the ladies of high social standing who came to pay calls.

'But I love to see her like this!' Uma cried.

'Like this?' Shakuntala laughed, looking down at herself. She stripped off her smock, of which she was really very proud, rolled it into a ball and tossed it into an armchair. 'You see, I was painting, but when Indira told me you are here, I came at once, that is why . . .'

Uma embraced her again: 'My own dear daughter.' Indira picked up the discarded smock and folded it neatly and silently. 'Thank you, Indira,' Madhuri said pointedly, but Shakuntala did not notice at all.

Uma, sitting in an armchair with her broad knees wide apart under her sari, looked round happily and said, 'How good it is to be with friends.' Indira thought, she has such nice hair, why does she not look after it properly.

'So now you have become a painter too, a great artist?' Shakuntala laughed and replied, 'Oh yes, very great,' looking at her mother, who failed to respond.

'Please paint me a picture too,' Uma said. 'I would like so much to have a beautiful picture of Siva and Parvati for my prayer-room.'

'I paint only in the modern style; I do not think this would be suitable for your prayer-room.'

Indira gave a well-mannered little laugh. 'Her pictures are so funny.'

'Because you do not understand, you say they're funny,' Shakuntala said.

'But Amrit also –'

'Oh, Amrit – he is just the biggest bourgeois of you all.'

'Where is Amrit, how much I would love to see him,' Uma said.

'Naturally, at this time of day he is in his office,' Madhuri said. 'He has a very responsible position.'

'And Raj? He will be coming home to India soon?'

'Yes soon, we hope ...' Why has he not written for so long, throbbed like a familiar little pulse in Madhuri's head. But, as familiar, came the immediate reassurance: he is all right, what can happen to a boy in Cambridge? It was such a safe place, where he could be exposed only to the best influences. She felt very comfortable about Cambridge. All the men in her family for the last two generations had gone there, all had come back polished and polite and ready to take up responsible positions. 'Yes,' she said, 'another six months and he will be home with us.'

Uma cried, 'How proud you must be of your sons! And dear Indira,' she said, turning to her with an affectionate smile, 'how proud she must feel of her husband.' Indira smoothed her sari over her lap and looked a little smug. Uma had an involuntary vision of her own Gulab sitting miserably in Esmond's flat. But it gave her, nevertheless, a glow of satisfaction to see Indira so fresh and well-tended and content.

She turned to Shakuntala and abruptly asked, 'Do you remember Narayan?'

'But of course, only the other day when Uncleji came we talked of him – he is so wonderful, such an Idealist.'

'Yes, yes!' Uma cried, and waited for Shakuntala to say more, which she did: 'Often now I think if only I had been cleverer or better, I too could have become a Doctor and gone out into the villages to serve Humanity. How wonderful such a life must be.'

'It is not suitable for a woman,' Madhuri said.

Uma did not hear. She was staring at Shakuntala, quite rapt; she cried, 'Really, you could like it, such a life?'

'But of course, what more can we ask but to be able to give ourselves for a great Cause?'

Indira said, 'You have paint on your cheek, Shakun.'

'Now that India is free,' Shakuntala said, and impatiently wiped her hand up her left cheek, 'the Cause we must work for is no longer her Independence but her Prosperity and Greatness.'

'Ah,' Uma said, smiling and thinking of herself as she had been at Shakuntala's age.

'The other side,' Indira said.

'And what better way is there than to turn one's back on the city with all its comforts and go out into the remotest villages to devote oneself to the cause of rural development?'

'How beautifully she talks,' Uma said. And she thought, how happy my brother will be when he hears of this: she is indeed the girl we want.

Madhuri said, 'It is talk only and nothing more.'

Shakuntala, who up to now had been looking exultant, the way she always did when she talked of these brave matters, at once assumed a hurt and slightly defiant air.

But Uma came enthusiastically to her defence. 'Ah, no, when it comes to the doing, she will do, I know it'; because she herself, in her own time, had both talked a lot and, when it came to the point, done all she could.

'If only there was something for me to do,' said Shakuntala, revived again and her voice quivering with a longing to prove herself. She too thought of Uma in those days and she added, 'In your time, Auntieji, all of you who wanted could help, you could all go to prison, but now – what can I do, when I am not a doctor nor a social worker nor,' she laughed as she said it, sounding not at all dispirited, 'good for anything at all.'

Uma wanted to cry, But there is something you can do! She wanted, here and now, to ask her to be the wife of Narayan. She thought how happy they would all be, Shakuntala and Madhuri and Indira, and she herself. She did not want to postpone that happiness – this is the moment, she thought. Already great joy was welling up inside her as she anticipated their reaction, first their surprise, then their joyful, enthusiastic assent: for they too would feel that this union was what was needed most in their lives, a beautiful climax. They would sit then with love for one another in their hearts and look radiantly together into the future.

Madhuri said, 'Shakuntala, please go to the bathroom and wash the paint from your face'; and to Uma she said, 'I hope there is enough sugar in your limewater?'

So then Uma did not say it after all, she felt the moment had passed.

15

Shakuntala greatly enjoyed Betty's party. She felt she was becoming quite an adept at parties, though this was only the second real grown-up one she had attended. She seemed to know practically everyone there, and they all remembered her and talked to her as quite one of themselves. What especially flattered her was that she was the only Indian girl present, all the others were Europeans. She found the men very polite and attentive, they all seemed to know how to talk to women, which was more, she thought, than most Indian men did (she remembered how awkward Amrit had always been with her friends, even though he had been to Cambridge). Only in one thing was she disappointed: she had always thought that all Europeans knew all there was to know about Culture and that their conversation was always intellectual. She enjoyed their conversation, very much, but she had to admit it was not intellectual. Nor did she find them particularly attractive; they were all rather too large and too red. Only Esmond was slim and handsome.

She was one of the last to leave. This was because she was enjoying herself so much that she noticed neither the time nor the general move to go. It was not till Esmond said to Betty, 'I think it's time I made a move on too,' that she thought of leaving.

She and Esmond found themselves out by the gate together. 'Lovely party,' she said, to which he answered, 'Yes, wasn't it,' rather absently, looking up the road.

She stood hesitating and a little awkward. There was so much she wanted to say to him. Most of all she wanted to talk to him about his unhappiness which she had discovered the other day at Betty's flat. She understood him so well and she wanted him to know it. Only in what words, out there in the dark after the party at which she had not had much opportunity to talk to him, in what words to tell him, while he was busily looking up the road, that she saw into his innermost soul?

Because nothing else came to her, and yet she felt it vital to make some communication to him, she said, 'What a beautiful evening,' but before she had finished saying it, he -- who had not expected any further communication from her and so had probably not even heard -- told her, 'Well, good night,' and swung off down the road.

Her father had lent her the car for the evening, so she had no trouble about getting home. But when she got to the car, the driver was not there, which made her suddenly very cross. She supposed he was sitting gossiping somewhere with the other drivers or playing cards. She put her hand on the horn and pressed viciously, but still it took some time before finally he came running. Then she spoke very angrily to him, told him that if anything like this happened again, she would tell her father and see to it that he was dismissed. 'Forgive me,' he said, 'I erred,' but he said it negligently because he had said it so often before.

She continued to feel cross and somehow dissatisfied. He has spoilt my evening, she thought, glaring at the driver's back. He pulled up short – 'Now what's the matter?' she asked testily; 'Bus,' he said, jerking his head towards the window. She looked and saw a bus with a line of people ascending it. One of the people in the line, tall and noble among the rest, was Esmond.

'Stop,' she told the driver; 'stop.' She sent him to fetch Esmond, and when he came, she said, 'Can I give you a lift anywhere, please?'

'That's awfully nice of you. If you happen to be going down near Sundernagar?'

She was not, but she said, 'Please get in,' and to the driver, 'Go to Sundernagar.'

'Well, that was a lucky break,' Esmond said, settling himself beside her quite comfortably. It rather surprised her that he did not have a car of his own. He was the sort of person who ought to have a car, a long slim one, blue-grey in colour. But perhaps it had gone for repairs.

'How is Gulab?' she asked, remembering that she had not yet asked him that evening.

'Yes,' he said, and there was a short pause.

But because this was the only point of contact she had with him at the moment, she said, 'I would like to meet her, I have not seen her in so long. Yesterday her mother came to our house.' Esmond took out his cigarette case and silently offered it to her. She shook her head. 'Do you mind,' he murmured, lighting one for himself.

'I am very fond of her mother, she is so close to us, almost like a real relation. The whole family is so close to us, that is, her uncle Ram Nath also ...'

'You're sure Sundernagar isn't out of your way?'

'It is quite all right. Of course, everybody admires Ram Nathji very much, he is a great man. He leads a more retired life now, but in our struggle for freedom he played a very big part, his name was known all over India and he was loved by millions.'

Esmond politely nodded as he brushed ash off his knee.

'And there is also his son Narayan – you must of course know Narayan?'

'I've met him,' Esmond said, 'once or twice.'

'He too is doing very good work. He is an Idealist like his father, he does not care anything at all about money or position, he only wants to do good and relieve the sufferings of humanity – do you not think, Mr Stillwood,' she said, turning towards him and looking at him out of earnest, wide-open eyes, 'that we should all be like that, to follow only noble and unselfish ends?'

'Oh, rather,' said Esmond. He leant towards the driver and told him brusquely and in Hindustani where to draw up.

'Oh, are we there already!' Shakuntala cried.

Esmond opened the car door and with one leg out, said, 'So nice of you, thanks most awfully.'

'Do you know,' said Shakuntala on a sudden inspiration, and her eyes flashed with pleasure, 'I think I will come with you for a minute, if I may. I would so much like to see Gulab again.'

He laughed, rather taken aback, this was so unexpected. But he said, 'Please do,' and then he laughed again, holding the car door open for her in a gentlemanly manner.

He knew that Gulab would be in bed already, though it was only half past eight. She always went to bed early, she knew of nothing else to do. He rather looked forward to calling her out.

'Won't you make yourself comfortable?' he said to Shakuntala, indicating the gaily striped little divan.

'What a sweet room,' she said with enthusiasm. It was like the other rooms in which she had attended parties, only nicer still. How lucky Gulab was.

'Gulab!' he called. 'I wonder where she could be?' He could not, however, suppress a little smile.

'Oh, I do hope she is at home!'

'I think she is; she doesn't go out much these days.'

'Because of the child, I think.'

'Yes, because of the child. Gulab!'

'Please do not disturb her. Perhaps she is putting the child to sleep.'

He strode into her bedroom; though the windows were thrown open, it was still thick and sensuous with her smell. He turned on the light, exposing her discarded clothes scattered about. 'Come on,' he said, 'get up.' She was lying fast asleep on the bed. She lay on her back with her arms spreadeagled. He stood above her and looked down at her, lying there so vulnerable and exposed.

'Get up, there's someone come to see you.' And when she did not move, he prodded her shoulder and felt his finger sink into her flesh. This gave him a peculiar pleasure and he did it again, harder. 'You've got a visitor.'

She sat up, clutching her shoulder. 'Mama has come?'

'No, someone else. Come and see.' He grinned and called in a mocking voice, 'Surpri-ise!' And when he saw her look anxious, added humorously, 'Oh you needn't get panicky, it's no gentleman come to rape you with unseemly eyes. It's an old friend of yours.'

Though she could remember no old friend, Gulab, still heavy with sleep, got up and padded on naked feet into the sitting-room. Where she stood in the doorway and blinked against the light.

Shakuntala rose from the divan and said, 'Are you surprised to see me?'

Esmond, much amused, watched them both. Shakuntala was smiling; she stood there, healthy and radiant and dressed up in good clothes. Gulab had on the old sari and crumpled blouse she wore in bed; she was dazed and drowsy, and she held up her sari across her bosom with one hand, so that she looked somewhat on the defensive.

Shakuntala laughed out loud and said, 'You do not even recognize me, I think?'

Gulab blinked. But then suddenly her expression changed. Esmond, watching her, was surprised: he had not seen his wife look like this for a long time, had indeed forgotten that she could look like it. Her eyes, always somewhat melancholy, lit up and flashed with pleasure, she said in a low happy voice, 'Oh, Shakuntala, how glad I am to see you.' The two of them embraced one another, while Esmond said, 'My, my,' and smiled tolerantly.

Afterwards the two girls sat on the divan together. Gulab held her friend's hand, she would not let go. Shakuntala felt slightly uneasy: she had not anticipated such a warm welcome. She had never been very friendly with Gulab, even though they had grown up together; she had always considered her very slow and stupid, and had often laughed at her. She remembered this now, and felt somewhat ashamed.

Gulab, however, did not seem to remember anything except a perfectly radiant and beautiful friendship. 'How happy I am to see you,' she kept saying, 'how good of you to come to me,' pressing the other's hand.

'Don't you think you ought to offer our visitor something?' Esmond said.

'No, please – ' Shakuntala implored, laying a restraining hand on Gulab's arm.

Gulab thought hard what she could offer her friend. There were no sweetmeats in the house, no home-made sherbet; Esmond kept only factory-made biscuits in a tin, and these Gulab felt ashamed to offer to a friend like Shakuntala.

'At least have a drink,' Esmond said.

Gulab said in a shocked tone of voice, 'But she does not drink.'

'Oh no,' Esmond said with a laugh, opening his cocktail cabinet. Shakuntala did not want a drink, but now she felt she had to have one, to justify Esmond. For the same reason she also had to accept a cigarette.

Gulab stared at her, but it was more in admiration than in condemnation.

Shakuntala asked as casually as she could, 'You do not smoke?' Gulab shook her head, while she continued to look at her friend with admiring eyes.

'I've tried so hard to corrupt her,' Esmond said, 'but her virtues are too deep-rooted for my little arts.' Shakuntala laughed, rather uncertainly, but Gulab gave no sign of having heard.

'You were always so clever,' Gulab said.

'Who, I?' Shakuntala said with an uneasy laugh.

'I always admired you so much – oh, how happy I am to see you, how good of you to come, it is like a dream.'

'Would you care to see our boy?' Esmond said.

Shakuntala got up at once; she felt as if he had come to her rescue.

'Of course he's asleep now,' he said, leading the way.

'How sweet he is,' she said, looking at Ravi asleep. But he did not take after Esmond at all; he looked just like an ordinary Indian boy. 'I think he takes after you,' she told Gulab, who then radiated pleasure.

'Only in complexion, so they say,' Esmond said a trifle crossly.

Shakuntala looked at Ravi again. She tried hard to find Esmond's features in him; she wanted to find them. 'You are right,' she said, 'only in complexion,' and did not notice that Gulab looked hurt.

'Well, come on, there'll be murder if we wake him,' Esmond said with a smile. He put his arm lightly across Shakuntala's back to steer her out, which made her heart beat fast.

'You have such a lovely flat,' she said. She did not sit down on the divan again because she felt uncomfortable with Gulab sitting so close beside her, so soft and warm and sensuous, fondling her hand.

'Yes, my wife's quite an interior decorator,' Esmond said, one corner of his mouth drawn up into a smile. Shakuntala looked at Gulab who, however, gave no sign of either assent or denial. Shakuntala felt almost indignant: never in one thousand years, she thought, would she be able to furnish a house in this manner; it is all his work, only his.

'She's forever thinking up something new,' Esmond said. Gulab stared straight ahead. 'Yes, Gulab?' Shakuntala asked.

'Colour schemes are her speciality.'

Gulab said, 'Now you must come often, often.'

'Of course,' Shakuntala said; but she felt that she sounded false and forced in contrast to Gulab's ardent sincerity.

'Have another drink?' Esmond said.

'No, I – ' She had already had two cocktails at Betty's party, she really could not take any more. But somehow she felt she had to, he was willing her to, as if he wanted to set her up as an example or prove something by her.

'Your friend,' Esmond told his wife, 'is a member of the W.W.O. You are a member, aren't you?'

Shakuntala nodded. 'I think it is so much fun.' And then she said, because that seemed what he wanted her to say, 'Why do you not also join, Gulab?'

'What should I do there,' Gulab said quite calmly, apparently unaware of Esmond's smiling look upon her.

'But there is so much to do!'

'Just what I'm always telling her,' Esmond said.

Gulab smiled and shrugged at Shakuntala. 'But you know how I am ...' Shakuntala knew very well: slow and stupid and quite unfit for the company of emancipated European ladies. Why did he marry her, she thought, why. And she remembered again his unhappiness, the lines of sadness she had seen on his face as he had turned from the bookcase that evening in Betty's flat. Her heart turned over with pity for him. She glanced at him, as he sat there between Gulab and herself. But now he was serene and smiling; that did not, however, make her feel any better. On the contrary, it gave her a vague feeling of dissatisfaction.

'You were always so brave and clever,' Gulab said.

Esmond said, 'Does one have to be brave and clever to join the W.W.O.?'

'Even as a child you dared to do everything – to me you were always like a great heroine, like the Rani of Jhansi, because you dared so much and were so clever.' She laughed and looked at Shakuntala with great delight out of her beautiful eyes.

Shakuntala also laughed, but more uneasily. She glanced at Esmond and said, 'I was such an ordinary stupid little girl.'

Gulab cried, 'Never!' She reached out her hand to fondle Shakuntala's knee.

Shakuntala got up. 'I think really I must go.'

'But you will come again,' Gulab said. 'Very soon you will come again.'

'Yes, I – '

Esmond said, 'I'll see you down to your car.'

'You must see Ravi when he is awake, how you will love him, he is so sweet.'

'Yes.'

'I will tell him about you, then he will love you when he sees you and he will not be afraid. When shall I tell him you will come?'

'Oh, soon,' Shakuntala said, stooping to enter the car door which the driver held open for her. When she had settled herself on the back seat, she looked out of the window and said, trying to sound more enthusiastic, 'Very soon I will come again.'

'Come when – come in the mornings, on Wednesday or Friday.'

Esmond stuck his head through the window. 'I say, are you coming to Agra on that W.W.O. expedition?'

Shakuntala had not known that there was such an expedition, but she said at once, 'Oh yes, it will be so nice.'

'See you then.'

'Yes, see you then.' She waved good-bye to Esmond and, just as her car drove away, remembered to wave to Gulab too.

16

It was while she was taking her morning bath that Lakshmi had this wonderful idea. Afterwards she hurried through her prayers, sitting before the little shrine in the corner which she had partitioned off with a curtain from her bedroom. When she had finished, she went into her husband's room because she wanted to tell him at once what she had thought of. She was much annoyed to find that he had gone out. Where has he to go to, she thought, that he should roam like a vagabond through the streets. She hated these vague, aimless walks of his. Once or twice she had met him by chance in the streets, and she had noted how odd he looked, walking with his head bent and an air of obliviousness about him. She had been quite ashamed to acknowledge him, and it had been almost a relief that he had failed, or pretended to fail, to recognize her.

She walked about her two rooms, slowly sipping the tumbler of tea she had prepared for herself. She wanted very much to talk to somebody about her new idea; it was almost painful to her to keep something so exciting locked up, uncommunicated, in her own head. For want of anyone to talk to, she even sat down to write to her eldest daughter. But even after she had written *Dearest Daughter, God give you his blessings, here all is well,* according to form, she found that she could get no relief through written words. To formulate her thoughts was so laborious that by the time they reached the paper, they were no longer her thoughts at all, but something alien and abstract. Talking even to her co-tenants, low as they were was better than this lifeless form of communication.

She went to sit out in the courtyard. On the galleries ranged above her, the other tenants were hanging up clothes, washing children, cooking breakfasts and packing tiffin-carriers. It was the busiest time of the day, just before children left for school and husbands for government offices. Nobody had any time to spare for Lakshmi; except for the widowed sister of an officer in the telegraph office, who had quarrelled with her sister-in-law five years ago and had ever since refused to help with any work in the house. Lakshmi called to her, 'Come down, sister, I have made some good pickles, I will present you with a jar.' The other came, and at once Lakshmi said, 'Yes, soon I think my son will come home.' When she had said this, she became quite enthusiastic: he would come home, they would make this advantageous marriage for him, he would take a large house and begin a flourishing practice in Delhi and she would go and live with him and his wife. At last she would again be ruling over a prosperous household. 'Soon perhaps our hard times will be over,' she said, but the other only asked, 'What kind of pickles are they?'

When Ram Nath came home from his walk, the first thing she said to him was, 'How many times have I told you, it will kill you to go walking so much on an empty stomach, a weak old man like you'; and then, 'I have thought out everything – when the husband sits still and does nothing, all duties come down on his wife. What we will do is this: we will go to Har Dayal and tell him we wish to arrange a marriage for our Narayan with his Shakuntala.'

Ram Nath washed his hands, letting the water trickle down from his wrists. Then he went to his study, and at once began to read from where he had left off the night before. Lakshmi followed him, she said, 'Har Dayal is an influential man, he will be able to do a great deal for his son-in-law.'

'You are always grumbling how I starve myself, but I see no signs of my tea.'

'You will go to him today, there is no sense in wasting any more time.' She shuffled off to get his tea, all the time thinking happy thoughts about the good times ahead, when Narayan should be married to Shakuntala and live in a big house with many servants. When she came back along the passage, there was Uma just entering the house, holding a little earthenware pot covered with a fresh green leaf. Her sister-in-law was the person she wanted most at this stage to see and consult with, and she took her opportune appearance as a happy omen that from now on all things would be well and go, for the first time since her marriage, according to her wishes.

'See here,' said Uma, holding up the little earthenware pot, 'I have brought you some buttermilk made from fresh curds.'

Lakshmi, holding her husband's tea in one hand, clutched her sister-in-law with the other and whispered to her urgently, 'I have thought it all out, Narayan must marry Har Dayal's Shakuntala.'

The Madrasi clerk from the first floor came down the stairs and along the passage, on his way out to his office. He looked very clean and morning-fresh, wearing his shirt with a slight suggestion of waist-line over his trousers and his moustache neatly trimmed, his hair smoothly oiled. Uma called out to him, 'Well, Mr Ayyer, when is the date for your daughter's wedding?' to which he answered with a shy smile and the hope that she would come and honour them with her presence.

'You take more interest in these people who are nothing to you than you do in your own family,' Lakshmi grumbled.

'It was very difficult for him to find a suitable son-in-law among the South Indian community here. He is a Brahmin, and he cannot afford a great dowry.'

'What do I care about such people – listen to me, is it not a good idea what I have told you?'

'Now, thank God, he has found a good honest hard-working boy, a Brahmin of course, a clerk in a warehouse with excellent prospects. This tea is for my brother?'

'Come in with me, we will talk with him together.'

When they went in, Ram Nath looked up from his book and told Uma, 'She has had a great new idea.'

'I know, she has told me.'

'It is good,' said Lakshmi, 'that at least one among us has ideas.'

The other two exchanged a glance and then Ram Nath said, 'Well, you can tell her if you like.'

'Tell her what?' Lakshmi said, getting cross and looking from one to the other.

'You see,' said Uma, 'my brother has also had the same idea.'

Lakshmi cried, 'And you have spoken with Har Dayal?'

'The letter,' Ram Nath said, 'tell her also about the letter.'

'Narayan wrote and asked his father to find a wife for him.'

'He wrote! And I, the mother, was not told!'

Ram Nath rubbed his hands and cackled to himself. He looked incredibly malicious.

Uma, however, was embarrassed. She said weakly, 'You were so worried about Narayan, we did not want to . . .' and was even more embarrassed when Lakshmi burst into tears. Ram Nath cackled more loudly.

'Be quiet!' his sister shouted at him. She embraced her sister-in-law very tenderly and said, 'Take no notice of him, he is just mad,' making fierce signs to Ram Nath over Lakshmi's shoulder.

Lakshmi buried her face in Uma's bosom and luxuriantly wept. 'He has taken everything from me, and now he even wants to rob me of my son . . .'

'Rob, rob, why rob?' Uma said, patting her vigorously on the back by way of comfort. 'On the contrary, he is making plans to give you another daughter in addition to your son – and such a good brave sweet girl, you will have much comfort from your son's wife, you will see.'

Lakshmi raised her head. 'And he has spoken with Har Dayal?'

'Not yet – first of course he wanted to consult with you – '

'Of course,' said Ram Nath gravely.

' – and then afterwards, if you give your consent, he will go to Har Dayal and they will speak of it together.'

Lakshmi wiped her eyes with the end of her sari. 'You brought buttermilk?' After she had drunk it, she said, 'I will go and speak with Madhuri myself.'

'Not yet,' Uma said quickly, 'there is no need yet. First let him speak with Har Dayal, the two fathers together – '

'The two mothers should speak together also,' Lakshmi said with dignity; 'these things are best discussed among women.'

'Very well,' said Ram Nath, 'then you may go and speak, I will not go at all. Why should I trouble myself?'

'I know very well, whenever you can throw a burden on to me you will throw it, it has been like this always, ever since the cursed day they married me to you.'

'Of course he will go,' Uma said. 'He will tell Har Dayal how much we love his Shakuntala and would like to see her as a daughter in our house.'

'Har Dayal knows very well the worth of our family, even though today we are poor and unregarded. His father's lands adjoined my Uncle's lands in Uttar Pradesh and always their women came to call on my aunt and her daughters-in-law – I remember very well how

they all sat together in the big inner courtyard and the servants brought sherbet.'

'The girl,' said Uma, 'is exactly the type of girl we want for our Narayan – she is strong and healthy and intelligent, and she does not care for conventional life, she is very idealistic.'

'They will be happy to be connected with us – they were very disappointed when our Gulab ... but I hear the boy later made a good match, a girl from the Mathur family of Tejaput, he must have got a good dowry with her.'

'Narayan will be happy with Shakuntala, I know, and she will be a great help to him in his work.'

'That is exactly what I was thinking: Har Dayal has many good connections, so that it will not be difficult for a son-in-law of his to establish himself in practice here. This marriage will be a great relief to me.'

'If you had heard her talk as I heard her the other day – I could hear behind her voice God crying out to me, "This is the wife born for your brother's son!" '

'I am sure Har Dayal will give a fine dowry with her, one lakh at least, besides great wedding celebrations – but we are not so much interested in that. What is of greater interest to us is his influence in the best circles, and also I know he has several pieces of property here in Delhi of which he will want to settle one on his daughter and her husband, so that they can live in comfort.'

'Live in comfort?' Uma repeated, and then she looked at her brother. He seemed intent on his book, though from the amused expression on his face, she knew very well that he was listening.

'And I also can at last, in my old age, have some peace and return to the life into which I was born. Oh, how happy I shall be to leave this house and all the people in it! It is a great hardship to me to have to live with such people – just think, only this morning that widow from upstairs came and said "what pickle have you made?" just like that she asked me, as if I were her servant.'

'I did not know,' said Uma rather uneasily, 'that Narayan wanted to come and live in Delhi.'

'What do you mean,' Lakshmi cried, 'you did not know? What is there to know? Does not everybody know that a boy, a wonderful great Doctor, who had to live out in the jungles because there is no one to help him on in life, that such a boy wants to return to the city to live in a decent respectable manner and have a car and a house like other doctors? This is just common sense.'

Uma looked, rather hopelessly, towards her brother. He had his

108

head still lowered over his book, but his shoulders were hunched up and he was silently laughing to himself.

'Sister,' Uma said, 'our Narayan is not like other boys.'

'Of course not, he is so much cleverer, that is known to all the world.'

'Yes, he is much cleverer and therefore he knows that worldly possessions such as cars and houses are of little worth.'

Lakshmi looked at her husband and cried, 'Those are your thoughts, not my son's! My son has sense in his head, he is a fine, clever, honourable boy, he will see to it that his mother spends the remaining days of her life in comfort and happiness.'

'In the Gita it is written – '

'Please do not tell me what is written in the Gita! I have heard nothing but Gita, Gita, Gita, all my life – when my husband went to prison, you came and told me how the Gita says that this is a good thing, when all my jewels were taken from me, my clothes, my property, when I had to come and live in this house with such neighbours, always the Gita said it was a good thing.'

Uma quoted with an air of grandeur: ' "That man attains peace who, abandoning all desires, moves about without attachment and longing, without the sense of *I* and *mine*." '

'Thank you, I have heard that many times, till now I am tired. Is there anyone who has abandoned more desires than I? What attachments to the world have been left to me? It is you, not I, who live in a large house with so many rooms that you do not know what to do with half of them. Please read the Gita for your own benefit, not for mine.'

'But Narayan's nature is such that he does not wish to be attached to these worldly things: he wants only to serve, so that he can develop his soul.'

'There is no need for you to come and tell me about my boy's soul. It is I who am his mother, it is given to me to read into his heart, not to you.'

Uma sighed and glanced again at her brother; but he was still bent over his book.

'I have heard enough in my life,' Lakshmi said, 'about serving and sacrifice, now I think it is time for me to enjoy some fruits of my sacrifice. My son, thank God, has some feeling for his mother, he will not, like his father, sit quiet when he sees her having to live in the same house with people who in better times might have been the servants in my father's house. He will take me away from here; you will see, all will be well if only you do not stand in his way with

words of duty and sacrifice, as you have always stood in my way.'

'No one has to say these words to Narayan,' said Uma. 'He feels them here in his own heart. That is why we think Shakuntala will be a good wife for him, because she too is the type of person who does not care for worldly possessions but wants only to do good in life . . .'

'What are you trying to tell me,' Lakshmi said with deep contempt. 'All her life she has lived in a big house with many servants, she has had all the jewellery and saris she wants – should she now give up these things because you tell her not to care for worldly possessions?'

'That is the type of person she is.'

'And Madhuri – do you think she would allow her daughter to live such a life? Would any mother allow her daughter to live such a life? No, Har Dayal will see to it that they are comfortable, no son-in-law of his need ever want. At last my Narayan will find someone to help him in his career and set him up in the world in a manner fitting to the family he has been born into.'

Uma inwardly sighed, but said no more. Ram Nath drank his tea with a rather ostentatious enjoyment.

Feeling for once victorious, Lakshmi cried, 'And it is only right that Har Dayal should help my boy! He is a well-placed man, he serves on many committees and lives as comfortably as his father did. What has he ever given up? When we lost everything, he kept everything, he and his wife and his children. My husband had to go to prison, so that Har Dayal afterwards might become an important man –'

'At last you admit that I have been of some use in life,' said Ram Nath.

'Now let him do something for us, it is time, I think.' And just in case Ram Nath should think she had really been paying him a compliment, she added, 'Let Narayan look to his father-in-law, since his own father has not sufficient love in his heart to help his son.'

17

Gulab said, 'And she looks so pretty, even prettier than when she was a girl.'

Uma nodded; she was pleased. She laid a finger on her lip with a coy little smile, and then she said, 'I will tell you a secret.'

'Please tell me too!' Ravi cried.

'You too,' she said and kissed him. 'It is this – now your Uncle wants to arrange a marriage for her with Narayan.'

Gulab, whose mind never worked very quickly, sat silent for a while, chewing her betel-nut leaf.

'Do you not think this is a good idea, my darling? She is just the right wife for him.'

'For Narayan? I see: you wish to arrange a marriage for her with Narayan?'

Uma nodded and kissed the tip of Ravi's nose. 'And when will we arrange for you, my most precious, when will that happy time be?'

'But this is wonderful!' Gulab cried. 'She will really be my sister!' A few minutes after she had said this, she realized that it might have come about earlier and in another, closer, way; then she hung her head and felt confused.

Uma, who realized very well what was going on in her daughter's mind, cried rather more heartily than she might otherwise have done, 'Yes, how happy we shall be!' But afterwards she thought, no, why should I help her out, so she said very deliberately, 'Once it was in your power alone, daughter, to unite our two families.'

Gulab hung her head down lower, but her face began to assume a defiant expression.

'I do not reproach you; I only want to tell you that you can undo what has been done whenever you want – today if you like: shall I help you to pack your clothes and jewels?'

With a determined if unsubtle effort at silencing her mother on this subject, Gulab said, 'But is it all arranged? Why have you not told me up to now?'

'Nothing is arranged yet. Your Uncle will go and speak with Har Dayal.' She wanted to get back to that other topic, but when she glanced at her daughter's face, she changed her mind. 'Yes, he will speak with Har Dayal and then we will see.' I am weak, she told herself, I ought to urge her: it would only mean giving her pain, like a doctor, a surgeon, so that in the end she need have no more pain. But she only said, 'I am happy that you like her so much, it is very important for the women in a family to love one another.'

'Oh I do love her,' Gulab said, raising her head again and speaking with a sort of passionate and joyful intensity. 'I have always loved her, so very very much.'

Uma kissed her daughter's hand. 'My darling,' she said. She thought, how can I hurt her, she is so good and pure, her heart so soft and loving.

'Soon perhaps you will have a new auntie,' Gulab told Ravi. 'How happy you will be.'

He thought it over for a moment, then he asked, 'What is my auntie's name?'

'Her name is Shakuntala and she is very beautiful, you will be so proud of her, you will walk with her at India Gate and everyone will look and envy you.'

'Is she as beautiful as my Mama?'

'No one is as beautiful as your Mama,' said Uma with decision. She looked at her daughter proudly and rather defiantly, as if daring anyone to contradict her. And indeed, it would have been difficult to think of anyone more beautiful than soft, luscious Gulab.

But as her beauty was nothing new or exciting to her, she never cared to hear it discussed. 'Your new auntie came to see you,' she told Ravi. 'She came in the night and she looked at you and she said how lovely my little Ravi is.'

'What did I say to my auntie?'

'You said nothing, you were asleep. Only you smiled in your sleep and then your auntie knew that you were happy to see her.'

'What does he want?' Uma said irritably, jerking her head towards the doorway where the servant stood, blankly staring. 'What do you want!' she shouted. He blinked once, a hood flickering over the empty eyes, but his expression remained unchanged. 'He is always standing looking, looking, looking, what does he *want*?'

Gulab shrugged her shoulders. She yawned, tapping the back of her hand several times against her open mouth. She never even noticed him; so many servants had come and gone since her marriage that for her they had ceased to have individual personalities, being no more significant than any other piece of property around the house.

'I do not like it, all these new servants and you and the little one alone here.'

'There he is,' Gulab said in a low voice.

'Who?' Uma said, and a few moments later she became aware of steps on the stairs. She was not, unlike her daughter, trained and tense to sense Esmond's approach.

Gulab thought quick, what did we eat, is there any smell of food, has Ravi had his bath. She said, 'Why is he early today?' resentful and unhappy because she had so much looked forward to being alone with her mother for at least another hour.

Uma, noticing her daughter's change of mood, became angry. She glared at Esmond and greeted him with, 'You are early today,' accusingly.

He was so much taken aback that, on the defensive, he said almost apologetically, 'My student is down with jaundice.' Only afterwards did he recollect himself sufficiently to assume his urbane and ironic manner; then he leaned against the wall, with his arms folded and his

elegant ankles crossed, and asked, smiling his lifted-eyebrows smile, 'Not in your way, am I?'

'Of course you are in our way,' his mother-in-law said irritably. 'You must understand that a mother and a daughter like to be alone sometimes so that they may talk together in peace.'

Gulab told herself, I am not listening, not listening, and combed Ravi's hair with great concentration.

'Awfully sorry,' Esmond said as urbanely as he could under the circumstances.

'What do you mean awfully sorry – if you are awfully sorry, then please go away again, this would show that you are really sorry and respect our feelings.'

'What *have* I done to make your mother so angry?' he asked good-humouredly.

'Angry, angry, I am not angry, I am only telling you truth!' She was almost shouting, but when she caught sight of her daughter's face, bent in agonized concentration over Ravi's hair, she tried to control herself. She got up and paced the room, swaying her head from side to side as she urgently told herself, be calm now, say nothing, she wants you to say nothing.

'I'll go away again, if you really feel so strongly about it.'

'Well, well, now you are here you may stay.' She stopped in front of him and surveyed him. 'It is not very often I see you.' For her own sake she would have scorned to avoid him deliberately; but for Gulab's she did it, and so she only came when he was sure to be out.

'Is that my fault?' he asked with another smile.

'It is not your fault, but it is as I told you – a mother and a daughter like to be alone together, it is only natural.'

'You look well,' he told his big, robust mother-in-law.

'What does it matter if I look well or not,' she said with an impatient toss of the head. 'I am just an old woman, whether I die tomorrow or the day after does not make much difference. It is the looks of these two, your wife and your son, you should see to.'

'They're all right, aren't they? I flatter myself I look after them very well.'

Uma pointed an accusing finger at Ravi and said, 'My grandson looks thin.' Ravi stared back at her with great, frightened eyes.

'Who, Ravi? *No*,' said Esmond, pronouncing the vowel very broadly and accompanying it with a playful, diagonally downward wave of the hand. 'He's just svelte – aren't you, my duck?' Addressed thus directly, Ravi shifted his eyes, grown even bigger and more frightened, towards his father.

'Of course not, Mama, you are imagining,' Gulab said. Rather ostentatiously she glanced at the clock: 'It is nearly time for his lunch, I will go and prepare his boiled vegetables.'

'There is no need,' Uma said sternly. 'He may eat the food I brought, it will be better for him.'

'He cannot eat such food,' Gulab intoned, not looking at anyone; 'it is too rich for him.'

'Nonsense!' cried Uma, determined to fight at least this minor battle. 'It is exactly the food a child needs, good strengthening food cooked in plenty of ghee! If you do not give such food no wonder my grandson looks thin.' She glared at Esmond, her head very erect and her nostrils inflated.

'But, Mama, I told you you are imagining,' Gulab pleaded; 'he does not look thin, he is only – ' but she could not remember the word Esmond had used.

'Well, perhaps just this once,' Esmond said good-humouredly. 'Because his granny brought it.'

'Not just this once, but always! Always a child needs this food!' She got angry again, and then she forgot Gulab's desperate pleading eyes. 'He needs such food, and he also needs to have his legs rubbed with oil to make them strong and his hair must be shaved so that it may grow luxuriant, and black shadow must be applied under the eyes to shield them from the strong sun, and in the night he must sleep with his mother so that she may comfort him if he wakes with bad dreams!'

Esmond crossed his legs the other way and smiled tolerantly. But Gulab said, staring straight ahead of her, 'Mama, your ideas are so old-fashioned; we are educating Ravi according to modern theory.'

Esmond smiled brilliantly at his mother-in-law: 'Doesn't it sound silly coming from her?'

'What do you mean? What are you saying against my daughter?'

'He is making a joke!' Gulab cried.

He smiled more and stretched out his hand towards Ravi: 'Come to Daddy, darling.' But as Ravi started up towards his father, Uma, sitting between them, intercepted him. She held his little body between her great arms and hugged him close, so close that it hurt him almost, though he kept quite still.

'You like your granny better than your Daddy?' Esmond affectionately inquired.

Uma shut her eyes and held him tight. You are mine, she willed through her tensed body; mine, mine, not his.

Gulab murmured, 'He does not see her very often.'

Uma wanted to shout then, I will take them both home with me, today, I will take them away from here.

Gulab said, 'Now go to Daddy, Ravi,' and Uma, feeling helpless and defeated, relaxed her hold and let him go.

Ravi said, 'Soon I will have a new auntie.'

'A new what, love?' Esmond asked.

'Nothing, nothing,' Gulab put in quickly. Instinctively she felt that she did not want him to know. What concerned her family was no concern of his, she did not want it to be.

He shot her a quick, intelligent glance – the same he always used when he was on the track of something she had done against his orders – then returned, tenderly, to his son. 'A new auntie, boy?'

'Her name is Shakuntala.'

'And a very nice name too.'

'She came to see me in the night when I was sleeping.'

'Came to see you ...? Oh – *that* Shakuntala.' He laughed and looked at his wife: 'And how, pray, is she to be his auntie?'

'There is no need to speak of it,' Uma said. 'Nothing at all is fixed yet, so what is the use of speaking of it?'

'Well, you seem to have been putting some ideas in my boy's head.'

'He is a child – only in play we spoke of it.'

'But of what?'

'You see,' said Gulab, heavily, because she did not like to tell him, 'Mama says they want to arrange a marriage for my cousin Narayan with Shakuntala.'

'Is that all? Why make such a mystery of it?'

'It is no mystery,' Uma said. 'Only I said there is no need to speak yet, before strangers.'

'So now I'm strangers?' But he turned it off lightly: certainly he wanted no quarrel, especially since he saw that she was so ready for one. All he said was, 'Sounds a queer match to me,' in an offhand manner.

'It is not your place to judge what is queer and not queer,' Uma pounced again. The way she said 'queer' was not quite right: it was not a word she would have used herself, she spoke it as one would pick up a strange thing between forceps.

Esmond threw up both his hands and said, 'Pax.'

'In India,' said Uma, 'it is the custom for sons-in-law to treat their mother-in-law with respect.' But she was much annoyed with herself: she felt that she was dribbling her righteous anger away in irritation and pettiness. She should have spoken out boldly and told him everything that was in her heart, and then taken her two treasures away. She felt ashamed for saying nothing, doing nothing; I am useless, she thought, I cannot even help my own daughter.

Gulab said, 'Mama, you said you must go to Uncle at twelve.' She hung her head and said in a low voice, 'Now it is twelve.'

I deserve it, Uma fiercely told herself; I deserve that my daughter should make up lies so that she may get me out of her house.

18

They had hired a coach. A beautiful maroon-and-cream-coloured coach, which was the private property of an enterprising Indian lady who ran a tourist service agency; there was a driver to go with it who was used to taking parties to Agra. He kept his eyes stolidly on the road and never turned round to see what the Sahibs and Memsahibs behind him were doing. When they stopped for any reason, he tactfully disappeared.

Shakuntala found herself sitting with the Billimoria sisters, who were very enthusiastic about everything seen on the way. Until Betty, sitting further down with Esmond next to her, said, 'The trouble with the Indian countryside is that it's so frightfully dull,' and then they kept quiet.

It was dull. There was only the road, running through the dry, barren, anonymous landscape. When they came to a village, it was always the same village, as dry and dusty as the surrounding landscape. Sometimes they ran the gauntlet of a row of village shops in which there was nothing to buy except the things the poor sell to the poor – wilting vegetables, lentils, soiled sweetmeats, weak tea in brass tumblers. Imperceptibly – dust unto dust – village and shops faded again into desert landscape, and sometimes there was a ruined mosque among the withered shrubs and stumps of trees. The sun became hotter every minute, making of sky and earth one vast white bowl of dust.

One or two ladies began to think that it would have been better to come in winter. Nobody had remembered that April could be so hot. However, they all kept in good spirits, for this was only the beginning of their three-day trip. They even sang some songs – English folksongs like 'Cherry-ripe, cherry-ripe', in which the Billimoria sisters joined in more heartily than anyone, and modern hit-songs, rather jazzy and erotic, at which Esmond sniffed in a disgusted manner and said, 'Well, if this is the folk music of today, God help today.'

Most of the time the road was empty, but sometimes they had to slow down for a herd of fat buffaloes or a bullock-cart piled high with dry grass. Occasionally shiny cars whizzed past, more tourists going to Agra.

At ten-thirty they stopped to eat their sandwiches. They unpacked their thermos-flasks of tea and bottles of boiled water. Esmond and Betty went to sit in the shade of a tree by the roadside, but the others stayed in the coach because that gave more protection from the sun. Shakuntala decided that she would prefer to sit under the tree. There was not much grass to sit on, and what there was was dry and prickly; no birds were singing, and the glare of the sun stabbed at the eyes like legions of needles.

Betty, looking nevertheless cool and fresh in a pink candy-striped dress, passed sandwiches to Esmond. She lifted the top-layer of each one to peer inside, saying, 'You like egg ones, don't you?' He did not appear to have brought any of his own.

'I have egg, too,' said Shakuntala, proffering her tin.

But he shook his head. He was reclining on the ground, his head supported on his hand, and allowing Betty to feed him.

Betty smiled and said, 'We've plenty, thanks.' She also stretched herself out and supported her head in the same manner as his and very close. He bent his face forward slightly and rubbed his nose against hers, just once. She wrinkled it and said, 'Nice.'

Shakuntala counted the sandwiches in her tin. She knew that European men and women behaved in a free way with one another, so she was not shocked. But she felt very strange: almost as if she were going to cry, which was ridiculous.

Esmond lay flat on his back and said in a deeply contented voice, 'Lovely to get away for a while.'

'Get away from what?' Betty asked.

'It is the change one appreciates so much,' Shakuntala said.

Esmond yawned, wide and lazy. 'Yes, the change.' He stretched himself and looked like a lovely long elegant cat.

Shakuntala lowered her eyes away from him. She sat facing the other two, cross-legged and alone, while they lay with their heads so close together. There was something almost like pain inside her; it was quite a new feeling for her.

'I know someone here,' said Betty, with a sly smile at Esmond, 'who would like a change a lot more radical than that.'

Shakuntala looked up. She was very much interested; so much so that for a moment she forgot about her misery. But Esmond turned his head away and said wearily, 'Why talk about it now.'

Shakuntala felt impelled to ask a question. She knew it was tactless and perhaps might offend him, but she had to ask it. She asked, 'You do not like to stay in India?' By this she meant many things. For instance, she meant: you are not happy with Gulab; and more than that, she meant: your life altogether is not happy, you feel lost and misunderstood? It was a question to which she felt she knew the answer – knew it oh so well and oh so deeply – but she wanted to hear it from him; she wanted it very much.

Esmond asked with his eyes shut, 'Got some water?'

Betty lifted his head and held the bottle to his lips. 'I'm feeling ever so maternal today,' she said. Shakuntala packed what was left of her sandwiches back into the tin and tied a string round the tin.

'Finished?' Betty said, and then she too drank, tilting her head far back as she did so. Shakuntala noticed that she had not even wiped the neck of the bottle with her hand.

Esmond tickled Betty's throat, very smooth and tanned golden-brown, with a blade of grass. At once she jerked her head forward again and water spluttered out of her mouth.

Shakuntala, to bring herself closer to them, said, 'Oh do let her drink in peace, she is thirsty.'

'Isn't he a mean pig?' She tweaked his ear. 'Enough of your school-boy tricks, you *you*, you.'

'I'm a me *me*, me?'

'And worse,' Betty said severely.

Shakuntala would have liked to laugh, to show them that she was easy and happy and could enjoy their banter. But there was an obstruction in her throat, just as if she had not talked for a long time, which would let no laughter get past it. She tied another knot in the string round her tin and looked down at her hands as she did so. It would have been best of all if she could have joined in their banter and also spoken witty and carefree things. But she knew she would never be able to catch the same tone, so that her contribution would sound quite false and out of place.

'Do you want me,' said Betty, 'to start telling you here and now just exactly what you are?'

'Heaven forbid,' said Esmond, and blew a crumb of sandwich from her cheek.

Shakuntala looked towards them, took in their fairness, their slenderness, he cool and crisp in his white shirt open at the throat and his white ducks, she in her pink candy-striped dress, both of them golden-haired, relaxed, graceful, easy. Shakuntala felt herself such a contrast to them; she felt herself heavy and dark and dull.

The Secretary of the W.W.O. stuck her head from out of the door of the coach and shouted over to them with a nervous laugh, 'Sorry to disturb the idyl *à trois*, but don't you think we should be getting a move on?'

Esmond and Betty, sitting side by side at the back of the coach, were rather gay. Betty sang comic songs – 'She was only the Milkman's Daughter' – in a stirring and sentimental manner, which made everybody laugh; she made Esmond join in the chorus. Afterwards he recited some comic verses: he recited them very wittily, stressing all the comic points with a sharp tongue, so that it was hard to understand why nobody laughed much, or at any rate not heartily.

'They are very good friends, those two,' one Billimoria sister whispered to the other. They looked at Shakuntala, sideways and rather slyly: 'You know them quite well, don't you?' Shakuntala had to tell herself how ridiculous it would be if she cried.

Betty stood up and shouted as though through a megaphone, 'Ladies and Gentleman, you are now approaching the historic spot where four pimps of three successive Moghul emperors met with an honourable burial. On the left you will see a pee-house for jackals.'

'She is very attractive,' the Billimoria sisters whispered. 'She has had many men friends.' They tittered behind their hands.

Shakuntala said sharply, 'There is no harm in men and women being friends. In Europe everybody is like that.'

'Of course: nowadays only people in India are old-fashioned about this sort of thing.' They looked at one another and smirked.

'And on your right,' declaimed Esmond, 'you will see the historic spot where Mr E. M. Forster first met Miss Adela Quested while she sat taking notes for her Social Science class.' But the laughter to reward him was not spontaneous.

Shakuntala felt sharp elbows digging slyly into her side. 'He is a real Don Juan,' whispered the Billimoria sisters.

'What?' she said loudly.

They looked round over their shoulders and then giggled secretly. 'Shshsh ... you know, Don Juan the Great Lover – it's an opera by Mozart.'

'And also,' said Shakuntala, loudly and proudly though she was feeling so miserable, 'a poem by Lord Byron.'

'He has a Hindu wife.' They said 'Hindu' with a real Parsi contempt, but remembering Shakuntala herself, added, 'An old-fashioned Hindu girl, who will never go anywhere out of the house to meet people. She is quite uneducated, she doesn't even speak English.'

Because she felt annoyed with the Billimoria sisters and needed to contradict and confound them, Shakuntala's first impulse was to defend Gulab and to point out that she was educated and came from a well-known and progressive family. But then she found that she did not want to speak in Gulab's favour; she herself was somehow annoyed with her. They are right, she thought, she is old-fashioned; she would never understand about Esmond and Betty, not the way I understand. She would think it was wrong for a man and woman who are not related to one another to be so friendly together.

'Our revered friend and companion, Mr Esmond Stillwood,' Betty announced, 'will now give an impression of an ex-Burra Sahib lapping his whisky-and-s. at eventide.'

Shakuntala thought, it is not wrong, it is quite natural and also rather beautiful. In Europe everybody does that, all men and women are friends together. She looked out of the window, out at the dust and sun, and the pain was sharper.

19

Madhuri sat with her hands folded in her lap. She looked demure and dainty. But her voice trembled with fury: 'How dare they,' she said.

Har Dayal paced up and down with his hands behind his back. He felt very uncomfortable and only dared glance at his wife out of the corner of his eye.

'And you just sat quietly and listened to him?'

He stopped still and spread his arms in a gesture of helplessness. He did not know what to say or do, not even what to think.

His wife, though, knew very well. She compressed her lips tightly in her sweet, finely-preserved little face; she wished nothing so much as that Ram Nath should be there now, so that she might show him her contempt. She longed to be insulting to him, to his face; vent finally the grievance which had been growing and growing ever since Gulab had not married Amrit. 'Impudence,' she said, 'such impudence,' all that grievance inflamed within her.

Har Dayal ran his hand through his mane of grey hair. He did not think it was right to be angry, but dared not tell her so. After all, what Ram Nath had offered was not an insult but, on the contrary, the greatest compliment one family could offer to another.

'And what did you say to him?' she demanded, and wished that she could have been there to say everything that was in her heart.

Har Dayal could not or did not want to remember what he had said. He had been so confused; so he had kept saying, 'Excellent; wonderful, wonderful, what honour you show us,' but had refrained from looking at Ram Nath, sitting there so still and quiet and saying in a soft voice that he wanted a wife for his son.

And just the day before, his old friend Professor Bhatnagar, who was something very important in the Ministry of Education, had drawn him aside, after they had met at a committee meeting to discuss cultural pageants for the Republic Day parade, and had told him that his son was returning shortly from the United States. 'He has been studying at Harvard,' Professor Bhatnagar had said. 'He has done very well there. Now he will probably join the Ministry.' Har Dayal had congratulated him on his fine son, and then Professor Bhatnagar had congratulated Har Dayal on his fine daughter. They had both been rather pleased. They were such old friends.

'Why do you not answer!' Madhuri cried, striking her little hand on the side of her chaise-longue.

Har Dayal did not know how to answer. He was glad that he had not yet told Madhuri about Professor Bhatnagar. If she knew, she would waste no time in going to the ladies of the Bhatnagar family and soon everything would be almost fixed up. But Ram Nath was his oldest, his best, his best-loved friend.

'Tell me what you said, what he said, I want to hear.'

'But I have told you,' he said miserably.

'You have told me nothing. You only said how he dared to come here with such an offer – '

'That was all.'

'But what did you *say*?' she cried.

He took off his spectacles and wiped them on the wide sleeve of his golden dressing-gown. He kept his eyes downcast as he did so, and heaved a sigh. He could not admit to Madhuri that at first, more than anything, he had wanted to say yes. Was this not the opportunity he had always sought – to give all he had to Ram Nath, to serve him and do good to him? He had always been so unhappy because his friend would take nothing from him. Now should he not be ready to give, willingly and happily, when the other was ready to take? But there was his other old friend, Professor Bhatnagar, whose son had done so well at Harvard . . .

Madhuri got up and walked away from him, beating her two clenched hands together so that her golden bangles jingled. 'Who are these people,' she burst out, 'that you should allow them to come here and insult us!'

'Why insult,' he gently remonstrated, 'why do you say so?'

'What else is it then – after all they have done to us, and now to come and ask for my only daughter for their son, who is nothing, a nobody – do they really think we would give her to such a man?'

'He has good prospects,' Har Dayal said limply and entirely without conviction.

'Prospects – what prospects can such a man have, living in the jungles like a savage, yes like a savage! Is it for such a life that we have given our daughter the best education a girl can get and have spared nothing to make her fit to become the wife of a husband of high position?'

'I do not think she wants such position, you know she is – '

'Then we must want it for her! She is only a child, she knows nothing, it is we who have to decide and think for her.'

Har Dayal kept quiet. She was putting him in a false position, making him defend something which he had really in his heart no desire to defend. His trouble was that he felt about this as she did. Only with him it was a very guilty feeling.

'Ah, if only I had been there,' she said. 'If only he had come to me with this fine proposition of his, I would have known what to say to him . . .' At this moment her woman servant came to tell her that everything was ready for her bath. Nothing, not even righteous indignation, could induce Madhuri to change her daily schedule, so without another word to her husband, she retired to her bathroom.

Har Dayal sat down in the cane chaise-longue his wife had vacated. He took off his glasses and wiped them and put them on and sighed and then took them off again. It was all very confusing and unfortunate. His thoughts strayed off to the ceremony he was going to attend in the afternoon. The President was laying the foundation stone of a new technical college and Har Dayal was going to sit on the platform with other dignitaries and also make a speech. He had his speech all ready; he had been, before all this happened, so much looking forward to making it. In the last few years he had learned to enjoy addressing audiences gathered together on some ceremonious occasion. He always felt when he spoke that he was very close to his listeners and that he was stirring them profoundly with the noble words he uttered.

He was glad that Shakuntala had gone away to Agra. At least this gave him a few days in which to settle his mind before speaking to her. Ultimately, of course, he must speak to her; it would have been against his principles not to be quite frank and open with her about all the offers that came for her. There had already been several others but as they had been quite impossible – the young men being in each case too unintellectual and too unremarkable, though from excellent families – they had only served as a cause for wit and laughter between father and daughter. Now he would have to tell her about Professor Bhatnagar's son, and about Narayan. Especially, his conscience told him, about Narayan. She would not, he knew, laugh at Narayan. On the contrary, Har Dayal's greatest fear – though he had not yet reached the stage of admitting it – was that Shakuntala would be too serious about him. He knew her idealist principles and feared that she might be eager to seize this opportunity of putting them into practice. Yet at the same time he was aware that he too should be eager to seize this opportunity of at last being able to give something precious and valuable to his friend Ram Nath, as a proof of his great love for him. But now Professor Bhatnagar's son was coming home to take up a high post in his father's ministry.

'And you sat quietly and listened,' said Madhuri, fresh from her bath. She was fragrant with the best soap and talcum powder, elegant in a meticulously pressed sari; but her fury had not abated.

Har Dayal got up and she arranged herself again in her chaise-longue. The woman servant let down the bamboo shutters which enclosed the adjoining veranda, so that the sun was shut out and the room became dim and cool. Fresh flowers had already been placed in their usual position on Madhuri's little table and on the mantelpiece. The brass ornaments – Nataraja dancing with many arms, a Jaipuri tray with ashtray, box and jug, none of which had ever been used, Ganesha the elephant god – gleamed and shone in evidence of regular and well-supervised polishing; so did the mosaic floor, each marble chip shining fresh as a sea-washed pebble. The cushions, liberally strewn about the room, sat plump and tight and smooth. On the floor lay grass mats in bright untarnished colours. Madhuri's little gold clock, inherited from her grandmother, ticked with precise little ticks.

'But when good offers came, you laughed and did not listen, and you taught your daughter to laugh also.'

Har Dayal, silent and miserable, let his hands hover over the flowers, but dropped them again to his side, realizing that his wife's flowers did not need rearranging.

'The son of a Minister, an I.C.S., such people were not good enough for you . . .'

He murmured in weak self-defence, 'They were not suitable,' more than ever glad that he had not yet told her about Professor Bhatnagar's son.

'And this one perhaps is suitable?' she shot out at once, sharp and contemptuous.

He turned, spread his arms, dropped them again to his sides. 'But my darling, I did not say yes.' He wished most fervently that Ram Nath had never spoken. Then there would be only Professor Bhatnagar's son to consider, and Madhuri would be pleased with him and not angry as she was now.

'Why did you sit and listen? Why did you not tell him at once, how dare you come to my house with such an offer?'

'How could I say such a thing? Even to ordinary people one must be polite, let alone to him – '

'Polite! Perhaps they were polite to us, to our son, five years ago?' To the woman servant she said, 'You may send the cook.'

'It was no one's fault,' he said, as he had said many times before. She did not even bother to answer this, but only inflated her delicate nostrils in the contemptuous way he knew and feared so well.

Amrit, bathed and breakfasted, plump and clean and satisfied, came breezing into the room and said, as he said every morning, 'Well, here's one more slave off to his galley.'

'One minute,' his mother said, 'I wish to speak with you.'

'Let him go to his office,' said Har Dayal. 'What is the use of bothering him in this matter?'

'What matter?' said Amrit. 'What's up? You are both looking a bit rattled, if I may say so.'

'My son has a right to know everything that goes on in the family. I only wish that Raj were here also to give me his support.'

'Has there been any letter from him this morning?' Har Dayal cunningly asked. However, much as she had been worrying about Raj's silence, Madhuri was not to be put off so easily. She said, as if he had not even spoken, 'I hope you are not suggesting that I should keep silent before Amrit?'

Har Dayal made a helpless gesture and said, 'Well, tell him,' turning again to the flowers and noting again with regret that they did not need his attention.

Madhuri told him. Amrit nodded and looked sympathetic. 'Of course,' he said, 'Narayan is a nice chap, none better, but – well . . .' he laughed, knowing what he wanted to say was understood.

'Please ask your mother why she is so angry,' Har Dayal said.

'Angry? Why angry? There is nothing to be angry about.'

'For lunch,' Madhuri briskly told the cook, 'cheese soufflé and cucumber salad.'

'We only tell them no in a nice polite way and there you are.'

Har Dayal, though he liked his son's easy attitude, felt uncomfortable. Only he knew how difficult it would be for him to say no. Ram Nath had not tried to commit him to anything; he had pointed out no advantages, had not tried to colour his mind and dispose him favourably, had only said quietly that he liked Shakuntala and that his son wanted a wife.

When the cook had gone, Madhuri said, 'But your father did not say no.'

'Of course not,' Amrit said, 'how can anyone say it straight off like that. You must wait, and then it will be understood.'

'What is there to wait for!' she cried. 'Who are these people that we must be so sparing of their feelings?'

Amrit and his father looked at one another. Har Dayal slightly shrugged his shoulders. Amrit looked amused. 'But, Mummyji,' he said, 'why are you angry?'

'Impudence,' she said, her head held high but her hands trembling; 'impudence to come to us with such a suggestion. After what has happened.'

'But what *has* happened?'

'That is a question *you* know best how to answer.'

'I?' Then he realized, and threw back his head and laughed, richly and unaffectedly. 'No, really, Mummyji, are you still harping on that? But you see, I have not died of a broken heart.' And he spread wide his arms to show her how very whole and unbroken he was. Indeed, no one could have been more so.

Indira came in and said, 'Amrit, what are you doing, you will be late for your work.'

'Mummyji is worrying about my broken heart.'

Madhuri threw a warning look towards Indira, but this made Amrit only laugh more: 'She knows all about it,' he said.

'All about what?' Indira said.

'About Uma auntie's Gulab and how she preferred someone else to yours truly.' Indira looked down; she was smiling but embarrassed.

'She does not even mind,' said Amrit. 'She does not think she has made such a bad bargain.' He laughed and slapped his thigh. Indira confirmed his statement by a radiant look of happiness.

'That is no reason,' Madhuri said fiercely, 'Why now we should give Shakuntala to them.'

'But nobody is giving Shakuntala to them, Mummyji,' Amrit said with great reasonableness.

Indira asked, 'Giving Shakuntala?' He told her and she said, quite shocked, 'But it is impossible. He is very poor and lives in a village.'

'Of course it is impossible, we all know that, 'Amrit said. 'But there is no need to be angry.'

Har Dayal's mind savoured the phrases he intended to use in this afternoon's speech: This occasion on which we are gathered together is yet another landmark in the cultural development of our country ... 'No,' he said aloud, 'this is exactly what I told your mother.'

'You told me,' she took him up immediately, narrowing her eyes at him, 'that it is impossible?'

Trapped thus, he kept silent. His mind hovered round a quotation from Matthew Arnold, which he decided after all to leave out: whatever quotation he might use would have to come from the Indian classics, preferably from Sanskrit; only such would be well received.

Indira settled herself on a stool at Madhuri's feet and tidily arranged her sari round her feet. She said in a rather matronly manner, 'It would be good for Shakuntala to be married.'

'Very good,' Madhuri said, 'if we arrange suitably.'

'There,' Amrit said humorously. 'Now they have started.'

Har Dayal smiled absent-mindedly, but a moment later wished he had not. 'Perhaps it is a laughing matter,' his wife asked him, 'that I should wish to see my daughter well settled?'

'It will change her in so many ways,' Indira said, complacent and wise.

'For you it has always been a laughing matter — when good offers came, you sat with her and laughed.'

'Yes, for instance, I never knew what you had against poor Ved Kumar,' Amrit said. 'Very decent chap, I always thought, and his family also have no flies on them, to use a homely phrase.'

His father said, 'My dear boy, he was quite quite unsuitable and your sister did not care for him at all,' in a somewhat blustering manner which, however, failed to hide his unease. He really ought to tell them about Professor Bhatnagar's son, he thought; but he put it off. He knew Madhuri would rush things, and then how would he face Ram Nath?

'Because you taught her not to care,' Madhuri said. 'What does a young girl know whom to care for, whom not to care for: her parents must decide this for her.'

Indira clasped her arms around her knees and looked dreamy. She wondered whether what her mother-in-law was saying held true in every case. She rather thought that she had begun to care for Amrit even before her parents had directed her to do so. She had, she thought, felt an agreeable flutter right from that first time when he had come with his uncle to look at her and they had all sat in the drawing-room and had tea.

'Whatever has she gone to Agra *for*?' Amrit asked.

'Yes and so alone,' Indira said with a tinge of disapproval.

But here Madhuri was on Shakuntala's side. 'I allowed her to go,' she said. 'I think it may be good for her to associate with an organization like the W.W.O.' Associate, that is, with Western ladies: Madhuri herself had always liked to associate with Western ladies. Even in pre-Independence days she had always had one or two English lady friends, with whom she had got on very well. She had entertained them at tea, serving them with thin cucumber sandwiches because they said that these made them feel so much at home.

Har Dayal pointed out, 'And can one ever see enough of the Taj Mahal?' Inwardly, he added, quite automatically, for his mind was still turned to the afternoon's speech, 'that noble pile which is not only a monument to a great queen but also to a great culture.'

20

Uma and Bachani were both very happy. They walked around the house, looking for dirt, of which they found plenty, and then shouting lustily for the sweeper. Uma even gave a few energetic rubs to the heavy brass door-fittings which had turned green with age and neglect. When they met in any part of the house, they would shake their heads at one another and say, 'What dirt, what filth, that sweeper is a lazy good-for-nothing,' and then they would shout for him in chorus. Best of all, though, was discussing what to cook. Food had regained all its glamour now that Gulab and Ravi were there to enjoy it. Although each detail of the menu of their three-day stay had already been settled, Uma and Bachani nevertheless could not deny themselves the pleasure of keeping it open for further suggestion and counter-suggestion. Every few hours one of them would think of something new to add and tell it to the other, which always gave rise to vigorous discussion. Bachani had already prepared three seers of ladoos which were now spread out on trays in the kitchen, large round and yellow and shining with ghee.

Uma came out on to the veranda where her brother sat. She stood behind him and looked out over the tangled garden, the ornamental lake stifled under patches of grass, washing slung between the statues. 'I will get a gardener,' she promised herself, 'a full-time gardener.' Everything should be made beautiful for her daughter and her grandson.

Ram Nath said, 'I had another letter from Narayan. He is coming next month.'

'Narayan is coming to Delhi?'

He handed her the letter which said, 'I have managed to arrange leave for next month. I do not know when I shall be able to arrange this again, so everything must be settled when I come home now. I have promised everybody that I will bring a wife back with me, so dare not return without one.'

Uma said, 'You have spoken with Har Dayal?'

This was what he had come to talk about. He did not want to fail his son, but neither did he want to press Har Dayal any further. He said, 'Is there no one else?'

Uma looked at him in astonishment: 'You are not telling me he said no?'

'Not exactly no – ' He made a vague gesture which he hoped would suggest Har Dayal's forced enthusiasm.

'Of course not,' she said energetically, 'he was, I am sure, very happy.'

'He pretended to be so.'

'You are imagining. What is the matter with you? Why do you speak in this manner about your friend?'

Bachani came out and said, 'Do you think they would like butter-milk with their food?'

'Leave me alone,' Uma cried and stamped her foot, 'can you not see I am speaking of important matters with my brother? He will be as glad as we are about this connection,' she told Ram Nath, 'why do you pretend otherwise ? Not buttermilk – afterwards we will make mango fool, she likes that very much!' she shouted after Bachani.

Ram Nath shrugged his shoulder and smiled a rather unhappy little smile.

'Why do you look like that, like a sick cat?' But she laid her great hand on his shoulder and tenderly massaged it. 'You will see, it will be such a happy marriage, our own youth will return with them.'

But Ram Nath thought of the way Har Dayal had avoided his eye while declaring, so heartily, how happy, how honoured he was by this proposal.

'Yes, and also I am happy that Narayan is coming because he will help us with my Gulab...'

'Help us with Gulab?'

'It is good for a family to be together, then all problems are more easily settled. I am glad you came today, now you too may speak with her. Please,' she said, and sat down beside him, 'tell her how she must leave him and come to me, help me in this as you have helped me in all things throughout life.'

Ravi came and sat on his grandmother's lap. He was sucking a ball of crushed ice which Bachani had flavoured for him with rose essence. He said, 'Swamiji is standing on his head.'

'Yes, my darling, he is doing Sirsana. It is a very great yogic asan; while he is doing it his spirit is mingling with the Infinite.' She passed her hand over his hair. 'How much he looks like our Narayan – when I look at him, it is as if our Narayan is a child again.'

Ram Nath also looked at Ravi, and his heart contracted. He re-

128

membered one night when the police had come to arrest him and before leaving he had gone to look at his son. Narayan, then three years old, had been lying asleep on his side, his hand under his cheek; he had looked so strained and earnest, his father had wondered what great troubles were in his mind. He had not seen him again after that for three years.

'But the eyes are my Gulab's.' For Ravi had large, liquid, dreamy woman's eyes, with a heavy silk fringe of lashes; whereas Narayan had always looked with eyes clear and black and alert.

She glanced at her brother's profile and said, 'Please do not be sad. You will see, everything will be well.' She laid her hand on his, encompassing it completely. 'Good times are ahead of us, our children will be happy.'

He smiled. 'You have been to the astrologer again?' Whereupon she took her hand away: 'You may laugh at these things, but I have had much experience of their truth and greatness. Everything is written in the stars, it is a very ancient science. "Like the night without a light," ' she quoted, ' "like the sky without the sun, even so the king without an astrologer wanders blindly on his way." This is written in the works of the great sage Varahamihira.'

Ram Nath said abruptly, 'Of course I know how often Har Dayal seems insincere, even when he is sincere, but this time I know he was sincerely insincere.'

'What nonsense are you talking?'

'It is no use being so stern with me. You cannot bully me out of my conviction.'

She placed both her hands with great firmness on to her mighty knees, and told him in a manner which was so emphatic that it was almost threatening, 'With old age your soul is shrivelling up. Your thoughts have become mean so that now you see evil everywhere. Even your friend is not spared your malice.'

Though amused at this description of himself, he could not let it pass without protest. 'If you had seen him ... it was so painful for him, in his embarrassment he did not know how to smile enough and tell me that he lived only to serve me.'

'Malice.' she repeated, but laughed in spite of herself. 'Your wife is right, your liver has turned quite black.' She took Ravi's hand. 'I will take this child away, in your presence he can learn nothing that is good.' She went into the house, and he heard her shout for Bachani to get two seers of milk quickly, to make mango fool for her children.

He was sad again, looking out over the tangled garden hot and dry under the sun. Not that he had, ever, expected anything from Har Dayal: but he had not thought that what he had gone to ask could have been construed as a favour. It had seemed to him that what he was putting to Har Dayal was a proposition equally agreeable to both of them.

He realized now that he had been wrong. 'I have lost,' he thought, 'my knowledge of the values of the world.' Once he had known them very well, all the different values belonging to different classes and different people. In rejecting those of his own class and position in life, he had not acted blindly. He knew that it was pleasant and comfortable to have money, privacy, and privilege: only he had exchanged these things for others which to him personally meant more. But he had never lost his knowledge of what the rejected values still meant to other people, to people like Har Dayal; and so, in dealing with such people, he had made allowance for them and had not asked of them things he would have asked of himself and of those he knew thought like him.

But now, it seemed, he had lost his grasp. She is right, he thought, my soul has shrivelled. In old age there should be some greatness, some wisdom. With him, he felt, it had happened otherwise: instead of expanding and taking in all the world, he had narrowed and could see only himself and his own path. Then he thought that perhaps in many things his wife was right. He laughed at her because she expressed her desire for wealth and position so crudely. But it was not really a desire that could be laughed at, because so many people had it. One had to adjust oneself to all these other people. Now he saw that he had forgotten how to do so.

Gulab was having her bath. The bathroom in which she was having it was as large as the biggest room in Esmond's flat. The marble was turning brownish and the coloured panes of frosted glass had been largely replaced by pieces of cardboard which were not tacked down too well so that some of them flapped loosely. Gulab languidly poured water over herself from a brass mug. There was no place, she thought, so good to have a bath in as her mother's house. Afterwards she rubbed plenty of oil into her hair. Esmond objected to oil – 'filthy habit, do you think I want all my cushions and walls patched with grease?' – so at home she could not apply it as liberally as she knew was good for her. It was cooling to the brain, she knew, and besides it smelt so beautifully.

Oh, but she was happy. All day she ate and slept and let Bachani massage her with sandalwood oil; in the night she and Ravi curled up together on a stringbed in the garden and they lay like that till morning when they woke one another up, all warm and drowsy, with kisses. Nothing marred their pleasure. Like Ravi, Gulab was capable of forgetting that Esmond was ever coming home from Agra and that they would have to go back to the flat. She had also managed to forget Esmond's strict injunction before leaving: 'You're to stay in the flat,' he had impressed upon her several times. 'No little excursions to your mother's house, understand? I don't want to come back and find that thieves have broken in and walked off with everything. So you're to stay right here to look after things, is that quite clear?' It was, but she had since allowed it to slip out of her consciousness. She did not want anything to spoil her stay with her mother, so she had chosen to forget. In fact, she had chosen to forget everything outside this house: she had managed to immerse herself so deeply in its pleasures that any thought of ever having to emerge from them could not reach down to her.

Uma vaguely sensed this. Of course she wanted her daughter to be happy; she never stopped thinking all day of different ways in which she could make her happy. But at the same time she wanted Gulab to be aware of the contrast between what was here and what she had in her husband's house. She had hoped that the sense of this contrast would undermine Gulab's courage so that in the end, when the three days were up, she would have no courage left on which to go back. But she had reckoned without her daughter's ability to submerge thought in the sensuous satisfaction of the moment. When it would come to going home, Gulab's reserves of courage would be untouched. And perhaps she would not even need them: she would simply go, by instinct, not allowing herself to think what she was going back to at all.

When Gulab emerged from her bath, Ravi was helping his grandmother to make mango fool. Both were squatting in the little covered veranda that led off from the kitchen, and while Uma strained the mangoes, Ravi sucked the discarded stones; his mouth was already stained bright mango-colour. Gulab sat with her uncle on the veranda. She liked sitting with him, she found him so restful because he hardly ever talked to her. She drank the tea which Bachani brought for her and ate the ladoos which were so fresh that they were warm and wet and juicy like an exotic fruit. She made noises of relish. Ram Nath listened to her. As always when he was with his niece, he had the sense of being near a great amorphous mass of sensuous life, of softness and sweet, cloying tastes.

It was with some reluctance that he remembered that Uma had told him to speak to her. Though he liked sitting with her, he disliked speaking to her. He felt it was impossible for him to make any contact with her; there was nothing in her to respond to the way he thought and talked. Five years ago, when she had wanted to marry Esmond,

Uma had urged him to talk to her, to use what Uma had called his influence with her. He had obediently talked; he had been very logical and coherent and intelligent; and all the time he had known that what he was saying was not touching her mind at all. Talking to her was, in fact, rather like sinking one's finger into a nice plump rubber cushion; one could expect to make the same amount of impression and one that lasted just as long.

'You see, daughter,' he said dutifully, in his piping voice which was as clear as what he said, 'your mother wants you to go away from your husband.'

Gulab had her mouth full of ladoo. She did not stop chewing. She was too replete with twenty-four hours of happiness to be easily assailable.

'We all think that you should go away from him,' he said. He did not look at her because her calm, chewing face tended to disconcert him. 'We think so because we know that you are unhappy with him. If there were any chance that you would ever be happy or at least contented with him, we would not tell you to go away from him. But we know there is no chance. He is a very different person from you and he does not understand you and the way you live and think, the way we all live and think. I think he should not be in this country at all because he in no way belongs here, but I do not want to talk about that. All I want to talk about is that it is wrong for you to stay with him. It happens very often that there are differences between husband and wife, that they quarrel and do not agree with one another. When these differences go very deep, it is better for husband and wife to part because otherwise they will begin to hate one another and that is very ugly. Do you understand me, daughter?'

She nodded, though her face did not lose its contented expression. She liked listening to him, she found this thin old man's voice soothing. And he was wrong in supposing that she was not taking in his words at all. On the contrary, she was very interested in what he said, especially about Esmond not understanding the way she lived. How clever of Uncle to know that, when she had never told him that Esmond did not like her to lie on the floor or eat with her fingers or rub herself with oils and unguents. She took a gulp of her sweet tea to wash down her ladoo. Yes, Uncle was right: Esmond did not understand. But she was so drowsy and honeyed with contentment that at that moment his lack of understanding meant nothing to her.

'Mama!' Ravi cried across to her, 'look, I am making mango fool!'

She kissed her hand at him and smiled. Uma shouted, 'How he is helping me, he is a very hard worker!'

Ram Nath said, 'You see, in such circumstances it is not wrong to

132

leave your husband. We are afraid that there is something in your mind' – though he knew it lay deeper, much deeper, than that – 'which makes you think it is a very great wrong for a wife to go away from her husband, because she belongs to him and it is his right to treat her in any fashion he likes. This is not true. No person has a right to treat another person in any fashion he likes. Please remember you are an individual being first and a wife only second.' He looked at her. She was still smiling at Ravi. She looked so happy, so deeply contented, that he was glad that she had not heard or not heeded him.

Inside the house a musician from the South, who had come to stay for a few days, was playing his veena. Deep, passionate notes throbbed through house and garden, and made Gulab sway her head and beat the rhythm out on her thigh. 'How beautifully he plays,' she said. She turned towards her uncle: 'When is Narayan to marry Shakuntala?'

'When is . . .?' he repeated, and then he laughed.

'I so much love weddings. All the music,' she explained, 'and the lights. My Ravi also will enjoy it.' She looked over at Ravi sucking mango stones and blew him another kiss.

21

They had meant to go to the Taj very early in the morning, before the sun got too hot, but it was nearly ten before they managed to start off. There had been delays over breakfast, for some of the ladies had suddenly decided that it would be fun to order scrambled eggs and liver, and Esmond had had to send his coffee back twice because it was too weak. And after breakfast the ladies had gone upstairs again to their rooms in order to touch up their make-up, and Betty had decided to change her clothes. It took her nearly half an hour, and they all stood about in the hotel lounge waiting for her, and the driver leaned against the coach and smoked a *bidi* cigarette. Esmond got rather cross, he kept looking at his watch and saying, 'What's the use of coming all this way if you can't even get ready in time.' When Betty finally turned up, she did not apologize for keeping them waiting, but she looked wonderful. She was wearing a tight-fitting cream-coloured dress, very cool, with a green belt and a green spotted pocket handkerchief. She looked round at them, smiled and said, 'Well, all set?' Esmond went quite red, he did not even look at her but turned to the others and said brusquely, 'Come on,' leading the way so authoritatively to the coach that they all immediately followed. Betty was left standing in the lounge; she stared after them, though she was still smiling, and then with a shrug she followed.

In the coach Esmond sat next to the Secretary; he explained to her how the architect of the Taj was said to have been an Italian adventurer, Geronimo Veroneo, while the others craned forward in their seats to listen. Shakuntala sat next to Betty. She would have liked to listen to Esmond, in order to learn something, but Betty kept talking in a loud and vivacious manner. Betty told her how once in the heat her make-up had started running – big red blobs of lipstick on her chin and tears of black mascara down her cheeks, so she said. She was carried away by her story, and soon she had herself streaming with rivers of colour, which she comically described. Some of the others began to listen to her too. 'My God, but I looked holy,' and she told how the whole town was running after her and rival priests tried to direct her into rival temples – 'and me only out to buy a little nylon doo-dah.' All the ladies who were listening to her were laughing, while all those listening to Esmond were nodding in an intelligent manner.

But when they got down in the parking space outside the Taj, they all began to look intelligent and composed, ready for the great architectural beauty that was about to be revealed to them. Shakuntala remembered the very first time she had come to see the Taj – she must have been about nine – and how her father, before they went in, put his arm round her shoulder and said, 'Now, darling, you are going to see one of the most beautiful things man has ever made, and I want you to look at it with great pride and wonder.' She had sincerely tried to do so, Daddyji holding her hand all the time and from time to time pressing it, so that it had been quite easy for her to keep her mind off the ices they were going to have after lunch.

Betty said, 'The picture postcards were right.'

'Of course, one ought to see it by moonlight from the air, then it is really wonderful,' said the Billimoria sisters. They had been telling everybody how once they had come to Agra by night in a specially chartered plane with a party of film people from Bombay.

Esmond said, 'Now you'll understand how no pictorial representation can really do justice to it.'

Shakuntala breathed a long-drawn 'Yes.' He looked round at her and addressed himself specially to her: 'Because, like every great piece of architecture, it is designed in relation to sky and earth, the very space, the very air, that surrounds it, and it must be seen in that relation.' She nodded, and looked again. 'It seems not to be standing at all but floating,' she hazarded, glancing up at him for approval. Which she got in the form of a smile: 'Doesn't it?' he said, and then they looked together, and she really felt herself rapt under the influence of great beauty.

They walked towards the mausoleum in a leisured way. Some of the ladies began to fumble with their cameras, but Esmond advised, 'Not now, later: first you must see and understand,' so they obediently packed them up again. Betty walked on one side of Esmond and Shakuntala on the other. The Billimoria sisters covered their heads with their saris to protect themselves against the sun; they looked at one another and laughed rather shamefacedly: 'We look like Hindu ayahs'; but it was better than being darkened by the sun.

Betty took Esmond's arm. 'I'm feeling good,' she confided to him.

'Don't say you're aesthetically sensitive, after all,' he said, but with an indulgent smile.

'After all what? Can't a girl enjoy a morning off without being accused of all sorts of unmentionables?'

Esmond told Shakuntala, 'Now you can see how English Betty is – she's ashamed of owning to any of the nobler emotions.'

'But of course she is English,' Shakuntala said, puzzled.

'And proud of it!' Betty crowed in a parody tone.

Esmond stuck out his other arm, invitingly crooked, at Shakuntala. She hesitated for a moment before she took it; her heart beat wildly, she had never before held a man's arm except her father's. Betty peeped round Esmond: 'Now isn't that cosy,' she said. Arm in arm the three of them walked towards the Taj. The Billimoria sisters, walking behind, smirked at one another.

When they reached the mausoleum, they had to take off their shoes. There were several boys guarding the shoes of visitors and they showed themselves very attentive to their party, ranging all their shoes in a row. But Esmond said sternly, 'Don't touch them, leave them right where they are'; to the ladies he explained, 'All they want is a fat tip for doing nothing.'

'What fat tip?' Betty said. 'Two annas?'

For the second time that morning Esmond turned red with anger. He fixed her with his eyes, very cold and blue now: 'When you have been in this country as long as I have, you'll perhaps begin to understand that these things are not a matter of money but of principle.'

'There,' Betty said with her most charming smile, 'I've done it again.' Shakuntala felt critical of her: it seemed to her that she behaved in an unnecessarily provocative manner towards Esmond.

He was a wonderful guide. He appeared to know everything and he vas prepared to explain everything, bringing out a great deal of hisorical and architectural information. Shakuntala felt she was really earning. Of course, Daddyji was also a very good guide, but even he was not as full of information as Esmond. She marvelled again how a foreigner could know so much. Many of the other visitors also joined their party in order to listen to him. There were even some villagers who stared at Esmond with round eyes and open mouths and were very attentive, though they could not understand any English. One neat little clerk in a dhoti and a clean striped shirt over it, holding a baby son in his arms, kept nodding and saying, 'I see,' and then he would turn round to the rest of his family – a meek, sleek, smiling wife and two huge-eyed daughters and translate for their benefit. Esmond was not in the least put out; he spoke loudly and lucidly and with a most becoming air of authority.

But when they came outside again, his shoes were missing. All the others had no difficulty in finding theirs, but his were simply not there. The attendant boys had gone and some others had taken their place; they assiduously helped him to search – 'brown shoes, Sahb? with buckle?' Quite a crowd collected round them, they stood and shook their heads and told one another that a Sahb's shoes had disappeared. Esmond passed his hand through his hair and said, 'But this is ri-diculous.' Everybody searched. The boys redoubled their efforts, they pushed one another and the spectators out of the way, every few moments they came and waved shoes under Esmond's nose – ladies' high-heeled sandals, villagers' boots, embroidered slippers – 'Is this it, Sahb?' He stood very straight and still, his lips in a tight line. Finally he demanded the whereabouts of the boys who had been there before. Their successors knew nothing: they came at a certain time, they went at a certain time, who was there before them, who after – of that they knew nothing.

'Who is in charge here?' Esmond said in an ominously quiet voice. A ripple of interest passed through the spectators and they moved in closer.

It seemed no one was in charge. Only an attendant was pushed forward, a venerable old man in a splendid red tunic, his hair and beard hennaed the orange colour which betokened that he had made the holy pilgrimage to Mecca. No, he did not know who those boys had been: boys came and went, every day there were different ones to look after shoes.

Esmond fixed the boys before him with a stern look: 'Then I must hold you responsible.' They were puzzled by his Hindustani, they shuffled their feet and grinned.

'Why are you laughing!' he thundered. At once they became serious and stared at him with large wondering eyes. The spectators looked from him to them, full of interest but showing no partiality to either side.

136

The old attendant interceded on behalf of the boys. These were good boys, for that he could vouch, one of them was his own sister's son.

Esmond ignored him. He looked over the top of the venerable old head and repeated in a loud voice, 'Who is the officer in charge here?'

There was, it appeared, a superintendent, but his office was shut, it shut at twelve o'clock on Saturdays and would not reopen again until Monday morning. 'This is ridiculous,' Esmond said, rolling the r very sharply. More people, those emerging from the mausoleum and those about to enter it, kept crowding round. Esmond was pointed out to them as the Sahb whose shoes were missing and all looked at him with interest.

It was hot, and time for lunch. The ladies in Esmond's party were getting impatient; moreover, they did not care to be the centre of so much attention. Only the Billimoria sisters and Shakuntala, however, were actively embarrassed. To them it was terrible to stand exposed as the target of public curiosity. Even Shakuntala – by her mother's standards so free and bold – hated being scrutinized at such close quarters by the sort of people whom she usually saw only through the windows of a motor-car.

'This is a matter for the police,' Esmond said. The Secretary of the W.W.O. touched his arm and timidly suggested that they should contact the police from their hotel. The other ladies hastened to agree with her: 'Your shoes'll be found,' they said, 'they can't just disappear like that'; they knew only too well that they could, but they were feeling both hot and hungry. Those among the spectators who understood English translated what was being said for the benefit of those who did not.

Esmond, standing tall and slim and angry, looked very much alone. There was, Shakuntala thought, great dignity in this angry solitude of his. The people grouped round him – the shabby spectators staring with curious eyes, the ladies in their bright summer dresses, the guilty boys, the old attendant in his splendid uniform – they all seemed insignificant before him, mere extra players. It was as if he alone were of any significance in the world, he and the hot sun, and behind him, a fitting background to his monumental tragedy, the Taj Mahal.

But Betty was laughing. At first it was only a giggle, which she even made some attempt to stifle, but soon she was laughing outright. She put one hand over her eyes and laughed quite without inhibition. Now all attention was turned to her, Esmond was no longer in the centre and everything returned to normal proportions. The ladies smiled with or at Betty, but the outside spectators watched her with great seriousness.

'I'm sorry,' she said when she had finished, and still gasping a bit, 'but how *can* I help it?'

Esmond gave her one look, only one. Shakuntala shuddered for her, but felt that she deserved it. Then Esmond walked away – the crowd of spectators respectfully parted – down the steps, along the path by the side of the canal. He walked on naked feet, but though the stones burning in the sun must have hurt him, he did not flinch; nor did he once look back. The ladies of his party followed him, feeling uneasy and vaguely guilty. They forgot to take photographs.

22

On entering Madhuri's house, Lakshmi felt at the same time bitter and triumphant. She felt bitter because Madhuri still had all the things – costly carpets, well-trained servants – which she herself had lost. But she felt triumphant because coming here proved to her that she still belonged to this world and was therefore many degrees above her neighbours. She wished they could have seen her – the mother of the Madrasi clerk, the widowed sister of the telegraph officer – how she was ushered into the drawing-room by white-liveried servants, how she sat on the sofa among the floral patterns of bolsters and cushions, her hands in her lap, her knees close together, still – in spite of all she had been made to suffer – a lady of good family.

It must have been some years since she had last seen Madhuri. She did not, however, feel strange towards her: she thought so often about her, spoke so much about her, that it was to her almost as if they had been meeting every day. And Madhuri had not changed much; only her hair was a bit greyer and her mouth a bit tighter. Lakshmi wondered whether Madhuri was thinking that she too had not changed. She tried to see herself as Madhuri must be seeing her. She had to admit that she had grown somewhat stouter in the last years; and her hands were not – surreptitiously she glanced at them – quite as smooth as was fitting for one of her station.

'Yes,' she said, 'thank God they are all well settled.' She was proud of her daughters; she felt they had – unlike her husband, unlike her son – done well in life. But it was not about them she had come to talk.

All the same, it was about them she continued to talk. 'My eldest is married to an officer in the Ministry of Education, he draws very good pay, they live in a big bungalow . . .' She did not quite know how to start about Narayan. Her main difficulty was that she did not know whether Ram Nath had already come to prepare the ground or whether she would have to start all afresh. He tells me nothing, she thought in an upsurge of irritation against him. Well, this time she too had told him nothing; she had come here quietly, secretly and quite of her own accord. She was pleased, thinking of this, because she felt she had for once outwitted him.

'My second is the wife of a big engineer.' As she spoke she watched Madhuri playing with her rings. Such beautiful rings – though she herself, Lakshmi thought with the same mixture of bitterness and triumph as before, had had even bigger ones. And she had had bracelets like Madhuri's, necklaces, everything. Ruefully she looked down at the glass bangles which now adorned her short, stout arms. 'They also are very well off, my daughter wears fine jewels and clothes.'

Madhuri yawned, tapping the back of her dainty hand against her mouth.

'They have many servants'; and Lakshmi also yawned, tapping the back of her hand against her mouth. She felt so ladylike.

'My third,' she was about to continue when Madhuri said, 'Last night I could not sleep at all, it was terrible.'

'You must be very tired. My third is married to a great businessman, he has excellent prospects and my daughter wants for nothing.'

'I would not mind being tired, but my head – ' She placed two fingers against her brow.

'It is aching? I will tell you an excellent remedy – please, just put your feet into cold water in which you have thrown a little turmeric, and after twenty minutes you will see there will be no more pain. Please call for a bowl now, I will direct you – with my own hands I will mix in the turmeric.'

'I cannot trouble a guest in this manner,' Madhuri said with a painful smile.

'What trouble is there – I am the mother of a Doctor, these things are nothing new to me.' And then she found herself on the right track: 'Yes, of course you must know, my Narayan is a big Doctor now, he has great chances.'

'He has a practice in Delhi?' Madhuri innocently inquired.

'Not actually in Delhi ... he is such a clever boy, he came first in his examination, all his professors said he will be one of India's greatest Doctors. Your Shakuntala, I hear, has finished with her College education?'

Madhuri rang the bell. To the servant who answered she said, 'Please tell Indira Bibi that I have ordered the car for ten-thirty.'

'You are going out? You should not go out in this heat, it will make your headache worse.' She was feeling rather thirsty but did not care to say so. Perhaps Madhuri had already ordered the servant to bring some sherbet. She remembered how it had been in her father's house, how when visitors came the servants had of their own accord at once brought sherbets and fruits and sweetmeats.

'It is a great thing to see one's sons and daughters doing well in life, it makes the mother's heart young again. Your sons are also well settled?'

'Amrit is in an English firm, probably he will be made Managing Director. Raj is still studying at Cambridge, soon he will come home and take up a good position.'

'I am happy, very happy. I will tell you frankly – I have always been sorry that nothing came of the match between your Amrit and our Gulab. Of course she does well enough with this Englishman, but a connection between our two families is something we have all of us always wished for.'

Madhuri, turning and turning the ring on her middle finger, said, 'You are, I think, no longer living in your old house?'

Lakshmi was taken aback for a moment. It was so long since anyone had asked her this question, so long indeed that they had left their own house. How could Madhuri have forgotten? 'We live in a smaller place now, what is the use of two old people alone in a big house? We are very comfortable.' She thought of her husband and how he would have laughed to hear her. Let him laugh, she furiously told herself; at least one of us must keep up the honour and dignity due to us.

She recovered herself and returned to the real issue. 'Thank God, there is still another way by which our two families may be connected.'

Madhuri rang the bell again: 'Tell Indira Bibi to be certain to be ready on time,' she told the servant.

'Our New India needs doctors so much, no one has better chances these days than a young doctor.'

'We still go to Dr Shlakas – of course he is getting old now, but still there is no one better than these doctors who have had all their training abroad. His son has now also begun practice; he returned from England only last year, but already he is doing very well here. Later he will take over his father's practice – it is good when a son is helped by his father in this manner.'

'Of course, my Narayan's father has also helped him a great deal and he will help him even more in the future – you know how much influence he has, how his name is respected everywhere, every day people come to our house to ask him for favours.'

'Please do not speak of people who come to the house to ask for favours,' Madhuri said, putting her hand to her brow in a gesture of weariness. 'This is a tale I know only too well. Often I ask, "Is this the Secretariat or is it my home?" And the committee meetings – the Ministers that come with their bodyguards and their big cars and chauffeurs – often when I come home from paying visits my own car cannot get into the house because my driveway is choked with other people's.'

'Exactly the same as I have in my house,' Lakshmi said. But her spirit was flagging: she felt suddenly very much aware that her sari border was frayed at the edge and even slightly torn at the bottom. It was the only really good sari she had left from the old days – a rich Bangalore silk, purple with a vast golden pallu – and she had per- suaded herself, when she set out, that its defects were invisible.

She asked, almost shyly, 'Your Shakuntala is at home, I think?'

'She has gone to Agra,' Madhuri replied with satisfaction. 'She has gone with a party of English ladies – now that she has left College, she has begun social life, it is such good training for a girl. Later perhaps we will send her to finishing school in Switzerland, together with the daughter of Sir Homy and Lady Fonwala – you must know them?'

Lakshmi nodded noncommittally. She was a little bewildered, she did not know why Shakuntala should have to go to school again now that she had finished her College, and indeed why there was no men- tion of marriage, even though Shakuntala must be almost twenty. She did not, however, care to put any questions. She remembered that Madhuri's ways had always been rather different from her own. As a girl, before marriage, Madhuri had sat quietly all day in the women's quarter of her father's house, stitching samplers, reading Bengali novels translated into Hindi, and practising on her sitar. But Lakshmi and her sisters had spent much time in the kitchens, had laughed and joked and sung, had dressed themselves up in gorgeous saris and jewels, sat on swings in the garden, rapturously enjoyed all the numerous weddings and ceremonies that took place in the family.

All the same, she thought, Madhuri was a mother. She must have the welfare of her daughter at heart; and welfare of a daughter could only mean a favourable marriage. Perhaps she had made no mention of this because no good opportunity had as yet presented itself; perhaps all she was waiting for was to be told of a good opportunity – 'My Narayan has always been a clever, hard-working boy: in his horo- scope it is written that he will go far in life.' There was something almost appealing in her voice; and she looked rather awkward and anxious, sitting there short and fat in her purple sari with the frayed border, her feet hurting in her only pair of shoes.

Har Dayal did not even recognize her. He came in and said, 'Oh, I beg your pardon, I did not know you had someone with you,' and was about to go out again when Madhuri stopped him with, 'But this is your friend Ram Nath's wife.'

Greeting Har Dayal, Lakshmi thought why does she call me only his friend's wife, am I not her friend too?

But all her doubts melted under the warmth of Har Dayal's welcome. How deferentially he apologized for not having recognized her, how cordially he greeted her, with what true interest he asked after her own welfare and after that of each one of her daughters and of her son, with what respect he pronounced the name of Ram Nath. She settled herself more comfortably between the bolsters and cushions. She was glad that she was wearing her Bangalore sari which was so beautiful and only a little bit frayed; and perhaps they would not notice her lack of jewellery – or if they did, ascribe it to a pleasant idiosyncrasy which made her lock all her ornaments up at home and come out adorned only with glass bangles. There were women like that.

'I am a little thirsty,' she confessed. 'It is the heat, I think. A glass of cold water . . . you will forgive me, but this is like my own home.'

Har Dayal, in ordering sherbet, was quite sharp with the servant. Madhuri only said, 'Is Indira Bibi ready?' Har Dayal began to talk rather fast, anxiously he asked particulars about her daughters.

In consuming her sherbet Lakshmi could not suppress a sound of relish. She had been so very thirsty. She replied to Har Dayal's questions with circumstantial detail and then she said, feeling at her ease now, 'And there is also my Narayan.'

'Yes, yes, yes,' he said, and he paced up and down, passing his hand through his hair, 'of course, of course, we hear great things of him.'

She folded her hands in her lap and crossed her ankles – her feet did not quite reach the ground – and said complacently, 'You will hear yet greater.' She looked from him to his wife: Madhuri was adjusting a bracelet, Har Dayal buttoned his coat and glanced down at himself as he did so.

'We are old friends, we are brothers and sisters,' Lakshmi said, 'why should I not speak out what I have come to speak today.'

Madhuri furiously rang the bell. Har Dayal cried at her, 'But what do you want?' 'Indira!' she cried back at him, 'three times I have sent to ask where she is!'

'Yes,' Lakshmi said, with her head on one side and a sentimental look in her eyes, 'my Narayan is thirty now, he has become a man . . .'

Suddenly to her surprise she found that Har Dayal had seized both her hands and was pressing them warmly; he was bent over her, he said in a rapturous voice, 'My dear friend, how good of you it is to come and see us in our home.' She was very much taken aback. His face was close to her, plump and round and the skin as soft as a woman's; he smelt of some kind of lotion, an expensive, artificially fresh smell.

At that moment she thought of her husband. She thought, you wizened old fool, see how this man who is almost your age has kept himself: see how he looks, see how he lives, and what have you got who have made so much sacrifice? But it was not with Ram Nath that she was angry.

Madhuri said, 'Ah, Indira, it is good you are ready, the car is waiting for us.'

Lakshmi turned round and thought, so this is the one who has taken our Gulab's place. Indira was, as always, neatly and elegantly dressed; she looked young and healthy and comfortably married. But when one conjured up the image of luscious Gulab to stand beside her, then it at once became evident that Indira was only of a very ordinary prettiness. Lakshmi conjured up that image as strongly as she could, and it gave her satisfaction.

'Oh, are you all,' Har Dayal beamed, 'going out together?'

'Have you your car with you,' Madhuri asked Lakshmi, 'or would you like us to leave you somewhere?'

Har Dayal cried, 'But now you must come often, often!' Everybody was standing, so Lakshmi got up also. She looked from one to the other, she was a little bewildered. There was still so much left to say. Perhaps they did not realize this, perhaps they had not yet understood what it was she had come to say.

23

They had done Agra Fort. They had done the Tomb of Akba and the Tomb of Itmad-daulah; they had done everything that they had been told was of any importance. Now they could truly say that they had seen Agra. Esmond had explained everything carefully and their minds were filled with vague but beautiful impressions of marble inlaid with jewelled flowers, of latticed windows, of arches and niches and sunken baths, of old trees and laid-out gardens and lotus fountains. Helped by what they had read or heard or imagined, some of them also managed to populate the scene with appropriate ghosts — veiled queens and silken courtiers and the laughter of lotus-eyed dancing-girls. Over everything there was always the sun, which they bore stoically.

But now even they were tired. They retired quietly to their hotel rooms – an hour to go till dinner – and began to address the picture postcards they had bought. The Billimoria sisters were quite frankly exhausted. They sank down on to their double bed and rubbed one another's temples with eau-de-cologne. Shakuntala was also feeling very tired. She could not help admiring the way these European ladies tramped around all day in the sun, passing from one historical monument to the other, and ended up smiling. There was Betty, with whom she shared the hotel room. Betty sat on a stool by the dressing-table, in a white nylon slip, putting polish on her nails. She was humming a little tune. She looked as if she had just had her morning bath and was getting ready for a long and exciting day.

When Esmond briefly knocked and came in, Shakuntala hastily threw her housecoat over her blouse and petticoat, but Betty merely crossed her slender legs the other way and continued to polish her nails. 'Hallo, Shahjehan,' she said.

Esmond said, 'Excuse me,' and he spoke only to Shakuntala, 'We're trying to fix up tomorrow's programme. Any ideas, bright or otherwise?'

'Good heavens,' Betty said, 'haven't we had enough programme yet?'

'Some of us,' Esmond told Shakuntala, 'would like to push off to Fatehpur Sikri straight away in the morning, but some of the others want to get some shopping in first.'

'Oh, I think it will be best to go early in the morning to Fatehpur Sikri,' Shakuntala replied without hesitation.

'I'm all for the shopping myself,' Betty said. 'I think I've seen about enough of splendours past and gone – the rest can go on rotting in peace, as far as I'm concerned.'

Without looking at her and in a voice meticulous with disdain, Esmond said, 'I was under the impression that we had come out here in order to see something of the past.'

Betty laughed in a quiet and unaffected manner: 'What an old prig you are.'

'So I can count you as one of the Fatehpur-ites, can I?' Esmond asked Shakuntala, his hand already on the handle of the door.

She nodded, but not very confidently, because she felt that by doing so she was somehow taking sides against Betty. She did not mind taking sides against Betty, but not so overtly, not in front of her.

When Esmond was gone, there was a silence which Shakuntala interpreted as being heavy with her companion's displeasure. After a while, however, Betty spoke, and her voice was as free and friendly as ever. 'You know, you mustn't let him bully you.'

'Please?'

144

'He really can be the most frightful bully, if once you let him.' Shakuntala felt uncomfortable. She began to brush her hair and hoped Betty would not say anything further.

'Ask his wife. You know her, don't you?'

Shakuntala answered reluctantly and somewhat stiffly, 'Her family and mine have been very close.'

'Well, she'll have a tale or two to tell.' She studied the finished nails of one hand against the light. 'Let me give you a tip.'

Shakuntala brushed her hair with great concentration. She counted one, two, three, four to herself, aiming at a hundred strokes.

'I'd say it was very bad policy to get interested in a man like that.'

Shakuntala laughed in a way calculated to make Betty think that she had no idea what she could be talking about.

'And if you do go in for that bad policy, then don't say yes and amen to everything he proposes. If you start that way, you'll finish up by not being allowed to breathe unless he gives you permission.'

At dinner in the hotel dining-room Shakuntala sat at a table for four with Esmond, Betty, and the Secretary of the W.W.O. Esmond was charming to her. He saw to it that her water-glass was kept filled, instructed her as to which were the best pieces of chicken and kept her entertained with stories of all the places he had been to in India and what had happened to him there. The Secretary also listened to him with interest and laughed at the right moments, but nervously. Both she and Shakuntala were made uncomfortable by the fourth member at their table. For Betty just sat and ate. She did not listen to Esmond at all, and when the others laughed at some particular humorous part in his narration, she would call to the bearer and select another piece of chicken for herself. From time to time she commented scathingly on the food – 'a relic of the British Raj, middle class and indigestible' – but in an off-hand way which showed no concern whether anyone heard her or not.

After the steamed pudding, Esmond proposed a walk in the garden. The Secretary excused herself – she had bought so many picture postcards, she had to start getting some of them off – so he gently grasped Shakuntala's elbow and guided her towards the door. Shakuntala's heart beat wildly: she felt somehow that going out into that garden was a fulfilment of the dreams she had had with her College friends, of their midnight talks together, their vague longings and expectations from an unknown life of infinite possibilities. Also she was much aware of the caustic look Betty gave them as they walked out together.

The garden was very romantic. It had trees and moonlight and a fountain. Esmond led her straight to the fountain, where water came out of holes pierced in a nymph and fell on a lotus leaf of stone. There was a garden seat of wrought iron, delicate and attractive if not very comfortable, on which he made her sit down. He stood and looked down at her, and smiled. She looked back at him. He said, 'Enjoying your trip?'

'Oh,' she said, 'I enjoy it so much, I do not know when I have enjoyed anything so much.'

He sat down beside her, sideways and on the edge of the seat. His arm was laid along the back, behind her but not touching her.

'It must be wonderful,' he suggested, 'to be seventeen.'

'I am nineteen.'

He laughed and she laughed with him, searching his face with eyes full of undisguised love and wonder. 'It is true,' she said, 'you look like Shelley.'

'I do?'

'Exactly . . . anyway, as I have always imagined Shelley.'

'He's your favourite poet?'

'He is now,' she boldly answered. He brought his hand lying along the back of the seat forward to touch her arm lightly with his fine, fine fingers. The minute touch released in her a series of quivers which were so ecstatic that they were almost frightening.

She seized his hand and said, 'I have always dreamt of meeting someone like you, all my life I have dreamt of it.'

Smilingly he withdrew his hand and put it up to touch her hair. 'And now you've met me, what do you want me to do for you?'

'Do not laugh at me, I beg of you . . . oh, Mr Stillwood, you do not know how I admire you and look up to you.'

'Mr Stillwood?'

'Esmond. Esmond, Esmond, Esmond – it is the most beautiful name I know.'

'What an intense young lady you are.' Casually he took his hand from her hair and laid it on her full, straining breast, tight in the deep-cut blouse. She shut her eyes in an agony of longing and pleasure and hardly dared to breathe.

After a while, however, he took his hand away and said, gentle and ironic, 'We're supposed to be going for a walk.' He stood up and held out his hand to her.

She rose obediently but rather sadly. Silent and with downcast eyes, she walked beside him.

'A beautiful night, a beautiful garden, a beautiful girl,' he said lightly.

'Because I am young and inexperienced, you do not take me seriously.'

146

'But my dear child, how seriously do you want me to take you?'

'I am not a child!' Then she said quickly and meekly, 'Forgive me, forgive me . . .'

'No, you can shout at me if you feel like it.'

'You make me ashamed. How can I shout at you when all I want to do is fall at your feet and worship you and serve you – '

'Heavens!'

'You laugh at me, you only laugh at me.' At last she burst into tears. Which was perhaps what he had been waiting for – at any rate he brought his handkerchief out very promptly and wiped her face in an expert manner.

'Shakuntala,' he said gently, 'you mustn't act like that.'

'Why should I lie to you? Why should I not show you how much, how deeply, how greatly I love you?'

'Shakuntala, please.'

'I do love you, from the very first moment I saw you I loved you. I cannot hide it any longer, if I do, it will break me, my heart will burst.'

'Hearts don't burst that easily . . . no no, I am not laughing at you, but do try and be sensible. Remember, your parents allowed you to come here because they trusted us to look after you – '

'How can you talk about parents now, what are they to me now, compared with what I feel for you?'

'All right then, think of your fiancé, what's-his-name – Narayan.'

'Narayan?'

'It's still supposed to be a secret, is it? But you see, I know more about you than you think, even your secrets aren't secrets to me.'

'I would never,' she declared, 'keep anything secret from you – on the contrary, I want you to look deep, deep into my heart and my soul.'

They had arrived back at the fountain. Moonlight streaked the curved sprays of water falling on to the lotus leaf. It was very quiet, only the sound of the water. The wrought-iron seat stood lonely.

'And Narayan?'

'Which Narayan – I do not know what you mean, I think you are just trying to make a laughing-stock of me. Why are you so cruel?'

'Darling,' he for the first time said, 'let's get this clear: you're supposed to marry Narayan, aren't you? After all, I have it more or less from the horse's mouth: my mother-in-law (the metaphor isn't altogether inappropriate applied to her) she's Narayan's aunt, she ought to know what's going on in her family.'

'Oh, that Narayan,' she said without interest.

'Yes, that Narayan – don't you think you owe him something too?

Why mess up things at this juncture, just as you're about to start your life together.'

This news meant nothing to her. She shrugged it off there and then. 'What do I care about him, about anybody or anything, when you are there?'

'Don't be so *extreme*.'

'Esmond, I know you are married and also you have a child, but I tell you all this means nothing to me. I only know you have come into my life and now it is my duty to give everything I have to you, to adore you and to serve you and to be your slave.'

He drew her closer and looked down at her, meeting her passionate pleading eyes with a look of tolerant affection. He said, 'You're so sweet.'

She whispered, 'Let me be your slave, please allow me, I want to humble myself before you.'

'I give up,' he said, and kissed her long and expertly on the mouth.

So that night he allowed her to stay with him, and her bed in Betty's room remained empty.

24

Lakshmi sat writing a letter to her son. She sat in her husband's study at his table, looking very serious with large spectacles perched on the end of her nose. Whenever she had to write a letter, she waited till her husband had gone out so that she could then sit in his study. She needed to concentrate hard. Her heart was full, but it was difficult for her to pump its contents out into the pen and on to the paper. She wrote, *We are all well, may God give you his blessings too. Son, do not worry at all, I am doing my best for you as a mother should.* Then she sat and thought; there was so much she wanted to say. She wished he were here so that she could say it to him. He would sit with her in the courtyard and she would tell him everything that was in her heart. Often they had sat like that together, she talking and he sitting by her. It did her good to talk thus freely. Though sometimes she had her doubts whether he was really listening with all the attention she could have desired. She would stop for a minute to glance at him for sympathy, and then she would detect in his eyes the same absent look she knew so well in his father. It always irritated her intensely. But when he was away, she did not think of this; she only thought of him as her own sweet beloved son, who sat and listened to her with all the attention and all the sympathy which her husband refused to give her; and she longed to have him with her.

She wrote, *I am taking active steps to fulfil your wishes*. But as soon as she had written it, she had again those doubts which all this time she had been trying hard to ignore. Of course, Madhuri had never had a warm nature – she had never kissed and giggled and held hands with her friends and sisters, as had been so very much the custom in Lakshmi's family (how else could one show one's affection and good-will?) – but this time, Lakshmi could not help feeling she had been especially unwelcoming. After all, it had been some years since they had met, one would have expected that a friend whom one had not seen for some years would have shown a more smiling face.

She would like to have told Narayan that everything was practically settled. She had been so sure, before she went to see Madhuri, that by her visit it would be. But now she was not even sure that Madhuri had understood her purpose. She thought she had spoken quite clearly enough, and yet Madhuri did not seem to have understood. So she could only write, *Soon I will write you another letter and then perhaps I will tell you some very good news*. But she was not quite happy because, hard though she tried, she could not be quite confident.

As she sat and thought of what more she could write, the memory of a conversation she had had yesterday with the widowed sister of the telegraph officer came back to annoy her. Her neighbour had inquired very politely after Narayan; but this had been only a convenient starting-point for the information that her sister's son was also a doctor, that not only was he doing very well here in Delhi, but they were on the point of arranging a most advantageous marriage for him, with a vast dowry attached. Lakshmi had not believed a word of it, but she had nevertheless felt humiliated. For there had been nothing with which she had been able to counter, no way in which she had been able to show that her son was one hundred times a greater doctor than the other's nephew and that the match they were arranging for him incomparably more desirable. She thought I have come to this now, that even people of this class can insult me. The memory of her humiliation automatically engendered bitter thoughts against her husband, and she wished he would come home so that she could reveal them to him.

When he did come, she ostentatiously put her hand on her letter to hide it. He said at once, 'You are writing to Narayan?'

'Perhaps now I am not allowed to write to my own son?'

He sat down and looked at her with amusement across the desk.

'How studious you look with your spectacles, I did not properly appreciate that I had a scholar for a wife.'

'What am I to do when everybody can come to insult me and tell me your son is a nobody.'

'Is this what your friend from upstairs came to tell you yesterday?'

'Please do not call such people my friends. It is bad enough that you put me in the same house with them.'

'Will you go away now, I wish to sit at my table.'

She shot out at him, 'What are you doing for my son?'

Since she was sitting in his chair, he patiently lowered himself on to the other one, drawing it up to the table so that they sat facing one another across his books and papers. She glared at him, fierce and bespectacled. He drew out a book and started to read it.

Rather to his surprise she began to cry. At the beginning of their marriage she had often cried, but for the last forty years she had mostly given it up. The tears clouded her spectacles, but she did not take them off. She wept, 'I am all alone, all alone with no one to help me.'

Because he was himself feeling helpless and unhappy, he was more vulnerable than he would otherwise have been. To hide this, he clicked his tongue in irritation: 'Must you sit there like this at my table – look, you are spoiling my papers with your salt water.'

She looked down and said almost meekly, 'It is not your papers, it is my letter'; she tried to wipe her tears from the sheet but only succeeded in smearing the ink.

'If Pitaji were still living he would not let me suffer like this.'

'But my dear woman,' Ram Nath said, both surprised and irritated by this unexpected mention of her father, 'he has been dead for over thirty years.'

'How terrible it is to have no one to turn to.'

Ram Nath stared at her across the desk. It was a long time since he had looked at her consciously in this way. She was fat and old and looked so lost and unhappy. 'At least take off your spectacles,' he shouted at her, for they were now quite clouded over with tears, 'how can you see anything?'

She took them off and he snatched them from her and began to wipe them.

'My poor son wants a wife,' she sobbed.

'I know,' he said, furiously wiping.

'Do something! For once in your life do something for your children!'

He shouted back at her, 'But what do you want me to do, for God's sake!' He got up and began to pace the room. Unconsciously he was tapping his fist hard and sharp against his chest. Her tears dried as she watched him. She was much surprised: she had not seen him do this for many years. Though it was a gesture with which she was very familiar. In his earlier days he had walked up and down, up and down like this for many hours, his fist all the time beating rhythmically against his heart.

'Sit down,' she said, somewhat alarmed. 'What is the use of exciting yourself, an old man like you.' As was to be expected, he took no notice but continued pacing, with his head lowered and his hand all the time tapping. She watched him anxiously. After a while she said, 'It is all right, you need not trouble yourself. I myself will do everything.'

A few moments later she said in a louder voice, 'I myself will do everything. Perhaps you are right, it is woman's work.'

'Please sit down,' she said desperately. 'What is the use of upsetting yourself? You will make yourself ill – I have no wish to be left a widow. I told you, I will do everything, you need not trouble yourself. I have already been to Har Dayal's house.'

At that he stopped still. 'You have been to Har Dayal?'

'Of course.' Now that she had succeeded in arresting his nervous pacing, she could afford to add, 'Since you would do nothing, of course I had to go, I owe it to my son.'

The silent stare he fixed on her was uncomfortable. She said defiantly, 'I was very well received. I drank sherbet.'

'What did you tell them?'

'Naturally such matters must be brought out with subtlety . . .'

'What did you tell them?'

'How can I remember everything that was said?'

He sat down again, wearily. 'You are a fool.'

'This is only what I have to expect. I do your work for you, and my payment is in insult.'

He thought of her sitting in Har Dayal's house. He could guess exactly how Madhuri must have received her. He felt himself getting angry at the thought of this reception of his wife; so he shut his eyes and told himself no, it is not right to be angry.

'We had much interesting conversation. They were so happy to see me.' She tried hard to persuade herself that this was true. Had not Har Dayal seized her hands and said how happy he was to see her? Yet she was uneasy, so she said more vehemently, 'They made me very welcome – it is good to have such friends.'

He had thought that nothing could really make him angry again. In his younger days anger had been his driving force. That was when he had work to do. Now he knew he no longer had any work; therefore he was calm and resigned and looked at everything dispassionately. It surprised him that he could not be dispassionate about this also.

'Madhuri left me at the bus-stand in her motor-car.' She sounded complacent, for about this at least she could be confident. Madhuri *had* left her at the bus-stand in her motor-car. It had been good to drive in such a large motor-car; if only certain people could have seen her.

He thought, it is ridiculous to feel like this. Har Dayal and Madhuri were not to blame. He had chosen to live in one way, they in another. It was not right that he should blame them for not wanting to accept his way. One should be proud enough to be sure of one's own value, he thought, not wait for others to estimate it.

'But why do you go there,' he said nevertheless, 'to let them insult you?'

'Insult me!' It was a shock for her; up to now it had quite genuinely not occurred to her to put such a drastic construction on her reception. She rejected the idea immediately and violently: 'How dare you say such a thing, when they received me with all honour and said not once but one hundred times how happy they were to see me...' By the way he looked at her she knew what he was thinking and imagining. 'You understand nothing,' she said. 'Of course we all know that Madhuri has not a very warm nature, but all the same she thinks of me as her dear friend, her sister, and welcomes me to her house as a sister.'

'And what did your sister say,' Ram Nath asked with a wry face 'when you kindly offered her your son?'

'How ugly you make everything sound – even of your own son you cannot speak with love and kindliness.' They looked at one another across the table. She said, 'What are we to do, where are we to turn to? He is our only son.'

He shrugged and answered, 'Why can you not put your trust in your God?' But he knew she had sensed his unhappiness and that it was no use trying to put her off its scent.

25

Everything was different. Or rather, it should have been different: the world had been transformed and yet, when for a moment she gave herself time off from her glorious thoughts to notice her surroundings, Shakuntala was surprised, and rather irritated, to find that things had remained obstinately and quite unreasonably the same. She had, she thought, always loved her home; but now it seemed to her dull and stolid. The furniture, the carpets, servants going up and down, Amrit setting off for work in the mornings, the parrot on the veranda: it was irritating to find that nothing should be different when her whole life had changed.

She found that her irritation was turned mainly against her mother. She had long since realized that there was nothing she and Madhuri had in common; and perhaps that was why, unlike other daughters, she had never really rebelled against her mother. There was nothing to rebel against. Madhuri's standards were so very different from those Shakuntala wished to impose on herself that she did not have to reject them in order to assert her own. She could regard her mother objectively, even admire her for being dainty and pretty and precise, because there was no danger of ever becoming like her. When Madhuri scolded her for being untidy and unconventional, she could afford to be good-naturedly amused, smilingly confess that her mother was right, that she really was quite, quite impossible: she could be thus tolerant because she had no intentions of changing herself and knew that her mother knew it.

But now it was different. Now she felt herself resenting Madhuri: perhaps because it was she who was responsible for the sameness of everything. It was the mother's personality that the house so uncompromisingly reflected, refusing to adapt itself to the daughter's changed condition. Shakuntala felt herself reborn; but Madhuri still insisted that she should be punctual for meals and hang her saris neatly on a hanger. For the first time in her life Shakuntala found herself thinking derogatory thoughts about her mother: she is petty, she thought, she understands nothing. Least of all would she understand about the great thing that had happened. She would apply, Shakuntala scornfully, bitterly thought, her own stupid little standards to him and me; she is incapable of grasping Beauty, Passion, Poetry. So when Madhuri scolded her for wearing a torn blouse, Shakuntala was rude to her. Madhuri was first surprised and then angry; she retired in a huff, and later behaved coldly towards Shakuntala to show her continued displeasure. Shakuntala did not care and was cold in return.

Her attitude towards her father, she found, had also changed (naturally, since she herself was quite a different person). She had always loved and admired him more than anyone else; she still loved and admired him, but in a different way. For now she pitied him a little, because she knew, and he did not, that she could never love him as much again as she had done; and also because he was old and his life was all finished and folded, when hers had just burst into bloom.

She was too much taken up with herself to notice that he, too, was not the same towards her. He was uneasy and, being uneasy, tended to be facetious and to clear his throat in a rather stagy mànner before talking to her. The fact was, he felt he had to tell her about Professor Bhatnagar's offer, and about Ram Nath's. It was not Professor Bhatnagar's offer that made him uneasy. On the contrary, he rather looked forward to telling her about the clever son at Harvard; they would discuss him together very seriously. But first he had to tell her about Narayan. What held him back from that was his fear of how she would react. He did not like to admit to himself how he wanted her to react; so he could not even try to guide her. The position was intolerably difficult for him; and though he was used, through his committees and other social activities, to dealing with delicate situations, it was rather different when they were so closely related to his personal life. He had a lot of tact, but tact, he realized, was not quite what was wanted here.

He was walking in his garden on a beautiful moonlit night. He could have been so happy. There was his gracious, spacious garden with lawn of succulent green (the gardener had had the hose on all day) and the tennis-court and white-and-green wicker armchairs and the rockery all laid out ready for flowers in winter. That afternoon he had been to such a charming 'At Home' to meet the Chief Minister of Uttar Pradesh State. Many of his old friends had been there – most of them Ministers now or Vice-Chancellors of Universities – and they had had gay, jolly conversation together. After a tea of vegetable samusas and rasgullas he had let himself be persuaded to recite some of his translations. He had been in such a mellow mood, till he remembered about Ram Nath.

Shakuntala was also in the garden. They met as she turned from the path by the tennis-court. Silently she tucked her arm under his and they walked affectionately side by side. Fragrant jasmine and ratki rani weighed heavily on the silver night. Har Dayal recited in a low and passionate voice, 'Wan is the moon, wan the white lotus and wan the cheek of the maiden longing for her lover.' His daughter pressed his arm. How well he understood; she wished she could have told him; she would like to have told him there and then, 'Daddyji, I am in love.' In love, in love. Her heart melted into the night, into the flowers and the moonlight. Har Dayal's voice came like honey: 'Now she dances before him, and sings, as he reclines wearied in the bower; the jewels flash in her girdle, bells ring from her ankles like the song of the swan.' Yes, she thought, in spirit I dance before him and sing. She wanted so much to tell her father. She was used to telling him all her finer emotions, sometimes even before she had quite felt them.

154

And Har Dayal could have gone on reciting for ever. He felt himself much moved by his own recitation. Poetry had such an ennobling effect, it made one realize all the beauty in the world and in one's own soul. But somehow, when he felt beauty moving in his soul, his thoughts always turned to Ram Nath. Perhaps because he had, from his student days, tended to associate all that was noble and fine with Ram Nath. He was silenced. He thought himself unworthy to partake of the purity of poetry because he was not behaving nobly towards his friend. So they walked together, he and his daughter, in a silence which for her was pregnant with a common understanding of all the wonder of the world and for him with guilt and unease.

'Shakuntala,' he said at last on a sigh.

She breathed back, 'Daddyji,' but hers was a sigh of rapture.

'There is something I must tell you.'

'Yes, my darling;' and more than ever she wanted to say and there is something I must tell you. Perhaps he had already guessed. She felt so close to him, it seemed to her that he must have guessed what she breathed out from every pore.

Then he told her and she was neither surprised nor interested. She said, 'I know.'

'You know? He has spoken with you also?'

'You mean Uncleji? No, it was not Uncleji ...' She dropped her hand from his arm and said nothing further.

'You know that I never wish to influence you,' he said uneasily.

'Daddyji, I hardly know Narayan, how can I – ?'

'It is true, you hardly know him.' He did not say, as he was aware he ought to have done, that there was opportunity to get to know him better. Instead he cleared his throat.

'Of course he is very intelligent and he is doing such noble work, I know that.'

'Very noble work,' Har Dayal said in a low voice. All the time he could not help thinking of Professor Bhatnagar's son, who would have a post in the Ministry and a good salary on which to live a life of culture and refinement.

'But I can only marry for love.' She put much expression into the last word, for it was spoken right out from her soul.

'Of course, of course, that is why – Let me not to the marriage of true minds,' he said desperately, 'admit impediments, but how can there be true minds when you hardly know one another?'

'Darling Daddyji, that is why I love you so: you understand everything.'

In his mind he told Ram Nath, you also would not like it that way – that we should arrange for them when they do not even know one another; these things must come by themselves, out of the hearts and minds of two young people. And perhaps, who could tell, she would care more for someone else – someone, for instance, like Professor Bhatnagar's son, whose background and education were nearer to hers, and who would enable her to lead the kind of life she was used to.

'It is true,' Shakuntala said, 'that I admire Narayan very much, as I would admire anybody who leads a life of idealism and sacrifices'; and she began to speak somewhat more slowly as she slipped deeper into the defensive, 'I also wish to lead such a life, of course – '

'But everyone,' he quickly cried, 'must choose his own path, is it not so?'

'You are the most wonderful Daddyji in the world.'

He took her hand and fondled it tenderly. 'You see, my darling, H. G. Wells, the great English author, has said that for every man there is his own sufficient beauty. It means that we must, each one of us, find that way of life which brings the greatest contentment to our souls, do you understand, my love? For without contentment of soul we cannot lead a good life. Let us say that Narayan has found his sufficient beauty; but does it follow that this will also give contentment to Shakuntala and enable her to lead a good life?'

'I think my ideals are different from his. Though of course I admire him very much ... Daddyji, I love Art and Beauty and Poetry, how can I give these things up as I shall have to if I go and live with Narayan in a village to do good to the poor?'

'You must never give them up, on the contrary you must base your life on them – '

'As you have done,' she said with an affectionate squeeze.

'I have tried to,' he modestly replied.

Shakuntala said, 'It is the same as with you and Ram Nath Uncle, I think.' He thought so too; had been thinking so all along. That was why he was well-fortified with arguments; for years he had been silently defending himself with them, till '47 and Independence had absolved him.

'Both of you were great Idealists,' she told him. 'But in different ways.'

Har Dayal shut his eyes and said, 'For him the life of action, for me the life of the spirit.' He opened them again to add, 'Who is to say which is the better? Narayan also has chosen like his father the life of action and you, my darling – '

'I have chosen like you, my own Daddyji.'

'Let us say that you probably will choose the life of the spirit, because as yet you are too young to have found your final path. But you care about things beautiful, about gracious living and the arts, this is obvious; and so it would be cruel, and not only cruel but also senseless, to plan a life for you in which you would not have opportunity to develop your taste for these things. Your Ram Nath Uncle,' he persuaded himself, 'would at once understand that if he knew you better. He would understand that though you greatly admire Narayan, as we all do, you cannot share in his life because it would be alien to your spiritual trend, you understand me, my darling? One day you will find your own mode of life and also,' his voice becoming a little unctuous as he thought of Professor Bhatnagar's son, 'the partner who will guide you in it . . .'

What then, in that romantic night, with their two spirits feeling so close together, prevented her from whispering into that sympathetic ear, 'Daddyji, I have found one already'? Only Indira coming towards them and saying with a timid laugh, 'But you look exactly like lovers.'

'In such a night,' Har Dayal said, sweeping out his arm and turning towards his daughter, 'Stood Dido with a willow in her hand Upon the wild sea-banks . . .'

'Merchant of Venice,' Shakuntala said with confidence, for they had had a production at College in which she herself had played Lorenzo.

Indira said, 'How wonderful you are to remember all this – of course I also had to learn it at College, but now I have forgotten everything.'

Har Dayal and Shakuntala refrained from exchanging a look, but each knew what the other was thinking; it made them feel very close. They were most satisfied with one another. Each felt truly understood by the other, and as understanding also implied justification, Har Dayal experienced a great relief. After a week or two he would tell her about Professor Bhatnagar's son.

'Shakun,' Indira said, 'will you come and help me put the new photographs into the album?' Amrit had lately bought a 750-rupee camera and had consequently begun to develop into a fairly keen amateur photographer, in which Indira enthusiastically supported him with her admiration. She had even encouraged him to enter a photograph in the *Illustrated Weekly* competition. It was called Mother and Child, and depicted the wife of the gardener holding her youngest baby and looking rather astonished. Indira had been surprised that it had not won a prize, for she had thought it very effective.

'I wish you would not call me Shakun.'

'Yes,' Har Dayal said with a smile, 'why do violence to such a precious name.'

Shakuntala, Shakuntala, Esmond had murmured, you have come to me like a fragrance of jasmine out of the pages of honeyed Kalidasa.

'They are such lovely photos – come, we will have fun together putting them into the album.'

'Oh, Amrit with his stupid camera . . .'

Indira would have vigorously defended her husband at any other time. But now she was too concerned with getting Shakuntala indoors. Not because of the photographs but because Madhuri had deputed her to speak to Shakuntala. She had not given her any specific instructions as to what to say, but Indira understood perfectly what was wanted. She was beginning to share all her mother-in-law's opinions, especially those regarding Shakuntala's shortcomings.

'No, darling,' Har Dayal said, 'photography may also be regarded as a form of art. A lesser form, it is true, since there is only limited opportunity to exercise the creative vision, but nevertheless one must concede it to be a striving for self-expression.'

'Not the sort Amrit does,' Shakuntala said decisively; which her father could not contradict. Anyway, he was anxious to go indoors and write a speech which he was committed to deliver next week at a centenary meeting in honour of one of the lesser Urdu poets. The composition of this speech had been weighing on him for some time, but because he had been feeling so worried, he had not been able to settle down to it with the ardour which he knew it required. It was only now that Shakuntala had relieved him of the better part of his worry that he felt really fit and free to round off suitably noble phrases on the poetic spirit.

'Or shall we just walk?' Indira said, cosily tucking her arm into Shakuntala's. Shakuntala did not at all want to walk with Indira who, she felt, would only spoil the harmony of the night and her bliss for her. What she wanted was solitude, to dream and remember and float on glorious feelings. She withdrew her arm and said, 'No, you see, I have work to do indoors.' Perhaps she would sit in her room and play 'Liebestraum' on the gramophone.

'What work? How can you have work now that you have finished your College?'

'Naturally I do not wish to forget everything I have learnt – on the contrary, I wish to learn and study much more. I must keep up my painting and my poetry, I cannot live without these things.'

Indira was not quite listening. She was thinking what to say and how to start on it. She wished, as Madhuri had asked her to do, to recommend certain virtues to Shakuntala, but it was difficult to put them into words. She tucked her arm again into Shakuntala's and said, to set the right tone, 'There is so much we have to talk about, do let us walk for a little while.'

Shakuntala laughed. Quite good-naturedly, for she was feeling superior. She and Indira could never, she knew, talk on the same level. Poor Indira. But she was prepared to let her talk her little talk. Perhaps she wanted to confide some mundane little matrimonial secret to her; maybe she was going to have a baby.

Indira was also feeling superior. She enjoyed the role of married woman giving advice to the young girl. She felt full of virtue and common sense. 'Often I think that we do not talk together enough,' she began. 'It is such a pity because there is so much we can learn from one another.'

'Please, Indira, do not talk nonsense. What could there be we could learn from one another when we are two quite different characters?'

Indira, unperturbed, continued as sweetly and reasonably as before: 'That is just what I mean. Because we are such different characters' – she conceded this as complacently as Shakuntala had proposed it – 'we should try to improve one another. For instance, I would like very much,' she said politely, 'to learn from you about poetry and such things –'

'And what do you think I should learn from you?'

Indira had hardly hoped to reach the point so quickly and exactly. But now it was reached, she found it was difficult to tackle. She knew very well what it was Shakuntala should learn from her, but did not think it was tactful to state it too directly. 'I always think,' she circumlocuted, 'that there is much we could both of us learn from Mummyji.'

'Oh my goodness,' said Shakuntala who was still feeling irritated with her mother, 'you mean how to fold saris and part the hair?'

Indira said gently, 'I don't think you are being quite fair to Mummyji.'

'I have known her very much longer than you have, and I do not think you can really judge whether I am fair to her or not.'

'I am sorry, Shakun, of course I did not mean to offend you . . . but don't you think it is nice always to look pretty and dainty and have your clothes in order and everything so smart and fresh?' Involuntarily she looked down at herself, at her crisp sari of such fine spotted organdie that the pink petticoat underneath was clearly visible.

'Such things are very petty. To care too much about them shows that you have a petty mind and are incapable of understanding great principles or suffering deep emotions.'

Indira inaudibly sighed. Shakuntala, as usual, was carrying the discussion into realms which were for Indira both unmeaningful and uninteresting. She had not come to talk of great principles and deep emotions; she never talked about such things. It was true, she sometimes did have deep discussions – for instance, at College she and her friends had had very intimate talks about the sort of husbands they hoped to marry, and now she and Amrit, in the privacy of their bedroom, occasionally discussed how many children they thought they ought to have (he said two, she three) and how to educate them – and she certainly enjoyed talking about the serious things in life in a common-sense way. But Shakuntala was always so vague, the things she said were quite remote from real life as Indira knew it.

'You and Mummyji are both the same, you are both so materialistic that you can think about nothing except clothes and tea-parties and going shopping in the car. Well, I do not care about such things, on the contrary I even despise them because I think they hamper the spirit.'

'No, please, Shakun, I think you are wrong, we do not care only about superficial things. But it is so important for a girl to always look nice and behave like a lady – you will realize this, I think, when you are married.'

'You do not think I would ever, ever consent to marry a man who wants me to behave like a lady?'

'All husbands want their wives to behave like ladies – unless of course they are a little peculiar and do not lead normal lives, like for instance Mr Ram Nath's son Narayan.' She gave Shakuntala a little sideways glance, wondering whether she had been told about that ridiculous offer.

'And what do you know about Narayan?'

'I have heard of him. Amrit often says how he has thrown away all chances in life.'

'Amrit says – and what does Amrit know? The only chances in life he can recognize are how to get more money and higher position in his firm. I will tell you: I would one hundred times rather marry someone like Narayan –'

'Shakuntala! You do not seriously say that you could marry Narayan?'

'And why not?' Shakuntala demanded in an almost blustering manner. 'He thinks like me – he does not believe in a merely commonplace life, he wants to give himself for something fine and noble . . .'

'Shakuntala, if you were to marry Narayan, I think your mother would die.'

'What nonsense you talk – what would there be to die about? Is it not better that I should marry someone who at least thinks like me

160

and has the same character than someone who Mummyji thinks is fitting only because he has a good safe job and goes to Club in the evenings?'

Indira was too agitated to listen or speak any further. She felt she had to go indoors immediately to inform her mother-in-law of this disturbing discovery which she had involuntarily made. Shakuntala did not notice her distress and was glad of her departure. Though she had spoken with some fervour, this was out of habit rather than conviction; the subject was not really very interesting to her. Indeed, no subject, except one, was at present really interesting to her.

26

Gulab knew that Esmond was in a bad mood and would be so for days to come. He always returned home, from a journey or even only from a dinner-party, in a bad mood. She understood that this was because the contrast between the enjoyment he had outside and the boredom he had at home was so striking. In a way she even sympathized with him. She herself could only resume her life in the flat by making herself forget the few days she had spent in her mother's house.

She lay on her bed in her room and waited for it to be night so that she could eat her dinner and go to sleep. Ravi was sitting on the floor drawing with crayons. It was very hot in the room but the only open space they had was a little veranda on which Esmond was sitting, and he wanted to read in peace. They had the fan on as fast as it would go, but it only succeeded in circulating a lot of stale air, laden with the intimately pungent smell of Gulab's body and clothes.

Both of them were distressed when Esmond, in a sharp voice, called for Ravi. They looked at one another and Gulab whispered, 'Go, my love.'

She could hear them talking out on the veranda. Esmond asked in a strict voice, 'What are you doing?' and when Ravi replied shyly that he was drawing with crayons, he said, 'Very good,' still strict. Probably, though, he was pleased, because he believed very strongly in children learning to express themselves through drawing.

'And what are you drawing?'

'I am drawing my Nani's house.'

'I see ... and after you've drawn your granny's house, will you draw your own house too, where you live with your Mummy and your Daddy?'

There was a short silence. Esmond said sharply, 'Well, will you?'

'I like to draw best my Nani's house.'

'Why?'

Again silence. Gulab lay tense on her bed. The fan turned and turned. Perspiration was trickling down her legs under the sari.

'Why?'

'I like my Nani's house.'

'But you like your own house too, don't you?'

'In my Nani's house there is a swing.'

'Yes, that's very nice. But this is your home, you know, even if it hasn't got a swing. You must always love your home better than any other place.'

'Nani's house is not my home?'

'No, of course not, you don't live there, do you?'

'Yes, I live there.'

'Don't be silly, Ravi. You live here.'

'I live in my Nani's house too. I sleep there with Mama on a bed and Bachani swings me in the garden.'

Gulab shut her eyes and thought how nice it would be to go to sleep. But she had not yet had her dinner and was hungry. Besides, she knew from experience that if she went to sleep now she would wake up in the night; especially as she had already had a long sleep in the afternoon.

She opened her eyes when Esmond came striding in. He held the book he had been reading closed in his hand with his long pointed forefinger stuck in to mark the page. 'Perhaps it wouldn't be asking too much of you to tell me just where you spent your time while I was away?'

Ravi picked up the piece of paper on which he had been drawing and held it up to his father. 'This is my Nani's house.'

Esmond looked neither at him nor at it. He looked only at Gulab. 'Surely you can give me some account of what you've been doing during my absence.' He had been speaking quite quietly and reasonably, but suddenly he thundered, 'Get up from that bed!' The piece of paper fluttered from Ravi's hand. He sat down on the floor and tried hard not to cry.

Gulab got up. Her hair had come down and lay straggling in a loose pigtail over one shoulder. She stood with her eyes downcast and her hands by her side.

'What sort of a slut's life is that to lie on your bed the whole day long? Answer me!' he screamed.

Gulab, without looking up at him, murmured, 'I was a little tired.'

'Is there any time when you are not a little tired?'

The servant appeared in the doorway. 'Sahb called?' Esmond looked at the book he was holding in his hand and then threw it at the servant. It missed; the man stooped down to pick it up, dusted it front and back and held it out at arm's length to Esmond. 'Get out of here!' Esmond screamed, snatching it.

The telephone rang.

'Telephone, Sahb,' the servant obligingly informed him.

Esmond strode out to answer.

'I had to ring you,' Shakuntala breathed. 'Only to hear your voice.'

'Oh, it's you. How are you?'

'Happy. Terribly, terribly happy.'

Esmond lit a cigarette and thoughtfully drew invisible patterns with the dead matchstick.

'I wish I could tell you in words how grateful I feel towards you for making me so happy ... Oh, Sumitra, how nice of you to ask me, I would love to come.'

'Hm?' Esmond inquired, biting the end off the matchstick.

'Mummy was just walking up the stairs. It is so wonderful to hear your voice.'

'My dear, you really mustn't expose yourself to such risks for my sake.'

'Risks!' she hollowly laughed. 'What risks? You do not know what I would not dare for you.'

'Look here, I don't want to sound abrupt but I have some people sitting here ...'

'Why must there be other people in the world? When there should be only you and I.'

'Yes, that would be very desirable, but as it is – you don't mind?'

'When will we meet?'

'I'll get in touch with you, if I may. Good-bye,' he said, 'it was awfully sweet of you to call,' and hung up rather quickly.

Gulab was still standing as he had left her. Ravi also was still sitting on the floor and trying not to cry.

Esmond flung his cigarette on the floor and crushed it viciously with his heel. 'This is a pig-sty and I'm treating it as a pig-sty. Why didn't you clean up in here while I was away? Didn't I tell you to get rid of all this filth?'

Ravi could hold out no longer. His mouth became twisted and big tears rolled down from his eyes. Esmond did not notice but Gulab did. She could not, however, move nor say anything to comfort him.

'What was there for you to do here while I was away that you didn't have time to mop up the pig-sty? My God, is the woman dumb? I asked you a question! Were you too busy or what were you doing? *What were you doing?'*

Gulab said in a low voice, 'We went for a short while to Mama's house.'

'I see.' He sat down on the edge of the bed. 'Come here,' he said quietly. She came and stood before him, but did not raise her head.

'I didn't by any chance forget to say that you were to stay here while I was away, and look after the flat?'

'Please,' she said, but hardly audibly, 'the servant was here.'

'Very nice. You left a fine responsible and trusted person to look after my clothes and books and papers. You were very clever.'

'Nothing is missing,' she murmured.

He jumped up from the bed and towered above her. 'Small thanks to you!' She made no answer, did not look up, tried even not to breathe. She could hear Ravi trying to stifle his sobs.

Esmond looked down on the top of her meek, still head. They stood very close to one another; they had not been so physically close together for a long time, and her pungent body smell maddened him. She is like an animal, he thought. He shouted aloud, 'Animal!' and then grabbed her upper arm and began to twist the flesh. 'You animal,' he muttered through clenched teeth, 'why did you go away when I told you to stay at home,' but he was hardly thinking what he was saying because all his consciousness went into twisting the flesh of her arm. He felt it soft and full in his hand and he twisted harder and harder. She had given only one cry of pain, which shock had forced out of her. After that she kept quiet; she did not want to frighten Ravi.

At last – neither of them knew after how long, was it only one minute or a full five? – he released her, and without looking at her strode out of the room. He felt himself much upset, and lit another cigarette to calm himself. Then he paced up and down the living-room with it, frowning heavily and from time to time shaking his head. He was greatly aware of the telephone which stood there black and silent; it reminded him of Shakuntala, and the thought made him feel cloyed and entangled. He picked up the receiver and dialled. 'It's me – Esmond,' he said. It was wonderful to hear Betty's voice; so cool, so rational. 'Well well well,' she said, and he knew that her trim eyebrows were lifted and she was smiling ever so slightly.

Afterwards he felt better. He sat on the little striped divan with his legs crossed. There was no sound, no sound at all, from Gulab's room. He was still holding his book, and he opened it and began to read. But after a very short while he shut it again and went out to where she sat on her bed, quite still and holding her arm.

If it had been anybody else, he could have said he was sorry. But not to her because he knew she would not understand such an apology. Probably she did not blame him at all. In that primeval mind of hers, he thought, everything is my right. So she sat quietly and only held her arm. Ravi also sat quiet; he was not crying any more, only kept his eyes, huge in distress, fixed on his mother.

Esmond thought of Betty. He thought of her pert little face and her laugh and the way her eyes challenged his. It was to her more than to Gulab, perhaps, that he said, 'I want a wife who's my friend and companion, not my slave.' Certainly Gulab made no response. He had not expected any; nevertheless he carried on: 'I regard my wife as an equal and I expect her to regard herself as such.' But it was no good. He knew she would not understand, and she did not.

So he turned to Ravi. 'Don't you want your supper, darling?' he said in his kindest voice. But Ravi also did not reply; he continued to look at his mother with his melancholy dark eyes. Angels not Angles, Esmond found himself thinking again; and he longed more than ever for a little blond boy with blue eyes who would be always gay and play rough-and-tumble games with his father.

Gulab found that she was no longer hungry. Now she wanted only to turn the light out and lie on her bed. But this was impossible because first she had to give Ravi his supper and then sit down with Esmond to their own. Ravi, she found, also was not hungry. He sat in his little chair and would not touch his food; so she had to eat it herself, gulp it down quickly and guiltily. She often did this, because Esmond was angry when Ravi would not eat. Afterwards she undressed him and put him to bed. Neither of them spoke one word all this time; but when he lay in his bed and she had turned out the light, they embraced and clung to one another. She could feel his body shaking, but she had to tear herself away quickly because Esmond was waiting for her to come and eat.

Esmond said, 'Aren't you hungry?' when he saw her picking at her food. She shook her head. 'That's a change,' he said, but quite good-humouredly; and when she made no response, continued with even more good humour, 'Usually you've got quite a hell's pit inside you.' She did not even hear him.

He stifled a sigh and helped himself to more macaroni and cheese. He felt himself to be in a pitiful position: the more so since there was no one with whom he could discuss it.

Nevertheless he forced himself to speak kindly to Gulab. 'What did you do all day today?' and in case she should think that this was the beginning of another scolding, added quickly, 'Don't you get bored, just sitting around and doing nothing?'

She did not answer. She was thinking of Ravi lying alone in the dark and being unhappy. She wanted so much to go to him, only to hold him and say nothing; but it was a strict rule that, once Ravi had been put to bed, he was not to be disturbed again. Even if he cried she was not allowed to go to him, so as not to develop a bad habit.

Esmond restrained himself from saying something sarcastic to her. He had to restrain himself very hard, for he was feeling greatly injured. Here he was trying to be kind to her, engage her in conversation, treat her as an equal; and she could not meet him even part of the way. There were, he knew, many other incompatible marriages; he had had much experience of them among his friends. But at least there was always some neutral ground on which the two parties could meet. They could, occasionally and in between their quarrels, converse about indifferent subjects, if not like friends then at least like strangers shut up together in a railway compartment. Or they could sit and discuss their incompatibility, and so get some satisfaction out of rationalizing their unhappiness. He was longing to do that. But with Gulab? She could understand nothing; talk to her, and her eyes – her beautiful deep sad eyes, which once he had thought full of all the wisdom and the sorrow of the East – remained what he had long since decided was a mere blank. It was like talking to an animal. An animal, he thought, I am married to an animal. Then he recalled his voice shouting 'Animal!' and the sensation that had flooded over him as he felt the flesh of her arm in his hand. He looked at her, her head bent over her macaroni cheese, and he felt her presence pressing in on him, her warmth, her softness, perspiration oozing like an unguent out of the smooth brown skin. To his horror he found himself wanting to seize her again and tear at her flesh and even to bite into her, to let his teeth sink deep into her soft body; to hurt her till he got some human response from her, even if it was nothing more than a cry of pain.

On a wave of disgust with himself and with her, he pushed back his chair and abruptly got up. His plate was still half full. Gulab showed no surprise; she did not even look up. He strode out on to the little veranda and paced up and down there. Up and down, up and down; it was a very small space. Out in the street servants from the neighbouring households had gathered to enjoy the evening air. They squatted by the side of the pavement and smoked bidis or chewed betel-leaves. A man with a little barrow had taken up his position under the lamp-post facing Esmond's house and did good business selling glasses of sugarcane juice.

He was trapped, quite trapped. Here in this flat which he had tried to make so elegant and charming, but which she had managed to fill completely with her animal presence. His senses revolted at the thought of her, of her greed and smell and languor, her passion for meat and for spices and strong perfumes. She was everywhere; everywhere he felt her – in the heat saturating the air which clung to him and enveloped him as in a sheath of perspiration; in the sugarcane juice, which the people in the streets were drinking and which he could almost taste, filled with dust and germs and too much sweetness; in the faint but penetrating smell of over-ripe fruit; everywhere, she was everywhere, and he felt himself stifling in her softness and her warmth.

He knew he had to get out of the flat quickly. He hurried into the bathroom, splashed his face with cold water, combed his hair, then into his bedroom to change his shirt. As he passed through the living-room, he did not glance in her direction though he knew she was still sitting there huddled over her plate. He walked straight through the door and down the stairs. He decided to take a taxi, defying the expense. He had to get to Betty quickly. She would give him a cool drink and he would talk to her and she would listen and understand. Perhaps they would make plans for his escape; perhaps she would be able to persuade him that it was easy to borrow money and book a passage and go back to England and start all over again. At any rate, just to be near her was already partly an escape: to be near her quick, lively mind and her quick, lively body, which was spare and cool and dry and smelt of hay like an English field in the summer.

After he had left, Gulab could at last go in to Ravi. He was still awake and his face was all wet; she could feel it wet in the dark. She held him in her arms and then he went to sleep, but she still stayed there holding him long after he had gone to sleep.

27

The anxiously awaited letter from Raj came at last. It contained the news that he had acquired an English fiancée. After the first shock, everybody was rather pleased. Har Dayal chuckled and said, 'The trend these days is towards internationalism, you know.' He had a committee meeting that morning, and he confided the news to one or two of the committee members who were his special friends, and they said the same thing. Amrit said, 'Good old Raj, didn't know he had it in him.' Indira was very thrilled at the prospect of an English sister-in-law and looked forward to the shopping expeditions they would make together.

Shakuntala was especially pleased because she felt that this event broke the ground for herself. Of course, Esmond would be a divorcé in addition to being a foreigner, but with the Hindu Code Bill and everything, who cared about that sort of thing these days? On the contrary, it was even rather glamorous and advanced to be a divorcé. For the first time she began to make really practical plans for the future.

It took Madhuri longest of all to be pleased. The idea of having a foreign daughter-in-law was still too new for her to be able to reconcile herself to it very quickly; and then too, she had been har-bouring some intentions for Raj in connection with an excellent and very rich family of Uttar Pradesh landowners (nothing definite yet – she and the ladies of that family had given one another one or two hints which had been pleasing to both of them, that was all). But when she remembered how many of the very best families had had foreign daughters-in-law brought into them; and how indeed it might even be regarded as a kind of hallmark, an indisputable witness to the fact that one had had one's sons educated abroad; and moreover, when she remembered how well she had always got on with English ladies – even at a time when there had not been many people who had been able to get on with English ladies – and how they had had tea-parties together and thought alike on many points; then really she had few regrets. And the photo Raj had sent was altogether reassuring. It was a tinted photo and showed a girl with a clear English complexion, nice blue eyes and a good forehead (Raj wrote that she liked sports and the open air). She was wearing a powder-blue twin-set and looked so neat and sensible. After studying the photo for a while, Madhuri was quite reconciled, and by evening she had propped it up on her writing-table.

There was this about Madhuri: she was small and she looked frail, she was not very well-educated and had not been out of the house much; but she knew how to arrange her life and the lives of those around her. The house was run entirely according to her plans: there was not a detail that she had not personally arranged. She was severe with her servants, but they stayed with her because they knew exactly both what to expect of her and what she expected from them. She had duly regulated every minute of their time, allotting to each his due share of work which had to be meticulously carried out. In this way she had managed to possess herself more or less of their lives. And she kept an equal, if less obvious, control over the members of her family. Har Dayal, in all he had done or not done in his life, might have thought of himself as a free agent, but a more detached observer could locate the mainspring of his actions elsewhere. Madhuri had at one time feared that he might follow the general madness and throw himself into the Independence movement, go to jail, give up his property and social standing. Certainly, given Har Dayal's predilection for making speeches and gestures, the danger had not been negligible; it had only been by exerting all her influence and bringing it to bear on the side of his other predilection for comfortable living that she had managed to counteract it. The balance had for many years been precarious, but she had always managed to keep it. Now, of course, all the danger was over, and she could enjoy the satisfaction of having successfully steered him into a safe and comfortable harbour. She could feel the same satisfaction about Amrit. Amrit was safe (not that there had ever been much to fear as far as he was concerned – that was why he was really her favourite child). He had the sort of job and the sort of wife and the sort of attitude to life one could wish for. And now Raj too. She looked again at the photograph, met that frank and sensible English gaze and thought that yes, Raj too was probably safe.

But there was Shakuntala. More than ever, now after what Indira had told her, there was Shakuntala. She sat on her upstairs veranda in the evening, with her hands folded in her lap and a frown cut in her forehead in a straight line above her nose. Gramophone music came from out of Shakuntala's room. Amrit and Indira were playing tennis, balls bounced round and plump and Amrit's voice, also round and plump, said, 'Oh, well-played' or 'Come on, Indi, you can do better than that.' Har Dayal came and sat beside his wife; he took her hand and said, 'So now, soon my darling will become a mummy-in-law again.'

Madhuri did not reply. She listened to the gramophone music from out of Shakuntala's room and her frown became deeper. Har Dayal gave her an uneasy sideways look: 'But you are happy, aren't you? you are not displeased? You see,' he told her, 'these days everything is international, all the old distinctions are going; that is, in marriage people do not care so much any more about caste or nationality.'

'Did you tell Shakuntala about – ?'

'About Raj? But of course, we all know, you yourself – '

'No, no, about that other thing.'

Har Dayal released her hand. He looked down at his own feet, wearing black-and-gold slippers with curled toes.

'I know you did,' she said in a hard voice. 'Indira warned me.'

'*Warned* you?'

The music stopped, but started again at once as Shakuntala turned the record. Madhuri pressed her fingertips against her temples in a gesture of exasperation. 'She has been playing for one hour now; she does not know what it is to think of others.'

Her husband murmured, 'She is so musical.'

Madhuri summoned her woman servant and sent her to Shakun-tala's room with the message that Madhuri had a headache.

'Yes, *warned* me. Thank God I have one person in the house I can trust. What need was there for you to speak of it to her? She would never have known, and then we would have been spared the trouble of driving out the stupid ideas which have now become lodged in her head.'

'What stupid ideas?'

'What stupid ideas – is that a question for you to ask who helped to put them there.' The woman servant reappeared. The music was still playing. The woman shrugged her shoulders and looked at Madhuri with a puzzled and unhappy expression on her face.

'What sort of a daughter is that,' Madhuri demanded angrily, 'who does not respect her mother's headache.'

'But she said no – she definitely said no,' Har Dayal broke out.

'I know she said no! This is what it has come to now – that I send like a humble petitioner to ask her to please turn off the gramophone on account of my headache and she answers me with no!'

'Not about that, about Narayan: she definitely said no.' Har Dayal sounded bewildered and almost shocked. He had thought that this matter was now decided and settled, that was why for the last two days he had been feeling light-hearted and had written an excellent speech for the centenary celebration of the Urdu poet.

'On the contrary,' Madhuri said peevishly, 'she definitely said yes. When Indira asked her, at once she said yes, I want to marry Nar-ayan, there is nobody else I wish to marry, only Narayan.'

'Perhaps Indira did not understand right,' Har Dayal said mis-erably. He found all his good spirits evaporating: and he really had been in such good spirits. There was that excellent speech he had written – one of the best he had ever done, it seemed to him – and there was the prospect of the English daughter-in-law who was to come to his house and whom he would teach all about Indian culture. Moreover, earlier in the morning Professor Bhatnagar had spoken to him over the telephone about a memorial to the founder of the Vil-lage Craft movement; at the end he had mentioned that his son was on his way to Europe where he would be spending a few weeks before coming home to India – 'He will be visiting Oxford, you know,' Professor Bhatnagar (himself an Oxford man) had said, 'and then over to Paris and Rome and Venice and all the old places . . .' 'Ah,' Har Dayal had said, and 'Ah, indeed,' had echoed Professor Bhatna-gar with the same nostalgia; he had added, 'We must get together when he comes back,' and Har Dayal had replied, 'Excellent, excel-lent.' Har Dayal was still smiling after he had put down the telephone.

But now all happiness was clouded again by the vision of Ram Nath sitting quietly and saying he wanted a wife for his son.

'Indira!' Madhuri's voice rang across the garden. It was a low soft voice, but they heard her at once and stopped playing. 'Will you please come up here for one moment – your father-in-law wishes to speak with you.' She leant back in her chair as if the process of calling had tired her. 'Now we will see,' she told Har Dayal, 'who understood right and who did not.'

Indira and Amrit, carrying rackets, were flushed from playing. Their eyes shone and they looked happy, healthy and vigorous, like an ideal couple in an advertisement for vitamin pills.

'Indira,' Madhuri said, her eyes fixed out into the garden where she saw one of her servants enjoying the evening air (he should have been on the back veranda polishing the cutlery: she would deal with him later) 'what did Shakuntala say to you about Narayan?'

'Oh good Heavens,' Amrit said, tossing his racket aside, 'did you call us away from our game to start that all over again?'

Madhuri withdrew her eyes from the malingering servant to fix them on her son instead. She said nothing, but her mouth was drawn tight.

'I mean,' he said in a tone which was at once blustering and placating, 'What is the use of talking so much about this thing? She will not marry Narayan, finished, we all know that – why then do we have to talk about it at all?'

Madhuri took her eyes away from him, slowly and deliberately, and looked at Indira. 'Yes?' she inquired.

Indira, caught between her husband and her mother-in-law, fidgeted. But Madhuri's gaze was very compelling. 'She said that she – '

'Yes?'

Indira swallowed. So did Har Dayal, while he studied his foot held out in front of him. Amrit sat down, with a scarcely audible sigh of resignation. The gramophone in Shakuntala's room played 'Liebestraum'. Madhuri looked at Indira.

'She said I wish to marry Narayan and go to live with him in a village.' When she had said this, Indira modestly lowered her eyes and hoped Amrit would not be angry.

Madhuri looked at Har Dayal with a half-triumphant expression which asked him what he might have to say now. But he had nothing to say. He drew in his foot and stuck out the other one and contemplated that instead.

'She may wish,' said Amrit, 'but that is a long way away from what she will get.' And for some unknown reason he laughed.

'But your father,' Madhuri said, 'wishes it also.' So now they all looked at Har Dayal.

'No,' he was forced to say, 'when did I say so.' He got up and paced up and down the veranda, his fingers fiddling with the dolphin-shaped buttons on his long white coat. 'I spoke to her myself,' he said after a while, 'and she said she did not wish it. She said she did not know Narayan well enough and felt no – no love for him.'

'But you feel so much love for Ram Nath,' Madhuri said dryly, 'that you persuaded your daughter to love his son.'

Amrit cleared his throat. Indira wished herself elsewhere. 'Liebestraum' started again from the beginning.

'I cannot understand,' Har Dayal said as much to himself as to his wife, 'why she should have said to Indira I wish, and to me I do not wish. She who is of such a frank open nature that she does not know even the meaning of deception.' By which he meant that he was sure that she would never deceive him. And he was sure of it. Had they not always taken delight in pouring out all their souls' treasures before one another, he and his daughter? Was it not he who had first taught her how many treasures the soul could store up?

'Excuse me please, Daddyji,' Indira said, 'but you know how she is. It is so difficult to find out what it is she wants to do. For instance, one minute she will say to me yes, Indira, I will come out shopping with you, and the next minute, when I am all ready, dressed and the car is waiting, she says no, I will not come, I wish to sit and hear the gramophone.'

Amrit struck his knee with the flat of his hand. 'Of course, you are right, she is just a silly kid who does not know her own mind.'

'This is true,' Madhuri granted, 'but it is all the more reason that we must see that she does not get any wrong ideas into her mind. I do not know why your father had to speak to her about this matter at all, there was no need for her to know – '

'But she said to me, definitely she said to me,' Har Dayal cried in some excitement, 'no, I do not wish to marry Narayan, I respect him and the way of life he has chosen but I care too much for other things to be able to share this way of life with him – these were her words!'

'She says so many words,' Madhuri said, 'really one cannot tell what she means.'

'But I know it is true! She is a girl who cares too much for the refinements of life, the beauties that come with sophistication, to be able ever to give them up.'

'You mean,' Amrit said, 'she likes good food and good clothes and plenty of servants and a car and a nice comfortable home to live in – how right you are.'

172

That was not quite what Har Dayal did mean, but he was too glad to have them agree with him to be able to contradict.

'Of course,' Indira said with her eyes wide open in surprise, 'everybody likes these things, it is only natural.'

'One can never expect Shakuntala to do what is natural,' Madhuri said. 'That is why I am feeling afraid and wish to have this matter settled now so that we need never hear any more about it.'

'But it *is* settled,' Amrit said. 'We said no, and it is all finished.'

'But *did* your father say no to Ram Nath?' Madhuri cried. 'Did you say no to him, clearly and definitely, so that he understood your meaning?'

Har Dayal was now only anxious to show himself on her side. Though he had not really as yet, it seemed to him, settled his own position in regard to Ram Nath's offer – he would, he promised himself, as he had already promised himself many times before, think it all out later – it was easier to pretend to his wife that he had. He wished he could have told her about Professor Bhatnagar's son right now. How pleased she would be! All her frowns would vanish, and she would be kind and nice with him again! He took her hand and smiled his sweetest smile. 'My dearest,' he said, 'please do not worry any longer, I will tell him definitely no. I will go to him and tell him, if you wish it so.'

'When will you go?' she at once asked, but allowing her hand to rest in his.

'Soon, very soon, as soon as I have time to go to him.' He hoped this would not be so very soon. It was pleasant to please his wife by promising to do her wishes, not so pleasant to have to fulfil that promise.

'Tomorrow?' she relentlessly asked. He could feel her hand ready to withdraw from his, so he said, 'tomorrow,' and she left it there, soft and small.

Amrit slapped his knees with an air of finality and got up. 'There, Mummyji, now you are happy?'

'How can one ever be happy with a girl like Shakuntala? It is so difficult to know what she will think out next to worry us.'

Amrit laughed and Indira echoed him. But Har Dayal said, 'No-no-no, now you will see, she will grow into a cultured young lady.' Soon, when all this was settled, he would talk to her again. He would tell her about Professor Bhatnagar's son and how he had done so well at Harvard and was now going to Oxford and Paris and Venice, and how charming and nice and suitable the whole thing really was. He was confident that she would allow herself to be guided by him.

'And I am sure the girl Raj is bringing from England,' said Indira, 'will also be a very good influence on her. We will all three go shopping and have so much fun together.' Madhuri made no comment, but her eyes strayed to the photograph propped up on her writing desk, and she looked complacent.

'And also,' Har Dayal said on a sudden inspiration, 'we will perhaps arrange for her to have some private tuitions. Sometimes I feel that her cultural background is not quite rich and full enough.' It really was an inspiration. He would say to Ram Nath her education is not completed yet, so it is too early to think of marriage ... 'I will speak with Mr Stillwood, there is no person in India better qualified to provide such a background, he will give her a good grounding in all aspects of culture, East and West. Together we will sit and draw up a programme, and then he will come in two or three times a week to guide her. I believe his fees are quite reasonable, considering the excellent service he gives.'

'And you will go tomorrow to Ram Nath?' asked Madhuri, who had not yet connected the name Stillwood with Gulab, and was ready to give her consent to her husband's plan if he followed hers.

'Yes, my dear, I will go.' (Her education is not completed yet, it is too early ...) 'Indira also may, if she likes, participate in these lessons, she also may learn much from them.'

'Certainly Indira will participate,' Madhuri said, 'the more she is with Shakuntala the better it will be for all of us.'

'So now I will get a bluestocking wife as well as a bluestocking sister,' said Amrit. Indira giggled. 'Liebestraum' had now changed to 'The Swan of Tuonela'.

28

Uma knew that her brother was unhappy, and it made her angry that she could do nothing about it. But, she felt, it was always so nowadays: she saw her dear ones unhappy and could do nothing. It was terrible for her to have to sit still and watch them being unhappy. She was not used to sitting still under such circumstances for she had always, all her life, rushed into action and done what it had seemed right for her to do. First she had prayed – for guidance, she said, though it must be admitted that the guidance had always taken the form of her own wishes – and then she had acted. But now, though she felt herself as full of energy and strength as ever, she could do nothing: not for Gulab, not for Ravi, not for Ram Nath, not for Narayan. She paced about her house all day, feeling her strength stored up inside her and unable to let it out. She quarrelled often with Bachani, who then went about looking gloomy and resigned and played to perfection the role of patient servant for thirty years in the service of a capricious mistress. Uma also talked to Swamiji, who read chapters from the Gita to her and then made her sing devotional songs with him. She enjoyed the devotional songs and the sight of Swamiji, so holy and good, playing the harmonium, his eyes cast up to heaven and his mouth very round as he sang. But afterwards she did not feel any better.

Though she was not much given to gloomy thought, yet it occurred even to her that their lives – that is, hers and her brother's – had somehow come to a standstill. It had all been so different once. Regretting the past was an activity she had never hitherto indulged in, so she was surprised when it occurred to her how different it had once been. There was her house – she was crossing the long room and looked up at the glass dome let into the centre of the ceiling, cracked now and opaque with dirt – and she felt sad when she remembered how it had once been. It was not the lost splendour she regretted – the carpets, the statues, the ivory elephants – not over the cracks and the dirt in the glass that she sighed. Things had been like this for too long already, so that she had almost forgotten that there ever had been carpets and statues and ivory elephants. But it was the life that had been lived in her house that she regretted. It seemed always to have been full of people and full of activity. It still was full of people – the Brahmins, the pilgrims, the social workers come to stay – but there was no longer any activity. These people who had come to stay did not really fill the house. They were just scattered individuals, camping down in odd corners. They regarded the house as a place to stay for a few days; so they did not bring their enthusiasm into it, they did not fill it with the spirit of their activities.

But once it had been a centre for the lives and activities of many people. They had come there to talk, discuss, quarrel, write letters, eat, sleep, compose speeches, form committees, plan campaigns. The office which they had had in the little room off the front veranda was always full of a lot of people sitting around and talking or using the typewriter, while the earnest young Secretary at his desk had looked perpetually harried, with a strand of very straight oiled hair fallen over his forehead and his hands full of files which he seemed forever to be in the process of arranging. They had all talked in loud and rather shrill voices, for they were all of them of an excitable nature. There had been frequent quarrels and, every day, a series of irritations, but nevertheless they had all felt very close to one another. Probably because they knew that they belonged together, for they were risking everything together and their future was so uncertain that they did not often like to think about it. Life sometimes did not seem to be quite real: everything was so temporary, they had been in prison the day before and they would be there again tomorrow, so the time in between was never quite real. They were restless and also perhaps a little unbalanced; they laughed rather more quickly and got angry rather more quickly than people do under ordinary circumstances. But their circumstances were never ordinary; life was always lived at a different pitch from that of people with no purpose.

Of course, nothing could ever be quite ordinary in any place where her husband was. He had always given the impression of being larger than life, so much so that everything he did and all the people he came into contact with were caught up in a kind of atmosphere of greatness. He did everything on a vast scale: this was implicit in his physical presence alone, for he was enormous, in height, in chest and thigh, simply enormous. When there were quarrels he outroared them all; he laughed louder, longer, and more heartily than anyone else; his anger too was louder, longer, and more hearty than anyone else's. His appetite matched his size and strength. She could still see him tearing up an oven-baked chicken with his hands and eating it with super-human relish. It was strange to think of such a man dying after·a hunger-strike. In a way she was glad that she had not been able to see him in his last days (he had been in prison and she in another prison, three provinces away): she did not want any other memory of him than that of the vast, striding, bellowing giant, bursting with health and strength.

Nothing was the same again after his death. And then afterwards, after '47, people just seemed to no longer be there, even those who had been there always through all those years. Some had died and some had got very old and some had gone to Pakistan. Some were now very important and no longer had time for anything except their official duties and positions. Some had gone to live abroad. And some had faded away, she did not know what had happened to them.

And Ram Nath. She could not and did not class her brother among those who had just faded away. But – oh, he was different. In those days he had come skipping into the house, and he had darted about like a bright, sharp little flame. He had always given the impression with his quick, jerky movements and his shrill, piping voice – which made the words come tumbling out so fast they seemed to be tripping over one another's heels – that there was great hurry, not a moment to lose, and the sense of urgency he conveyed was so infectious that everyone began at once to plunge into activity as feverish as his own. But now when he came, he came quietly and sat on the veranda; and

176

she sat beside him and talked to him and made him drink tea. Where had it all gone to, all that fire and enthusiasm, all that quickness and action? They were now like any other two old people with nothing more to do. But she did not feel old. She did not feel old at all. It puzzled her, when she noticed it, that life should have withdrawn from her and her house and her family. And, being puzzled, and unhappy, there was only one person she really wanted to go to, so she went to him.

But he was not alone. Har Dayal was with him. Uma was surprised to see Har Dayal there; it was not often that he paid them a visit. He was one of those friends whom through a lifetime one always thinks of as a great friend, but whom one hardly ever sees. Now perhaps he had come to talk about Narayan and Shakuntala. She was glad and so at once forgot her sadness.

Har Dayal was much relieved when she came in. It had been embarrassing sitting there with Ram Nath, though nothing so far had been said. He had had what he wanted to say all ready; he had thought about it the whole night (she is so young, she needs more education, she cares so much for Culture). But everything broke down when he approached Ram Nath's house. Not from nervousness about the coming interview – that was there too, true, but he had steeled himself and coached himself so well that he had, in setting out, been almost quite confident of himself. But when he approached Ram Nath's house, his confidence quite suddenly left him. Because this was so unexpected: he had had no idea that Ram Nath lived in this sort of district. Ram Nath had shifted house many many times during the past thirty-five years. On the rare occasions when Har Dayal had gone to see him during that time, he had found him always in make-shift quarters. But there had been a sort of charm about these make-shift quarters. Usually they were situated in a part of some decaying villa, which for all its decay still bore traces of its past gentility. So Ram Nath lived in rooms noble and spacious enough, even though the floors were cracked and the distemper on the walls in poor health and there was hardly any furniture. It was a respectable poverty, bohemian, intellectual; so much so that, on returning home, Har Dayal had almost regretted his own opulent surroundings, feeling a sort of nostalgia for that bohemian atmosphere where people constantly walked in and out, incessantly talking, and there were piles of papers and ill-kept files.

But there was nothing bohemian about Ram Nath's present quarters. This was a centre of lower middle-class life – a kind of life with which Har Dayal had never had any contact. He knew only the lives of the rich and, to some extent, through his servants, of the poor: the classes in between were an unknown quantity to him. He could not imagine how Ram Nath – who had been to Cambridge, was an intellectual and came from a leading Uttar Pradesh family – could fit in here among these rows of little food-stalls and hawkers with push-carts, the women out for their shopping with babies on their hips and shopping-bags made of gunnysack with a picture of Gandhiji printed on in red, adolescent boys playing volley-ball, Sikhs in short underpants squatting casually in doorways and combing their beards. When Har Dayal's long blue car parked outside Ram Nath's tenement, many children crowded round and touched the shining chromium lines and had fun looking at their own reflections in the windows, till the chauffeur drove them away. Har Dayal, emerging from out of the car, felt odd and out of place; he knew himself to be an object of great curiosity in his beautiful white clothes cut of the finest cloth. The children greeted him joyfully, 'Salaam Sahb!' they shouted and nudged one another, while Har Dayal murmured some embarrassed acknowledgement and hurried into the house. He walked straight through the little dark passage into the courtyard, and then he stood and looked up and round, for he did not know where to go. Many women were gathered on the verandas which ran like galleries round the house; they were all busy working, cleaning their vegetables, sifting the day's supply of lentils, hanging up washing, with their saris tucked in a business-like manner round their waists. They looked somewhat bedraggled, for they had not yet had time for their baths, but they seemed gay enough, calling across to one another in loud familiar tones. Some of them stared down at Har Dayal with interest, but most of them spared him only an indifferent glance thrown over their shoulders as they reached up to peg newly washed clothes on the line. Nobody seemed inclined to help him as he stood down there in the courtyard, not knowing where to go and hesitating to ask the women. At last the widowed sister of the telegraph officer, sitting rocking herself in a rocking-chair and fanning herself with a bamboo fan, called down to him, after she had carefully inspected him, 'You have come to see Lakshmi Bahin's man?' He worked this out and then assented. She directed him, and he walked back into the little passage, which was empty except for a servant in striped pyjama-trousers who lay asleep on the lowest step of the stairs. From upstairs came the sound of many taps running and clothes being pounded; someone was singing a hymn. There was a strong smell of South Indian cooking. Har Dayal called softly, 'is anyone there?' and at once upstairs two dogs began to bark furiously. The servant, however, did not wake. Both embarrassed and a little frightened by the loud noise the dogs were making – which was growing every second in ferocity – Har Dayal opened the door nearest to him and peeped round it. There immediately was Ram Nath, sitting at a table reading a book.

But by that time Har Dayal was no longer ready and prepared. He could only sit and make small talk and feel miserable. Ram Nath was rather quiet, which did not make – though Har Dayal had had much practice at it – small-talk easy. He longed for someone to come in, to come between him and his friend, because feeling embarrassed and guilty and also miserable, it was more than he could bear to be alone with Ram Nath, who was the cause of these feelings. But there was no one else – Lakshmi, it appeared, had gone to see her second daughter's mother-in-law for the day – and Har Dayal was trying to make up his mind to go away and perhaps come another day. Or write a letter – he thought, yes, that was what he would do, write a letter (she is so young, she cares so much for Culture). But on his return home Madhuri would at once ask him, 'Have you told him?' and how was he to evade her? Then there was Professor Bhatnagar, whose son would soon be home . . . With all this troubling him, he found it very difficult to sit and talk of indifferent things; nor could he, he felt, sit and say nothing, though Ram Nath seemed to be quite prepared to do so.

Uma changed everything. She was so happy because she thought Har Dayal had come to arrange about Narayan and Shakuntala, and she greeted him with a warmth which at once made him feel better. 'Ah,' she cried, 'how good it is to see our friend in my brother's house!' and she gratified him with looks of love in which she enveloped both him and her brother.

But Ram Nath said, 'Yes, he has come to tell us that it will not be possible for Shakuntala to marry Narayan.'

Uma sat down rather heavily, and the sadness with which she had come returned tenfold.

'Is it not so?' Ram Nath asked Har Dayal, who looked at the ground and said in a muffled voice, 'My friend, please let me explain what I have come to say.'

'Why explain – what is there to explain? You will tell me that she is too young and that they do not know one another and that you want her to have more education. And I will say yes, you are right, and so it is finished.'

There was a short pause. Till Uma said sternly, 'Have you offered any refreshment to our guest?' and then she went out to wake the servant.

When she returned, she said, 'When I came here I was so sad, I was thinking how it was in the past, how often we were happy though they were such hard times. It is true what is written in the Gita, "Whatever pleasures are born of earthly things are only sources of sorrow, they have a beginning and an end." So true, so true'; and she sighed a great sigh of sadness and resignation.

Har Dayal echoed that sigh and then quoted in his turn, '"Time doth transfix the flourish set on youth And delves the parallels in beauty's brow; Feeds on the rarities of nature's truth, And nothing stands but for his scythe to mow." '

Uma asked with interest, 'Is this also from our old writings? From the Upanishads perhaps? There is so much truth and wisdom in our old writings – this is because they were written by men so holy that they lived only in the spirit and did not care at all for the body and the things of this earth. How I love to hear their words, it is like communicating with a pure spirit and so we get very near to God. Please say again what you quoted just now.'

Har Dayal said it again, in his most beautiful voice. Ram Nath said, 'It was written by a very holy swamiji called Shakespeare.' Har Dayal looked rather ashamed.

'Well, why not,' Uma said, 'in England also I am sure there are very holy men. And Shakespeare was a very great writer, he is famous throughout all the world.'

'I also often think about the past,' Har Dayal told Ram Nath in a voice that was almost appealing. 'About Cambridge and our youth together and how we read Shakespeare and Shelley and Wordsworth.'

'Oh that past,' said Ram Nath with a smile. 'It is so remote, often I wonder whether it was not in a previous life.'

'But to me it is so near, so near!' Har Dayal cried. 'How I remember and cherish those years – do you remember how we sat round the fire in your room and read aloud to one another from the English poets and had toasted muffins?'

'Toasted muffins?' Ram Nath said, wrinkling his nose as one questioning some very outlandish and unknown thing.

'It must be something to eat,' Uma rebuked him, 'do not be so stupid.'

'It is when I think about those years that I realize how great is my debt to you. It was you,' he said, putting his hand on the table and stretching it towards Ram Nath with the palm turned upwards in a very affectionate gesture, 'who first opened the portals of the world for me.' And then he felt again that familiar sensation which always came over him in the presence of his friend – the desire to shout, let me do something for you, let me serve you. He would like to have told him please take my car, keep it for ever with the chauffeur, I myself will walk home; and he would really like to have done it. But then it struck him again how he had just failed Ram Nath and refused

180

him the only thing he had ever asked of him. He withdrew his hand, and looked down at the ground and felt very much ashamed; wishing it were only possible. But it was not possible, he knew, so there was nothing for him to do but to feel ashamed.

'Yes,' said Uma with a sententious sigh, 'when we are old we dwell too much on memory.' But then the sententiousness cleared away, her eyes shone and her voice was almost youthful: 'I was thinking today of that time when you came out of jail – in '20 or '21 it must have been – and everybody came to welcome you and everybody wanted to stay to eat with you. I myself was in the kitchen, and I kept sending Bachani and the cook to the bazaar to get more and more food – I think never in my life have I cooked so well as on that day! And then when it was all ready and you were sitting down to eat, then the police came to re-arrest you and straightway you went back to the jail.'

'Your memories are not very happy ones,' said Ram Nath.

'Oh yes, I know, we were sad then, but when I look back on it now, I do not know how it is, but there seems to have been as much happiness as there was sadness. How busy we always were, and how we talked through the days and the nights! Sometimes I think that in those days we never slept or rested, there always seemed to have been work for us or friends come to talk.'

Har Dayal drank the tea that had been given to him. It came in a thick crockery cup with a bit chipped out at the rim. He did his best to hide this chip both from himself and the others, though he suspected they would think nothing of it. 'What excellent tea, excellent,' he murmured as he drank.

'No,' Uma said, sipping her own, 'it is terrible tea, I think he did not use fresh leaves, the scoundrel. And there was also that time when the police came to raid us and your papers were in the house, they were lying in a folder on the sofa. For hours then I sat on that sofa and I pretended that my labour-pains had started, though I was not even pregnant. How can anyone tell a woman whose labour-pains have started to get up from the sofa?' She threw back her head and laughed merrily out of her full, round throat.

Har Dayal smiled in sympathy. But he was beginning to feel more and more melancholy. It was a familiar melancholy – how often he had felt it in the past, whenever he thought of Uma and Ram Nath and people like them and the full exciting lives they were living. He had felt then that somehow the main stream of life was passing him by and he was washed up on a ledge like some almost inanimate jellyfish. And though he had assured himself that he too was doing important work in upholding, as he put it to himself, standards of culture and refinement, yet he had never been able to stifle that feeling of missing something great, something vital. As it happened, events had proved him – and Madhuri – right, so that now it was he who was very much caught up in the main stream, it was now for him that there was always work and friends come to talk. But when he was brought face to face with the memory of that past, the old melancholy came back.

'And I was thinking,' Uma said, 'what has happened to us, why are we today so – so . . .' she caught her brother's eye and he smiled and said, 'It is senile decay.'

'Oh, your sister is senile and also decaying?' she demanded; but then returned at once to her previous tone: 'I do not know how it is, but today our houses always seem to be empty, I do not know where everything has gone, our work, our talk, our friends . . . where *are* all our friends?' she asked, looking at Ram Nath as if she were expecting him to give her an immediate and precise reply.

Which in a way he did, by pointing out, 'Well, here for one is Har Dayal.'

'Yes, he is here. How good it is,' she said again, 'to see you with us,' but she no longer sounded so happy as she said it.

He looked down at the thick crockery cup which he held empty in his hand. He wanted very much to explain himself. There was so much he would like to have told them, and somehow everything became mixed up, so that he wanted simultaneously to justify himself about the past in which they had gone to jail and he had not, about the present in which he was busy and important and they were not, and about Shakuntala. Many things occurred to him that he wanted to say, but he could not get them out. He had an uneasy feeling that his words would sound false, mere words with no love nor truth behind them, even though there was in reality, it seemed to him, so much love and truth inside him; and also he was afraid that Ram Nath would say again, My friend, what is there to explain? and then there would be nothing left for him but again to feel ashamed.

29

Esmond said, 'The Kavindravacanasamuccaya has 525 stanzas, none of which, we can say with certainty, was composed later than A.D. 1000.'

'How old our literature is,' said Shakuntala, admiringly.

Indira was likewise prompted to assume an expression of admiration. She sat with her hands folded in her lap and her head slightly on one side, to give the impression that she was listening with interest. Actually, though, she was thinking of other things. She was admiring Esmond's bush-shirt, wondering where he had got it. She would very much have liked to buy the same for Amrit. Most of all, she was thinking of what her mother-in-law had confided to her in the morning. Madhuri and Har Dayal had had some talk, and afterwards Madhuri, her neat small face aglow with satisfaction, had called Indira and told her about it. It appeared that Professor Bhatnagar, from the Ministry of Education, had a son who had been studying at Harvard ... Indira cast a covert glance at Shakuntala; she was so happy for her.

'The Sūktikarnāmrta of Çrīdharadāsa, son of Vatudāsa, can be dated at *circa* 1205.' Esmond also was thinking of other things. He was thinking of Betty, who was going back to England. She had said, 'Why don't you pack up and come along?' and then, 'I'll lend you the money, if that's what you're worried about.' It had sounded so easy as she said it.

Shakuntala, remembering her English literature course, said in a professional manner, 'This is earlier than Chaucer, I think?'

'Very much earlier,' Esmond said, a trifle wearily; he did not like to be sidetracked and she had been sidetracking him continually. But he was conscientious about his job. 'Chaucer's dates are *circa* 1340 to 1400.'

'How awfully clever of you to remember so many dates. Of course, I am very fond of English literature but I can never remember any dates. That is why I always got rather low marks in history.'

'The Sūktikarnāmrta contains excerpts from 446 poets, most of whom came from Bengal.'

'Is it not strange,' Shakuntala said, 'that most of our poets come from Bengal? Tagore, for instance, and so many others. Why is that, do you think, Mr Stillwood?' She enjoyed calling him Mr Stillwood in front of Indira. It gave her such a lovely feeling of complicity, of an intimate understanding between herself and Esmond; the more intimate because it so completely excluded Indira, who sat there blithe and unaware.

'But Munshi Premchand is not Bengali,' Indira rather surprisingly contributed.

'Munshi Premchand is not a poet, he is a writer of short stories and also of novels. But even writers of short stories and novels are mostly Bengali, for instance Bankim Chandra Chatterjee. Why, Mr Stillwood? I often ask myself this question.'

'Yes, well, it's a very interesting one, and we'll have to go into it some time or other. After the Sŭktikarṇāmṛta, the next anthology of Sanskrit lyrical poetry is the Subhāsitamuktāvali.'

'What long, long names,' Indira sighed.

'Really, Indira, you talk like a foreigner. Mr Stillwood does not find them so difficult to remember.'

'It's arranged according to subject matter – love, fate, sorrow, and so on.'

'Love and fate and sorrow – that I understand very well. But what is so on?' She looked at him mischievously with a little smile which suggested a lot of things.

'I am sorry, Mr Stillwood,' Indira said. 'We keep interrupting you, it is very bad of us.'

He smiled at her: 'Yes, isn't it? We really ought to be getting on a bit faster than this. As I was saying, then, it's arranged according to subject matter and there's an especially interesting section on – '

But here a servant came to say that the Memsahb would be very pleased if Mr Stillwood would take tea with them when the lesson was finished.

'How very kind of your mother-in-law,' Esmond told Indira.

'Not at all,' she politely replied, 'it is a great pleasure for us.' She and Madhuri had already agreed, after they had been first introduced to him, that Esmond was very, very nice. Of course, Madhuri had at first been extremely suspicious of him, for was he not her own Amrit's usurper and so the cause of all her grudge against Ram Nath and Uma? But after meeting him, she found it impossible to hold anything against him. It was, anyway, she told herself, not his fault because he could have known nothing of the previous arrangement. He was quite innocent of any duplicity, so there was nothing in the way of her whole-heartedly approving of him. She was very glad that these lessons had been arranged. Shakuntala could derive nothing but good from a teacher of such charming manners and refinement.

'But what were you saying, please, about an especially interesting section?' Shakuntala asked.

'Yes, there's an especially interesting section on poets and poetry which gives us definite information about a number of authors.'

'I see,' she said in a somewhat flat voice; but brightened again: 'That is really as it should be, because poets and poetry are so much connected with love and fate and sorrow, aren't they?'

'Now the arrangement of the Subhāsitamuktāvali has your approval, perhaps I may carry on?'

'Shakun, really we should not interrupt so much.'

'You are not cross with me, Mr Stillwood?' and she looked at him with eyes rather more romantic than the presence of Indira should have permitted.

'The Sārṅgadharapaddhati was written in 1363 and contains 4,689 stanzas.' Without Betty, life in Delhi would become intolerable for him. At least she always managed to stir him up into liveliness, even when she exasperated him, as she so often did. She was the only person, he felt, who understood him. He could be himself with her, he could relax; he did not have to be over-polite with her as he did with other ladies, nor did she expect him constantly to be clever and tell her things about art and literature and India.

'Compiled in 1363 by the son of Dāmodara, it is perhaps the most famous of the anthologies.' Of course, he enjoyed talking about art and literature and India: it was, he felt, his true vocation. But one must sometimes relax from one's true vocation.

'Why is it so famous? Is it the best of them all?' Shakuntala intelligently asked.

'No, it certainly can't be called the best but it just so happened that it's become the best known. Look here, I hope I'm not boring you? You see, what I'm trying to do is give you a background of facts and dates. Once you've got that background, we'll have some basis on which to discuss aesthetic values.'

'What question can there be of boring,' Indira replied. 'It is so interesting. Really I feel I am learning so much – don't you too, Shakun?'

'Mr Stillwood, it is only as I already told you, that I have not much brain for facts and dates. But I care so much for aesthetic values.'

'If you'll be patient just a bit longer, we'll be getting down to them sooner or later. Well then, after the Sārṅgadharapaddhati, there's Vallabhadeva's Subhāsitāvali.' It was not only from his vocation that Betty allowed him to relax. It was also from his wife. The strain of living with Gulab was becoming more and more intense. He was like the tiger who has once tasted human blood: for, since that day when he had twisted the flesh of her arm, he felt himself wanting, almost irresistibly wanting, to hurt her again. Often, when he lay on his bed at night and knew her to be sunk in what he thought of as her animal sleep in the next room, he imagined himself dragging her down from her bed and beating and squeezing and pounding that soft, abundant flesh of hers. He would dwell on the scene and the sensation it gave him with such relish that he quite forgot himself, losing his identity of the man of culture, courtesy and refinement; so that, when he returned to his normal self, he hated her more than ever for bringing him to such a state. And then, hating her, it started all over again as he imagined what he would like to do to her.

And Betty had said, quite casually, 'Why don't you pack up and come along? I'll lend you the money.'

'Then there is Srīvara's Subhāsitāvali, and that brings us up to the fifteenth century. And also, I'm afraid,' he said, looking at his wristwatch, 'to the end of the lesson.' He always kept meticulously to his set time. He had learnt from experience that, if he did not, ladies were apt to keep him long beyond the hour for which they paid him.

'Oh no!' Shakuntala cried. 'We have only just begun.'

This was an exclamation he knew well, so he only smiled, while he gathered his papers together and popped them firmly into his brief-case.

'Yes, how quickly the hour has gone by,' Indira said courteously. 'Shall I go and see if Mummyji is ready to receive us?'

'Yes, please go,' Shakuntala at once encouraged her. Then they were alone and Shakuntala heaved a big happy sigh: 'At last!' But Esmond was more busy with the clasp of his briefcase than was quite necessary.

'How wonderful it is to have you here! If only that Indira did not have to sit with us.'

'What a charming girl she is.' He meant it. So neat, so courteous: he could not help thinking that if he had to take an Indian wife, why could he not have taken someone like Indira. With such a wife, he was sure, he could have lived happily. Moreover, she probably came from a rich and influential family who would have helped him, so that he would not have had to sit and teach Culture to silly girls.

'Oh she is so stupid, I am sure she understands nothing of what you say. She is very insensitive.'

'At any rate, she's got a good sense of dress.' Which was more, it seemed to him, than could be said of Shakuntala. Shakuntala, he had already thoroughly noted, always looked rather slatternly. Even her nails were not as clean as they might have been. How he hated slatterns – whether they were of the bohemian variety, such as Shakuntala was aspiring to be, or of the just lazy variety like Gulab. Gulab, always it came back to Gulab. She obsessed him and made his thoughts wicked and vicious.

'Oh, do you think so? I think the saris she wears are always so dull. But why are we talking about stupid things? When there is so much for us to say.'

'You shouldn't despise a sense of dress. It's a most important asset for any woman to possess. After all, women are supposed to represent the more decorative aspects of the species – '

'Esmond. My love, Esmond.'

'Shakuntala, do remember this is your father's house and I'm here as your tutor.'

'Why are you so cold and distant with me? You have not yet given me one kind look, not one word of love. What is it, Esmond? What have I done?'

'Done, done,' he repeated irritably; but then checked himself. Though he wanted nothing so much as to tell her to go to hell and leave him alone, he felt he was not in a position where he could do so. For one thing, he was her tutor now and her father paid him money (which he very badly needed); so he had to be, apart from anything else, at least polite to her. For another, he had allowed her to sleep with him, an act which to her, he had enough imagination to realize, was of unspeakable significance and which she expected to have far-reaching consequences. Betty had already pointed out this aspect of things to him, with some relish: 'You've got yourself into quite a mess with that little girl,' she had told him, while stroking his head which lay in her lap. 'To you it was all nothing – just a poke in the eye for your poor pal Betty, because you were cross with her' – here she had tweaked a few hairs playfully but nevertheless painfully enough for him to say, 'Ow!' – 'but to her it was the beginning and the end of the world. And now the very least she expects from you is a frightfully long and even more frightfully unhappy love-affair, with everything laid on.' He would have done anything to cancel out that moment of weakness at Agra: but there was nothing now that he could do. He was trapped in her love for him; and being unable to break out brutally and by force, as he would like to have done, he had to proceed warily, extricate himself gently somehow. At any rate, he had to soothe her, use sweet, soft words: 'My dearest Shakuntala, don't you see what an awkward position I'm in? Your father has called me here because he trusted me, and whatever my feelings for you might be, I have to suppress them as long as I'm in his house.'

'Do you call our love an awkward position?' she sadly asked.

He thought, the position is ridiculous, the pleasure short; it came unbidden into his head so that he wanted to laugh, though he did not in the least feel like laughing. The pleasure is short, the position – 'Why do you deliberately misunderstand me?'

'I have not yet heard one kind word from you, not since Our Night, not one sweet look have I had from you.'

'But, Shakuntala, do try and be reasonable. How can I betray your father's trust?'

'Why can't you go to my father and say to him boldly, "I love your daughter and she loves me, and already we have consecrated our love." '

'And then?'

There was a short silence. Shakuntala turned her hands palm upwards and examined them; she said in a low voice, 'Daddyji says I am not to marry Narayan.'

'How does that help?' Esmond replied curtly.

After another short silence, still looking down at her hands, Shakuntala murmured, 'Even in India there is such a thing as divorce.'

'Do please come, Mummyji is already waiting for us.' Indira's voice was bright and cheerful, she herself was bright and cheerful, standing smiling in the doorway, beautifully un-intense. Gratefully Esmond got up to follow her.

Madhuri sat in the drawing-room, so gracious, so charming amid all her lovely possessions. A great calm came over Esmond as he watched her dainty hands deft among the tea-things, and the well-trained servants bending over him with sandwiches and biscuits tastefully arranged on plates of finest china. A little antique clock ticked, the teacups tinkled, the ladies' golden bangles gently jingled. Esmond sat there, slim and elegant, stirring his tea with a tiny silver teaspoon. All his worries left him and he was at peace. This, he felt, was where he belonged, in an elegant drawing-room, taking tea with elegant ladies. His whole mood changed, he was suddenly gay and carefree and oh, so light of heart. Instinctively his little finger – like Madhuri's, like Indira's – crooked as he raised his teacup to his lips to gently sip from its brim. His voice became softer and more melodious and all sorts of delightful gently witty sayings dropped from his lips, each word a little gem which he polished and caressed as he passed it to them with a respectfully intimate self-deprecating little smile.

They were delighted with him, he could feel it, and it made the very best in him come out. He told them, smilingly and with a great sense of style, one or two amusing and appropriate anecdotes – told them, for instance, of the time when he had taken tea with Lady Sohan Lal and how, when she had cut the cake, it was found to be uncooked inside – oh, what embarrassment, what silent tension in Lady Sohan Lal's well-appointed drawing-room as her guests nibbled at their cake and pretended to one another that they did not notice anything. Madhuri and Indira laughed gaily, with a laughter as harmonious and as well-bred as the clink of the silver teaspoons against the thin china cups. They were all three feeling very friendly and even intimate together. Madhuri and Indira told him about Raj's fiancée and showed him the photograph; he held it at arm's length, scrutinizing it carefully though respectfully, and then nodded and said, 'Yes, obviously very County'; which, though they did not know what it meant, sounded nice enough. They were also tempted to tell him about Professor Bhatnagar's son and would have done so if it had not as yet been held a great secret into which even Shakuntala herself had not been initiated. So instead they talked about clothes. Indira asked him, quite naturally and without any shyness at all, about his bush-shirt; and he, taking the question quite as a matter of course, told her – after taking a very little bite out of a ginger biscuit which he held at its very edge so delicately that he was hardly holding it at all – where he had got it and how much it had cost. He further gave her all sorts of tips about the best places to get gentlemen's clothes, and from gentlemen's clothes they passed to ladies' clothes, discussing the comparative merits of various silks – Madhuri liked Benares silks best, Indira had a preference for Mysore and Bangalore – the art of colour-combination and whether the best prints came from Bengal or Assam. They were all charmed with one another, and the presence of Shakuntala did not intrude upon them at all, though she sat silent and gloomy, refusing tea and all refreshments, with her hair straggling loose over her shoulders, in her sari of too bright a green contrasting with a blouse of too bright a yellow.

Esmond thought if only it could always be like this. Then how he would love India, he would feel at home here and never want to go away, and Betty's casual, 'Why don't you come along?' would not trouble, would not tempt him in the least.

30

Lakshmi's reaction to Har Dayal's refusal, when it was imparted to her, was very different from what might have been expected. It was Uma who told her the news, and she palliated it as much as possible: 'He feels his daughter is too young and perhaps he is right ... when one has only one daughter there is never great hurry to make her marriage, it is only natural.'

But Lakshmi would grant no palliation. And instead of, as Uma had expected, being downcast and unhappy, she became suddenly quite energetic. She reared up her head and swayed it from side to side indignantly: 'So now perhaps our family is not good enough for them?'

'There is no question of not good enough, it is only as I told you – '

'Leave off! There is no need to tell me, I can read far enough into their black minds. But I will tell you something else and it is this – never would I have consented to such a marriage, for I know very well that it is their family that is not good enough for us, nor their daughter for a boy like my Narayan!'

Uma was too pleased to have her take up this comforting attitude to want to contradict. Though she could not really agree: Har Dayal's refusal had made no difference to her feelings for him and his wife. She was sad, but not resentful.

'In my father's house there were many more servants than in the house of Madhuri's father, and my marriage celebrations and those of my sisters were one hundred times more costly than the marriage celebrations of Madhuri and her sisters. This was well known in all the province. And it was also known that in their house there was never sufficient food cooked – if there were two guests only, the whole household had to go hungry: whereas in my father's house, twenty guests could come and sit and eat every day in the year and still there was enough left over for the beggars that came to the door.'

Uma nodded noncommittally. She was sitting at her spinning-wheel and concentrated on drawing out the thread. She had never gained any very great proficiency in spinning though she had had, in Gandhiji's days, much practice at it. Nowadays she rather neglected it, which made her from time to time feel guilty. The fact was, the work was rather too slow and too sedentary for her, whose disposition did not easily lend itself to slow and sedentary pursuits. But today she had deliberately brought out her spinning-wheel – how ashamed she had been to see it so dusty and neglected – because she felt she needed the discipline which it imposed. She was displeased with herself: her thoughts had become so discontented; they kept straying back to the past instead of dwelling wholly and gratefully, as she felt they should have done, in the present. So now, besides sitting down to spinning, she spent two hours in the mornings in prayer and afterwards she sat with the Swamiji to discuss the state of her soul with him and listen to him reading from the Gita.

'And now this Madhuri thinks we are not good enough for her,' Lakshmi said with a laugh so scornful that to her mind it at once pulverized all Madhuri's pretensions. 'I noticed very well that when I went to her house she did not welcome me in the way it is right to welcome a friend whom one esteems. She did not even offer me sherbet until I asked for it myself, for I know very well what is due to me and I will not sit quiet when people do not offer me the respect that it is their duty to show me.'

'Before the Lord,' said Uma, still fresh from her session with Swamiji, 'what respect can any of us claim, when before Him we are all smaller than the smallest of all the insects. When Lord Krishna showed himself in his True Form before Arjun, even that great hero

190

cried out in fear and the hair stood up on his head. "The worlds tremble and so do I," he cried. Before Him, then, how can any of us stand and say respect is due to us.'

'That may be, but Madhuri is not the Lord Krishna and when I come to her house it is her duty to offer me sherbet. Oh yes, now they think they are very great, but who is it, please tell me, who has made them great?' The question was rhetorical, but nevertheless she paused in order to give the answer, which she intended to supply herself, greater effect. Uma's thread suddenly snapped, and she had to exert all the patience which prayer and contemplation had stored up in her in order not to give in to her impulse to seize the wheel in her strong hands and fling it at the wall.

'It is we and people like us who made them so. It is by climbing up on our suffering that they have now become like peacocks.'

Uma patiently began to insert a new cotton thread. Pleased with her own patience, she looked rather smug as she did so.

'We sacrificed everything in order that Our India might be free –' Uma was so startled that she dropped the thread: Lakshmi had always hitherto so carefully disassociated herself from the Independence struggle – 'for years we sat in prison and parted with all our jewellery, so that now they may have the right to look down on us. Narayan's father gave all his youth and all his strength –'

'Yes, yes,' cried Uma, delighted to have Lakshmi speaking good of Ram Nath for once, 'what has he not done, what has he not given for Our Country, when has he ever spared himself, so that India might enjoy her freedom!'

'He was always a fool. What need was there to give everything, when others who today call themselves great men gave nothing?'

'Ah, sister, in life one must always give, give, give, but it is sinful to look for material rewards. In the Gita it is written that "To work alone thou hast the right, but never to the fruits thereof." Our reward must lie in the peace of the soul only.'

'Yes, yes, but I am sure that Har Dayal's soul has peace also. What soul would not have peace with so many costly possessions and so much respect and honour everywhere? And now how he may laugh at us for giving everything, when it is for him who has sat still and done nothing that we have given! And have you seen how he looks – like a woman, with his skin so soft and his beautiful clothes, and he smells like a woman too, God only knows what it is he puts on himself to smell so. And that poor old fool I have sitting at home . . .' She sighed and, gathering her sari about her got up. 'I must go to him – if I am not there to see to him, he will even forget to take his food, that is the sort of man they have married me to.'

'He is very spiritual,' Uma said, turning her wheel.

'Yes, when people have nothing and are nothing, then it is said about them that they are spiritual.'

All the way home she indulged herself in indignant thoughts about Har Dayal and his family. Shakuntala, she was now quite sure, was certainly not good enough for Narayan, and she wondered how they could ever have entertained the idea that she was. Her indignation made her very proud and fiery and she sharply scolded an old peasant woman, who sat next to her in the bus, for taking up too much room. And when she got home, she at once charged into a little cluster of servant-boys, who stood gossiping about in the passage, and sent them about their business so energetically that they went scattering helter-skelter in all directions. 'And see that those stairs are cleaned up!' she shouted at no one in particular. 'Such filth – how can people like us be expected to live in such filth!'

Then she advanced into Ram Nath's room, her face flushed, her bosom heaving up and down. 'Enough now of your Har Dayal! Because he is your friend, I must give my boy to his worthless daughter?'

'He is coming home next week.'

'Who is coming home next week?'

'Who, who – the Lord Krishna, who else.'

'Yes, to blaspheme and to make a mock of your wife, you are first-class at that. I do not know what sins I committed in my past lives, but certainly I am punished enough for them in you.'

'But this is nothing compared to the punishment you will get in your next birth for not showing due respect to your husband. Do you not know that it is written, even if your husband is a frog, it is your duty as a wife to worship him?'

'I am sure a frog would have dealt better by me than you have done. Enough of such talk now!' she cried, beating her fist on his table so that all her glass bangles jangled. 'He has become an idiot in his old age and now he wants to make me an idiot with him.'

'Poor boy, poor boy, to come home to such a mother,' said Ram Nath, gravely shaking his head.

She stood quite still and gaped at him. Suddenly her expression changed. 'What do you mean?' He pursed his lips and continued to shake his head. 'He is coming home – my boy, my Narayan, is coming home to me?' she said in a trembling voice, hopeful and expectant as a young bride.

'I think I will write and tell him do not come, both your parents have become idiots.'

'How do you know? Has he written? What does he say?'

'He wrote last week.'

'And you have not told me?' But she had no time now for the recriminations which another time she would have directed at him in no uncertain manner. Her mind was already busy with all the preparations that would have to be made – the sheets to be brought out for him, the towels, the strings of the spare bed to be tightened. She wondered whether they could afford to have the room in which he would sleep whitewashed at their own expense: the landlord, scoundrel and exploiter that he was, would certainly not do it, that she knew, however hard she might press him. And at once ten seers of green mangoes must be bought, so that she could make mango pickle for him – 'Thank God I have enough jars with me,' she suddenly told Ram Nath, who could not guess what she was talking about. 'Perhaps, too, I will get some lime – he is fond of lime pickles, too.' She was already outside in the passage, shouting for the servant and fumbling for her money: he must go to the bazaar at once, no time must be lost.

Ram Nath, left behind in his still room, almost admired her for her great preoccupation with pickle jars and spare sheets and the servant to be sent to the bazaar. There might be something ridiculous in it – as he so often found pleasure in pointing out to her – but, on the other hand, could any great preoccupation, whatever it might be with, be thought ridiculous? It meant, after all, participating whole-heartedly in the affairs of life and that, he was beginning to feel, was the most important thing of all. He was beginning to feel so because he had lately come to realize that he had allowed life – or, what came to the same thing, his interest in it – to withdraw from him. His past, as Uma had reminded him, had been so full; and his present was nothing. He had lost contact – not with the world of affairs, of politics, meetings; he did not mean that, because that he had relinquished deliberately – but with all the world, all life. Daily he walked through the streets but was not part of them: the children playing, the milk-seller pouring his milk in a long stream as if it were to be measured by the yard, tomatoes squashed in the dust, women suspiciously squeezing the vegetables offered to them by the shopman and turning them over and over in their hard hands, bullocks squatting in the road and quiet men sitting on wooden benches outside the food-stalls – daily he walked past them but with no more feeling for them than if he had been walking through a vacuum.

Lakshmi reappeared in the doorway, some sheets over her arm. 'And do not talk to my boy about such people as Har Dayal with his Shakuntala. He will just laugh in your face and say, "Is this the best you can think of for me? I can find such Shakuntalas for myself, even in the jungle."' She held a sheet up to the light so that the rents in it

193

could be clearly seen. 'Tchk, tchk,' she clicked her tongue, 'do you expect my boy to sleep on such sheets when he comes home to his mother?' She withdrew again to sit in the courtyard and sort out her sheets there; which would also give her the opportunity of letting the widow from upstairs know that her son, the great Doctor of whom she had heard so much, was coming home to visit her.

And it was not only with the streets and the people in them that he had lost touch. It was also with those close to him, his family and his friends. He sat in his room and did not allow any other life to touch him. Even Uma – he felt guilty when he thought of her anxiety about her Gulab and how he only gave her even as much as his sympathy when she prodded him into remembrance. That was it: he just did not remember. He walked as in a daze, lost even he did not know in what thoughts of his own, and then he did not remember other lives and what he owed to them.

There was Narayan in his village. When he thought of him, he thought of him with love and tenderness and perhaps also some pride; but, he had to admit it, he no longer felt very close to him. He had always accepted the fact that a son's life is independent of his father's; but in the last years he had forgotten that, in spite of that independence, the father is still responsible to the son and owes him something. So that now when Narayan – for the first time – called on him to do something for him, he could not do it because he had allowed himself to lose touch. It was no use being angry with Har Dayal. It was with himself he should have been, and now was, angry. Har Dayal, unlike himself, still knew how things went in the world and what sort of person it was right for his daughter to marry. He had kept in touch. So that there was no more point in laughing at him, with his Committees and his importance, than there was in laughing at Lakshmi. Committees and that sort of importance were an integral part of contemporary life and as such, however ineffectual they might be in themselves, they took on some significance.

Lakshmi, full of energy and busyness, returned to tell him, 'There are many better ones for my boy, only let me manage.' She would go and speak to her second daughter's mother-in-law – together they would sit down and go over all the families with eligible daughters they could think of. Already she was looking forward to it. 'In this house, it is clear, it is the woman who has to manage everything. O Ram,' she sighed, but she was nevertheless very happy. She had already managed to acquaint the widowed sister of the telegraph officer with the great news of Narayan's coming. Now she would find occasion to sit and work in the courtyard and drop some more bits of information to her. Perhaps she would edge in a hint of coming marriage celebrations, of a great match for her son; though it was rather early.

He did not know how it had happened that now he should find himself so cut off. He had not envisaged his retirement like this. Rather he had thought of himself as reading and contemplating, and through reading and contemplation reaching further down into things and understanding them. But far from understanding, it appeared that he had even lost sight of them. There was so much; such an abundance of life: he had always had that feeling, but he had always been too busy to sit still and think about it. Even in prison he had been too busy because his thoughts had been taken up too much with what was going on outside the prison, to which he knew he would within a certain time return. So he had always put it off, telling himself, when I am old I shall think about it.

He had travelled in third-class railway carriages, with peasants and priests and prostitutes; had tramped through the jungles in his journey from one village to the other, and seen eggshell dawns breaking over a landscape of dust and dry thorns. He had penetrated into the narrowest lanes in overcrowded cities, stepped absent-mindedly over naked children with silver anklets and haggled with fat money-lenders who sat cross-legged on ther stringbeds and scratched their testicles. He had known all the smells and sounds and sights of the day and the night: and he had always promised himself that one day, when he grew old, he would sit and think about that deep thrill which they gave him and would ferret out their meaning. Well, he had grown old: and up till now he had not even noticed that he had ceased to notice them.

31

It was Gulab who answered the telephone, and she was extremely happy to hear Shakuntala's voice, which she recognized at once. Her sad face was flooded by a smile which was quite rapturous and she said, 'Oh, Shakuntala, how sweet, how very very sweet of you to ring me.'

First came a somewhat uneasy laugh and then Shakuntala's voice fidgeting through the telephone: 'Yes, I wanted to know how you were.'

'We have not seen one another for too long.' Gulab squatted down on the floor, ready for a long telephone conversation. Unfortunately Esmond came in to spoil her pleasure: 'Who is it?' he asked at once, and stretched out his hand for the receiver.

She hugged it closer in a quite possessive manner which was also affectionate, so that it looked as if it were a live thing she was thus hugging; she said, her hand over the mouthpiece: 'It is for me. My friend Shakuntala.'

Esmond shrugged; but he did not leave the room. Instead he sat down on the little divan, with his arms folded and his legs crossed, swinging one foot, waiting.

Gulab turned her face away from him; her smile had now gone. 'I am so grateful to you for telephoning to me.'

'How are you?' Shakuntala said again; and then, rather quickly, 'May I just speak with your husband for one minute, please?'

Gulab said, 'You wish to speak with him?'

Esmond silently held out his hand for the receiver.

'Yes,' said Shakuntala, with another embarrassed laugh; 'about our lessons. You know, he is my teacher now.'

'I know.' This was the first of Esmond's outside activities in which she had ever taken any interest. She had been longing to ask him all about his visits to Shakuntala's house, what had been said, how did Shakuntala look, were there many servants, whom had he seen there . . . but of course, she had asked nothing, nor had he talked.

She sat, quiet and resigned, waiting for him to finish. She noticed that he was not very pleased; his fingers drummed on the little telephone table. 'Very well,' he said in the end, 'half past five: if you really think it's necessary.'

'No, please wait!' Gulab cried, as he was about to hang up. 'Let me talk!'

He handed her the receiver, saying dryly, 'I think she's hung up.'

'Hallo,' Gulab said; and 'hallo, Shakuntala?' she called with an edge of desperation in her voice.

She replaced the receiver quietly. Probably Shakuntala had made a mistake, and would ring again within a minute.

Because she had to wait for this call, she stayed in the living-room, even though Esmond was there. But it was he who, after a minute, went. She had begun to notice that nowadays he stayed in the same room with her as little as possible. Not that he had ever particularly sought her company: but he had not minded lingering in her presence, if only to scold or at least jab at her. Lately he neither scolded nor jabbed. This should have been a relief to Gulab, who had never asked for anything better than to be left alone. But it wasn't: for she felt, though nothing was ever said, that there was something worse there in his mind against her than even his scolding and jabbing. She did not know what it was, nor could she sit and think about it. But lying in bed at night, she could sense it, a cloud brooding in the darkness, stifling them in that small flat. And in the day she also felt it, lurking in the corners, enveloping them both; even when he had gone out, it remained to oppress her with a weight not quite of fear but of unease. Ravi also seemed to be more quiet than usual nowadays, and he looked smaller and more pinched somehow.

She had been waiting patiently for some time, but the telephone remained quite silent. Probably Shakuntala would ring her at some other time; or perhaps she would even come to see her one day, unannounced. What a pleasant surprise that would be.

She heard Esmond leave the flat. It was ten to five now: he must be on his way to Shakuntala's house, since he had arranged to be there at half past five. She would have liked very much to send a message of love and friendship to Shakuntala: but certainly not through Esmond.

She got up and stretched herself and went to where Ravi lay sleeping in his cot in Esmond's room. It was very hot; all the noonday heat had accumulated into a solid mass which lay heavy in the air and pressed on the walls and ceiling, so that they seemed almost to bend and close in under the weight. Ravi's hair lay matted on his forehead and his shirt was soaked through with perspiration. Noiselessly on her naked feet she left the room and went into her own, where she sank down on to her bed. It was so hot and so still; all the world seemed to have swooned into a stupor.

Lying there, she derived some pleasure from thinking about Shakuntala. It was an escape from the hot, close, modern and ugly little room to think about her: for she saw her in a beautiful moonlit garden with smooth lawns all silvered and scent of jasmine and perhaps a fountain plashing, cool and liquid. Shakuntala was young and beautiful and smiling. She was gay and happy, because she lived in her father's house where she had all the things she wanted, and one day she would marry a charming young man from her own community whom her parents would choose for her, and then she would go to live in his house where she would also be gay and happy, because there too she would have all the things she wanted. Gulab smiled with pleasure when she thought of all this: it was good to know that so much happiness existed.

But the flat was so hot and still; tensed, somehow, and uneasy, as if there were something there hidden and waiting. She went again to Ravi's room, but he was still asleep. She would have liked to wake him; she felt so alone. But he did not sleep well in the night nowadays, so it was good for him to sleep as much as he could in the day. She

197

looked at him, kissed him, and went back to lie again on her bed. If only there were some noise, some household noise with which she could feel comfortable and familiar, so that she would not have to lie there, listening to the silence. In her mother's house there was always some noise: Uma shouting and Bachani answering back, water running as some of the guests took their baths, upstairs Swamiji singing hymns, from the kitchen the pounding of spices ... but here in Esmond's flat not even a tap to drip, a mouse to rustle, in the hot afternoon.

At last she heard some movement in the kitchen. That must be the servant come to start cooking the evening meal. She was glad even of his presence. She would ask him to make her a lime water and put some ice in it. It made her feel happier, the thought of that iced drink that would soon be running down her throat. She called him – 'Bearer!' she called (she had never yet found out his name – there had been so many servants in the last years, she had given up calling them by name). Lying there on the bed, she said, without turning her head, 'Bring me lime water,' and yawned, widely and rather luxuriantly because she was looking forward to her cold drink.

Suddenly she felt again the silence. It was like a presence in the room. She turned her head and saw that the servant was still standing in the doorway. He stood and looked at her stretched out on the bed. 'Hurry!' she said. 'What are you doing? I am thirsty.' But he only stood and looked. The silence swelled up so monstrously that it seemed as if it were going to burst and bring forth the terrible thing lurking underneath it.

Then he moved. She watched him from the bed. She watched him moving towards her and she saw that his eyes were fixed on her and then she noticed that his lips were moving and some sounds were coming out. She did not recognize the sounds. He never stopped looking at her and she never stopped watching him. When he came nearer, he stretched out his hands. His lips were still moving and he was repeating the same sound over and over again. He was very near now and she recognized that what he was saying was, 'My dearie, my dearie.' His hands were held out like a sleepwalker's. One hand he laid, very reverently, on her breast, where it came swelling out of her low-cut blouse; he was still saying, 'My dearie, my dearie.' For a moment his hand lay on her flesh and she looked down at it because she could not believe it, though she felt it there.

But the next moment she leapt up. She stood pressed against the wall and her whole body was tensed to attack. Her eyes were like fire. She advanced a step towards the servant, who at once drew back; her plump shining brown arms flailed the air. Then she flung back her head – mouth open, exposing all her sharp, strong teeth and the pink expanse of palate and tongue – before jerking it forward again to spit at him. She spat in one great spurt of rage. The servant gave a choked exclamation of both fear and surprise and put up his hands to shield himself from the evil she was spitting at him. All her softness and beauty had been transformed into one ball of tigress fury. The servant stood with his hands covering his face and his thin body trembling inside his dirty cotton clothes. She was yelling, 'Out, out, get out, filth!' slowly advancing upon him, so that he had to retreat backwards. When he reached the door, he turned suddenly and fled, quite silently.

She flung herself across the bed, face down, and pounded it with her fists. Her whole body was squirming with revulsion. She tore at her hair and let out loud screams of fury to give some release to the rage that was throttling her. And then, when at last it was all spent, she lay there with her bosom heaving up and down, and she wanted to be dead because she felt so defiled. The place where he had laid his hand was like a sore, something diseased and shameful beyond all cure.

For this was the one thing that had always been feared. This was the fear that made her scurry as quickly and as unobtrusively as she could through the open streets and sit cowering in buses: the fear that some stranger might look at her and desire her. Now the great defilement had happened. It was such a terrible thing in itself, such a depth of degradation, that it could hardly be made worse by the fact that it had been a servant who had defiled her – someone whom she had not thought it necessary to consider human, so that it had seemed quite natural to her to have him passing in and out of the room while she lay on her bed with her sari slipped down from her breasts. No, the fact that it had been a servant could not make the shame worse, because it was already the worst shame there could be.

Gulab was never, in anything, undecided. Probably because she did not form decisions about anything but followed whatever her instinct dictated to her. And just as before her instinct had told her that she must, whatever he might do to her, stay with Esmond since he was her husband and therefore her God, so now it told her that she must leave him. She was quite sure about it: so sure that she did not have to sit and reflect about it at all, but could at once start getting her things out, ready to pack them.

It was a husband's right, so her instinct told her, to do whatever he liked with his wife. He could treat her well or badly, pamper her or beat her – that was up to him, and it was not her place to complain. But in return there was one thing, only one, that he owed her, and that was his protection: it was his duty to see that she was safe in his house and that no stranger could cast insulting eyes on her. Esmond had failed in that duty; so now he was no more her husband. Nor she his wife: since she considered herself defiled, she could not remain in his house any longer but had to return, as was the custom, to her own people.

She flung things indiscriminately into a suitcase, whatever she could find – crumpled saris and freshly ironed ones, her jewellery, blouses stale with perspiration, Ravi's shirts and socks, her scent-bottles. Bachani could sort it all out later and come to collect whatever had been forgotten. She did not think about anything as she thus threw her things together. The silence of the flat no longer oppressed or frightened her, for she no longer noticed it. She did not know where the servant was and she did not care. The flat and everything in it meant nothing to her: it was now only a place which she and Ravi were leaving. Certainly she was not frightened: she knew that nothing more could be done to her. She was aware only of one sensation and that was of the touch of the servant's hand. All her consciousness, as she went about pulling out clothes and flinging them into the suitcase, was concentrated on that one spot where her chest began to rise and swell into her bosom.

She did everything quite correctly – crammed the lid over the overflowing suitcase, locked it and then went to phone for a taxi – though she was hardly aware that she was doing it. She went and woke Ravi. He began to cry, twisting the corners of his mouth downwards, as he always did when he got up from afternoon sleep. But she said, 'We are going to your Nani,' and then he kept quiet, though he was still too drowsy to get excited.

She stood by the door, her suitcase at her side and Ravi in her arms; her sari was pulled well over her head to shield her face so that no one could look at her. She did not speak to the taxi-driver, only motioned her head towards the suitcase which he then picked up. She followed him down the stairs, a silent shrouded figure. She left the door open; the flat meant nothing to her any more, it was dead, finished, so how could she be expected to shut the door and lock it and worry about Esmond's possessions.

In the taxi she sat as close as possible in the corner, with her sari still covering her, and he did not raise her eyes even once, because she did not want to look at the driver's back. Ravi also sat quite still. That spot on her breast still engulfed all her awareness. Soon now she would be in her mother's house, where she would bathe herself and scrub and rub at it with soaps and oils. When she thought of her mother's house, her tension eased somewhat. She did not feel glad at soon being there; she felt no emotion at all about it, only an impulse that drove her there to her inevitable destination. She was going to her mother's house and she would be staying there always – she knew it but did not feel about it. It was her fate, and she accepted it without emotional comment, in the way one should accept one's fate.

When the taxi stopped outside the house, she walked straight in, with her head covered and her Ravi in her arms. The taxi-driver walked behind her with her suitcase. Bachani was squatting on the front veranda and sifting lentils. She stopped dead when she saw Gulab; her mouth opened and her eyes grew round in astonishment and her hand, with a black grain which she had picked out of the lentils still held between thumb and forefinger, froze in mid-air. Gulab walked straight past her, so did the taxi-driver with the suitcase. She ran after them, holding the platter with the lentils, and shouted, 'So at last they have come!' Uma was just coming down the stairs; she looked down and saw her daughter and her grandson and the suitcase, and her heart turned right over in joy.

Gulab said, 'Please pay for the taxi.'

32

Esmond was not, as Gulab had thought, on his way to Shakuntala's house. Shakuntala had planned a shopping expedition, during which he was to meet her, come across her, that is, as if by accident. He very much disliked her plan, but had not been able, on the telephone and with Gulab beside him, to extricate himself in a satisfactory manner. Now, walking down the road to the bus-stand, he was in a bad mood. It was still very hot and the streets were empty. He tried to keep in the shade but there was not much shade, since the district was a newly built-up one and the trees were still very young and naked. Nobody but a fool, he thought grimly, would go out on such an afternoon. A fool or a lover. He certainly did not feel like a lover. Gulab behind him and Shakuntala before him: and all he wanted was to be free.

There was a bus-shelter, but it had been constructed in such a way that all afternoon the sun could penetrate into every corner of it. Each time Esmond had occasion to stand there, his temper rose against the municipal transport authorities, and he even made resolutions to write a terse but pungent letter to the newspapers, the text of which he had worked out long ago. There was no one else, that afternoon, standing under the shelter: probably a bus had just left and he would have to stand there in the sun, waiting till another bus came, perhaps ten minutes or twenty or – one could never know – thirty.

Delhi might be tolerable, he thought, as he so often did, if one had sufficient money. Then one would be able to afford a car and not have to stand in the sun and wait for buses that ran to an erratic timetable. Moreover, he thought, his mind automatically turning to other grievances which lack of money made him endure, one would not have to sit and give lessons to stupid women and be grateful for the money they paid one. Oh yes, with a nice private income life in Delhi could be more than tolerable. There would be parties, amateur theatricals, concerts, tennis, outings to places of historical interest. He shut his eyes. It was almost too much to bear thinking about, the way things could be if only one had sufficient money.

And no wife. At least, no wife like Gulab. It always came back to that same thing. She, even more than lack of money, strangled his life and his personality. If it were not for her, he could always be gay and carefree and charming, could always be as he had been that day when he had had tea with Madhuri and Indira.

The bus came and he got on. There were only a few people inside and they stared at him, as people on a bus always did, wondering why this white sahib did not travel in his own car. And as always, to meet their stares, he kept his head held high and looked proudly into the distance; in this way he had managed to persuade himself that he did not care.

He sat and stared out of the window, wearily. He was so tired of it all: the ramshackle huts which served as shops, the wilting array of fruits and vegetables and sweetmeats, the old men who sat on broken stringbeds and puffed at their hookahs, the dirty bullocks, the dirtier dogs snuffling around for refuse, the hordes of naked brown children with huge eyes and charms tied round their necks with black string: so persistent, so monotonous, drenched in eternal white sunlight; and always, encompassing everything and holding it in its vast bowl, the Indian sky – an unchanging, unending expanse of white-blue glare, the epitome of meaningless monotony which dwarfed all human life into insignificance. There was no romance about life in India, Esmond knew; only for tourists, he thought bitterly, who clapped their hands in delight over what was, he knew, only shabbiness and poverty repeated to a point where the spirit yawned at the boredom and futility of it all. How he longed for England where there were solid grey houses and solid grey people, and the sky was kept within decent proportions.

Gulab behind him and Shakuntala before him; and lessons, with the money in an envelope afterwards; and outside eternal shabbiness wrapped in eternal heat and sky. And now Betty was going away; which was the final push into despair. But it was just at that point, that point of final despair, sitting there in the bus among passengers who stared at him and wondered why he was not travelling in his own car, when his life seemed to him only a waste and a bitterness, it was just then that he made his decision which was like a great blessing suddenly descending upon him so that everything was changed and renewed and instead of misery there was happiness lifting him beyond all the things that lay dead-weight and apparently inescapable on his spirit.

Because he realized – or perhaps at last openly allowed himself to realize – that Betty was right, and that they were not, after all, in any way inescapable. 'Pack up and come along' – why not? Why ever not? When he realized how easy it really was, he felt like laughing out loud: what a fool he had been, what a fool, not to have realized it before. There was only this to do: get the money for his passage, pack his things and go. It was so easy – even the money was easy, because he had part of it and the rest Betty would lend to him. He would sail on the same boat with her. Already he saw himself playing tennis with her on the ship, both of them radiant in white tennis-clothes. They would sit at the same table for meals and make many friends. For three weeks they would be so gay. Everything would be left behind and he would be happy all day long and light-hearted. Already he felt happy and light-hearted. The bus and the heat and the shabbiness meant nothing to him any more because soon he would be free of them. Free of everything. He threw back his fine golden head and felt happiness welling up inside him.

Shakuntala had asked him to meet her in Janpath, by the long row of cloth and shoe and toy and haberdashery stalls which had become middle-class New Delhi's most popular shopping centre. Just now, though, there were few people about. The shopkeepers squatted cross-legged inside their stalls and yawned. As Esmond strolled by, peering into each stall to see if he could find Shakuntala, the owners stared back at him with bleary, uninterested eyes; they were not much concerned whether he bought anything or not – soon now the crowds would be coming and then business would begin in earnest.

He felt so young and sprightly. He had not felt like this for many, many years. Life was beginning again for him: he was young yet, young. There were three perfect weeks ahead of him on board ship. And then – oh, he was young, and he had wits, and charm, and one could always (couldn't one?) make an agreeable living in England. He had a sister there, and an aunt, and Betty was very well connected. There was nothing whatsoever to worry about; at any rate, he did not worry. He revelled only in his new sensation of youth and freedom.

Life could be, would be, *was* wonderful. There was nothing to regret. Not even, at this stage, Ravi ... One day perhaps he would have another little son, a merry fair-haired little boy (Angels not Angles). He felt so happy and light-hearted that even when a beggar accosted him he drove him away with the greatest good humour.

He found Shakuntala sitting in a shoe-shop. She had already had piles of shoes taken out and they lay in a heap around her – flimsy, dainty, decorative sandals, red and gold, black and gold, green and gold. Her rather large but well-formed foot was stretched out, and she watched critically and with concentration as the shopman fitted yet another sandal on to it. Esmond stood and looked at her, smiling with benevolence. Really, she was quite nice-looking and in a few years' time, when she had been married to everyone's satisfaction and had learned how to dress and be a lady, she would be nicer still. He could see her as she would appear in the weekly social magazines, smart, smiling, dressed in perfectly good taste with just a few artistic touches to make her daring and different.

'Hello there!' cried Esmond. She looked up and saw him standing in the doorway, smiling and golden. Her Shelley, her Ariel. Her eyes lit up, but she said in a tone which was almost measured, 'Why, what a coincidence, what are you doing here'; though this was probably unnecessary, since it was not likely that the shopman understood enough English.

'Come on,' cried Esmond, 'I'll buy you a Coca-Cola!'

'But I am buying shoes.'

'Hang your shoes!' and they both laughed as they urged her up and out, hardly giving her time to push her feet back into her old sandals. The shopman was left behind, philosophically tidying away his goods.

They stood outside a stall, which displayed an array of coloured bottles, and sipped Coca-Cola through straws. She looked radiantly up at him and he looked radiantly down at her. Both of them were so happy. The first stream of bicycles was just coming out of the offices, and shoppers began to parade up and down the row of stalls.

'Now again everything is all right,' she said.

'All right?'

'Yes, now you are again my Esmond.'

He laughed and took her empty bottle from her. Gaily he flung an eight-anna coin towards the shopman who tested it by tossing it on the counter.

'You see,' she said, 'no one trusts you.'

'It's that villainous look of mine.'

'Only I trust you. I trust you with everything. With my whole life.'

'Darling,' he said; perhaps a trifle absent-mindedly, but nevertheless with true affection. He was young again and oh, so charming, and a romantic young girl was madly in love with him.

The crowds in and around the stalls were growing denser. So was the traffic in the road: and there was an avalanche of bicycles, and cars hooting, and bullock-carts and a policeman under a parasol flinging out his arms, now in this direction, now in that. The hot day was finished; now it was evening, time to live again, stroll along by the shops, meet friends, sip iced drinks.

Reckless with happiness, she took his arm. She did not care who saw her: soon, anyway, everyone would know. Soon they would be together for ever, openly before all the world, beautifully. He brought his hand over on to hers, laid so trustingly on his arm, and pressed it. He too did not care who saw. He did not care nor fear about anything any more. He was young and free, and it was good to feel oneself loved. Behind them came a boy with a tray, urgently offering them, 'Any hairpins, combs, safety-pins, elastic?'

They were being jostled right and left by the crowd of shoppers. Most of these were women – great, heavy Punjabi women, who had eaten well for many years, sisters and sisters-in-law, with their children and adolescent daughters who had stiff pigtails down their backs and dreamy eyes and breasts just budding. The mothers moved forward resolutely, in consolidated blocks, not caring where or whom they jostled and pushed, only intent on their own business, which was buying the best at the cheapest price possible. They peered suspiciously into each shop from which the shopkeeper – already busy serving several other parties of shoppers – cried hospitably, 'Please come, please come, please command me!' On the outside of the pavement stood the transitory tradesmen – men with little barrows on which were piled towels or children's red slacks or slices of watermelon, all offered at competitive prices. Hawkers and beggars pushed through the crowd, choosing their prospective clients and fastening on to them with perseverance. Progress in all that crowd was difficult, but no one was in much of a hurry. In the roadway traffic grew denser and denser, cyclists were now six abreast and the cars hooted insistently and even the men who rode on top of the bullock-carts had wakened up. The swinging doors of the coffee-houses were constantly opening and shutting and one could see that inside all the tables were crowded.

Shakuntala took a deep, deep breath, which she felt she had to take or she would stifle in such a sea of happiness. She knew now that life was more wonderful, a hundred times more wonderful, than even she had suspected. It was not the moment, nor was she the person, to hide such a sentiment, so she told him, 'Life is wonderful – wonderful!' letting her hand slide from his arm down to his hand which she firmly and fearlessly held as they made their way through the crowd.

The fat healthy pushing women, the beggars, the obtrusive hawkers, the noise, the heat, the smell: these things did not, as they usually did, jar on him, indeed he hardly noticed them; for he knew that soon there would be only sea and sky and gentle games of tennis. So he allowed his hand to stay in hers and he answered her, with an affectionate smile and looking down into her eyes, which at that moment, so large and shining and brimful of joy were they, reminded him of Gulab's eyes as they had been when he was first married to her – 'Yes, it's not so bad, not such a bad old thing.

Printed in the United States
By Bookmasters